GAYLORD S

PRIZZI'S GLORY

OTHER BOOKS BY RICHARD CONDON

PRIZZI'S GLORY

RICHARD CONDON

E. P. DUTTON NEW YORK

Published in the United States by E. P. Dutton,
a division of NAL Penguin Inc.,
2 Park Avenue, New York, N.Y. 10016.

Published simultaneously in Canada
by Fitzhenry and Whiteside Limited, Toronto.

Library of Congress Cataloging-in-Publication Data
Condon, Richard.
Prizzi's glory / Richard Condon. — 1st ed.
p.   cm.
ISBN 0-525-24689-4
I. Title.
PS3553.0487P69   1988
813'.54—dc19   88-10194
                            CIP

Designed by REM Studio

3   5   7   9   10   8   6   4   2

Richard Condon, author of **PRIZZI'S GLORY** (E.P. Dutton)
Photo credit: <u>Playboy</u>

For the memory of
John Huston

Seeking good fortune
As we rise from the mud,
'Tis often we're paid
From a purse filled with blood.
THE KEENERS' MANUAL

You can make a fresh start with your final breath.
BERTOLT BRECHT

PRIZZI'S GLORY

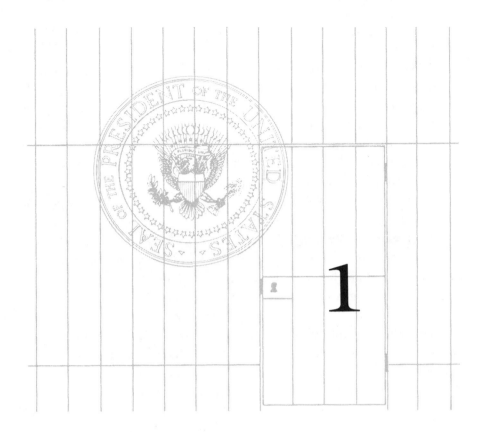

1

Early in December 1985, a rotten day weatherwise, Charley Partanna, CEO of the Prizzi family, sat behind his desk in the St. Gabbione Laundry, the family's executive offices for street operations, in central Brooklyn, and listened, over the sloshing roar of the laundry vats turning outside his office door, to a proposal by Sylvan Robbins, president of the hotel company that ran the three Prizzi casinos in Atlantic City.

"This is it, Charley," Robbins said. "Believe it. The wave of the future. Could you ever *conceive* of such a thing? A credit card for slot machines?"

"I don't get it, Sylvan."

"No more coins, no costs for cash security, handling, counting, wrapping, and guarding coins. No theft."

"Sylvan, please, tell me how it works."

"The player just sticks the credit card in the machine, coded to the value he wants to play for, and pulls the handle. If he hits a payoff, the recording inside the machine makes a sound like a bunch of silver falling out, but nothing happens, nothing comes out. But the card gets credited with the win, or, if he loses—ho, ho, ho—the card shows a debit. It can save the Prizzis about five million three a year on all the machines they have out."

"Jesus. Modern science. But a lot of romance is gonna go out for the players."

"I should put them in?"

"Not only put them in, send me all the dope so we can put them in at Vegas and all the other locations. You done good, Sylvan. If this really works, we're gonna give you another quarter point."

Charley didn't depend only on outside inspiration. He checked out every operation zealously so that his middle management would know that he was on top of every one of their opportunities and all of their problems. At four in the afternoon he had an appointment with the chemist in Matteo Cianciana's shit division to test batches of a new delivery of *cinnari* that had just come in from Miami and to supervise cutting it into dealer lots.

At half past six he had a meet with Girolama "Jerry" Picuzza to evaluate one of the new convenience orgy opportunities that they were testing out at eleven locations around town. If the orgies continued to win money the way they were going, he would recommend to Don Corrado that they go national.

Jerry Picuzza was an old-timer who ran vice and pornography for the Prizzis, and, being the old pro that he was, he had built up the orgies into something that really looked like it could hit. He had set up a regular schedule in four of the boroughs and in eastern New Jersey and southern Connecticut. He circulated a weekly chain letter to prospects, and it was really building membership. Sessions were held every weeknight, although special bookings could be arranged for Saturday, a slow television period, as well as patently promotional "brunch" orgies, with door prizes, on Sundays, at selected locations.

Jerry picked him up at the chemist's at seven o'clock. They had dinner at a small Sicilian joint on West Fourth Street, a nice, clean place with white tablecloths and white-haired waiters who wore old-fashioned tablecloth aprons. In the entire restaurant there wasn't a ketchup bottle in sight. He liked the atmosphere, but Charley hated to eat out because, no matter where, the food was never as good as the food he cooked himself—and they charged too much for it.

"Hey, how about this *farsumagru?*" Jerry asked. His cousin owned the place.

"Where's the salami?" Charley asked with harsh justice. "Where's the parsley?"

They drove uptown in Charley's beat-up Chevy van. They got to the site just before eight-thirty. The action began at ten; and Jerry felt that within four months they would have to add an extra midnight session. The site was in an apartment house at Seventy-fourth and West End Avenue that was owned by one of the realty companies of the Prizzis' Barker's Hill Enterprises.

"This ain't our top orgy unit," Jerry said. "This is what you call a nice middle-class orgy opportunity."

"We got other kinds?"

"What the hell, Charley: poor people are Americans—they gotta have a little fun of their choice, too."

He rang the bell at apartment 7E. A very large man wearing a white jacket and pressed black trousers over his muscles opened the door. "Good evening, Mr. Gibson," he said to Jerry Picuzza. "Miss Coolidge is expecting you."

They went into the large, heavily carpeted living room, entirely free of furniture, with about two dozen cushions placed on the carpet around the room. "Miss Coolidge is in the viewing room," the man said.

"We get sixty-five bucks a head from people who just like to watch," Jerry said. "One hundred and ten bucks a head from the players, plus they both gotta pay a membership fee and an initiation fee. After all, this is a club. Also, we sell alla them refreshments, mostly pot, some coke, and a little booze. The players don't know the watchers are watching, and neither side knows that both of them are having their pictures taken in case it should ever come up that we need the shots to negotiate something."

"Good thinking," Charley said.

Jerry opened a door and they went into a room with tiered chairs facing a one-way glass partition. A beautiful, willowy young woman, severely dressed in a black skirt and a gray blouse with high ruching at the neck, was testing the lighting in the main room when they came in. She stood up abruptly. Charley felt a jolt of high voltage electricity run through his body, starting deep inside and spreading out simultaneously to the roof of his head as if a horned ibex had leaped from his stomach and had crashed into his skull. He had to take a step and a half backward because of the sudden force of an instant erection. He knew he had never had such an instantaneous reaction to seeing a woman. He couldn't understand it. Nothing showed on her. The high collar of her blouse came up under her chin almost, and he couldn't see her legs because she was standing behind a sofa, but if anybody asked him to bet, and he never bet on anything, he would bet that she had absolutely gorgeous pins.

"Good evening, Mr. Gibson," she said.

"This is Claire Coolidge, our manager for the site," Jerry said to Charley. To Miss Coolidge he said, "Whatta the bookings look like tonight?"

"Thirty-eight players, sixteen watchers," Miss Coolidge said.

"That ain't all we got going for us," Mr. Gibson said to Charley. "We got exotic book sales. We'll make them an individual videocassette of their action for an additional two-fifty, and the membership is beginning to show a lot of interest in S and M equipment."

They left the site at 9:10 P.M. and drove back to Brooklyn with Jerry talking numbers all the way. "Figure this, Charley," he said. "At this site alone we are taking down $4,180 from the players and $1,040 from the watchers plus the refreshments, which average about $800, and that's only from one session a night."

"Not bad."

"Wait! Popular demand is gonna make us move up to midnight matinees. Eleven sites are working tonight and they work five nights a week."

"Very nice."

"But that's nothing. When it goes national, we'll have seventy-four national availability cities with an average of three sites per city, each one holding seven sessions a week. You can't beat it for a money-

4

maker. This can be the biggest thing since crack and hula hoops. The public is really going for it."

"You done good, Jerry. And if we go national, we're gonna get you a piece of the action."

"Jesus, Charley. That is terrific."

"Who is the girl?" Charley asked. His tone was mild, but that wasn't how he felt. His heart began to kick at his ribs as he asked the question. He had been absolutely knocked out by the girl. She was one of the most beautiful women he had ever seen.

"What girl?"

"The girl—the orgy manager. Is she a hooker?"

"A *hooker*?" Jerry seemed shocked. "She's got the worst case of the straights of anybody ever worked for me. She's an outta-work ballet dancer."

"Whatta you mean?"

"What I mean? She couldn't get any work at what she does so somebody sent her to us and she was so straight I figured to myself this is exactly what we need to run the retail side. I took out the hookers I had in the other ten operations and I put in straights and business went up twenty-three percent."

"How come?"

"Straight people don't approve of orgies. They show it. That provides the necessary feeling of guilt which the players and the watchers gotta have."

"That's very tricky."

"You gotta know my side of the business, Charley."

"She wants to be a ballet dancer?"

"Go figure it. I am paying her five hundred bucks for a twenty-hour week but I know all she's doing is saving up so she can quit me and go back to being an unemployed ballet dancer."

"That's the way you figure it?"

"No question. I got her replacement all lined up."

"When she quits, tell her to call me."

"Yeah?"

"Maybe I can get her a job as a ballet dancer."

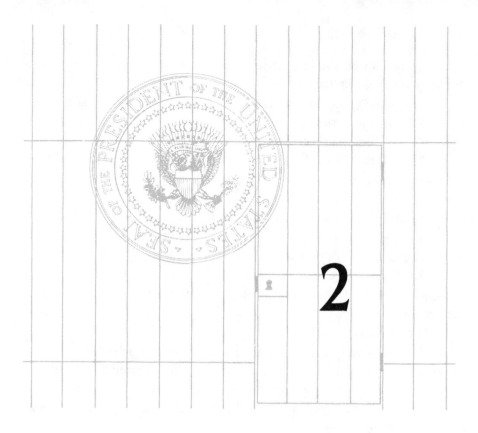

2

By February 1986, when Claire Coolidge called Charley, he was forty-nine years old. He had spent half of December, all of January, and a week in February agonizing as he waited for her to call him. Charley could go along for months, even longer, without falling in love, but when he did it was as though he had been dumped into a giant Cuisineart, whirled around, and chopped into so many small pieces of anxiety and doubt that he might as well have never gotten out of bed in the mornings. He couldn't do anything to bring her to him any faster than the route originally planned with Jerry because if he told Jerry again to tell her to call him that would be giving Jerry information that he didn't need to know because then if Jerry used the information on Charley, thinking he was playing on a weakness to get himself an advantage, Charley would either have to fire him, which would cost them

6

money, or have him zotzed, which would lose them the best flesh-fantasy man in the business.

So Charley waited it out and suffered. He lost eleven pounds, and although he knew he would gain it back after she called him, he had a tailor put alterations in one of his suits—both of his suits were made of dark blue serge—so that it wouldn't be hanging on him when he met her again.

Charley's ordeal happened a couple of times a year, less than when he had been fifteen years younger, but he put so much into his idealization of each girl as she happened to him that he couldn't remember the process of having it happen to him—he only knew it had all started in the back row of a Loew's in South Brooklyn with Vito Daspisa's sister Tessie.

Charley Partanna was not a womanizer, not a lady-killer, but his susceptibility to beautiful women went beyond Mother Teresa's susceptibility to the poor. For the past nineteen years, when a new woman happened to him, as lightning happens to trees when it strikes, he hated himself for a few seconds because all during the nineteen years, excepting for the few months he had been married to what's her name, he had been engaged, on and off, to Maerose Prizzi, a *great* beauty and granddaughter of the *capo di tutti capi* in the entire world, so, as it kept working out, he was always a little ashamed of himself.

Now Claire Coolidge had happened to him. How could it be? He was forty-nine years old, approaching the half-century mark. Could it be possible that this could go on until he was a little old man like the don and the women whose beauty he admired would laugh at him? "Why me?" he had asked Father Passanante during confession. "God created beauty" was all the priest would tell him. "He must have meant you to enjoy it." He only gave Charley two Hail Marys and one Our Father as penance.

After eight or ten years, Maerose could tell almost before he knew it himself that he was in the grip of his destiny—he knew she could tell, because she threw dishes and small furniture around—but she was very busy assisting her Uncle Eduardo at Barker's Hill Enterprises so she never had the time to bring it up. He dreaded the day when she would have the time. He liked Sicilian women, but most of the time he wished Mae wasn't so intense.

.   .   .

Claire Coolidge called him at 10:21 A.M. on February 16, 1986.

"Yeah?" he said into the phone.

"Is this Mr. Partanna?"

His heart leaped. Was this her? It sounded like her, although he wasn't that sure of his memory for voices. It had been a very short time that they had been together and that he had heard her voice, but this had to be her because the only other woman who had his private number was Maerose Prizzi and it certainly wasn't Mae. "Yes?" he said cautiously into the phone.

"This is Claire Coolidge." His gasp cut into his throat and scalded his lungs. "Mr. Gibson suggested that I call you about the possibility of an opening in your ballet company."

What the fuck kind of a thing was that for Jerry to tell her, that he owned a ballet company? "Oh, yes, Miss Coolidge," he said, as if he had been searching his mind and had finally made the connection. "Maybe we could set up a meet."

"Pardon?"

"Let me look," he said into the phone, but there was nothing he wanted to look at except her. "Ah, are you free for lunch today, Miss Coolidge?" Good luck. He held on tightly. Jerry had said she was very, very straight, and he hoped to God that the implied intimacy of the question would not offend her.

"Yes, I am, Mr. Partanna."

"Let's say the Russian Tea Room at one o'clock." The family owned 486 restaurants in New York and had the linen and towel concessions in 7,492 others, so why did he say the Russian Tea Room? He had never been in the Russian Tea Room. He wouldn't even recognize the food—maybe they only sold Russian tea. "Do you know where that is, Miss Coolidge?"

"Two blocks north of the New York Ballet Company. One o'clock. Thank you, Mr. Partanna."

Charley hung up and called Eduardo Prizzi's secretary. Eduardo's name had tremendous clout everywhere, from the halls of Congress to restaurant reservation desks. "Miss Blue? This is Charley Partanna. Do me a favor and call the Russian Tea Room and tell them I gotta have

8

a nice table for two at one o'clock. Then ask Mr. Price if he can fit me in between four and five."

"Can you tell me what you want to see Mr. Price about?"

"The ballet."

"*Ballet?*"

"Where they dance on their toes." Edward S. Price (Eduardo's legal name) was on the board of directors of everything. He would know how to handle this.

He put on a hat and coat and left the office. "I'll call back later," he told Al Melvini.

"Whatta you mean?"

"What do I mean? I'm going out."

"Oh. Hey, listen, Charley, if you're going near it, could you pick me up a tube of Preparation H? My air cushion is leaking."

"I can't, Al. I'm busy. You duck out and get it."

"Who'll man the phones?"

"Drop dead, Al." Charley dashed out of the laundry, got into the van, and drove to his apartment at the beach. He showered, powdered, applied a deodorant so strong that it could also have been used as embalming fluid, put on fresh underwear, his second set of the day, then immediately took the underwear off because it had blue and pink polka dots and if, by a miracle, he had to strip down with her that afternoon, he didn't want to give the impression that he was frivolous. He rebrushed his teeth, gargled with chlorophyll-packed disinfectant, took liver salts because he had read in a woman's magazine that the liver was where bad breath started, combed his hair, brushed it, then dressed in the blue suit with the slenderizing pencil stripe that he usually only wore to meetings with Eduardo Prizzi. Either Eduardo could set the ballet job direct or he'd know somebody who could do it. Why did he always read magazines whenever he had the time? Why hadn't he read books on the ballet so he could give this woman the feeling that he had some idea of what he was talking about?

When he was ready to travel, it was ten minutes to twelve. He started for the door, then wanted to yell at himself. He was a Boss. Why didn't he have a car and a driver like the other Bosses so he didn't always have to worry about the fucking parking every time he went into New York? But he knew the answer. If he had a car and a driver, he would be expected to have an entourage, and if he had a lot of guys hanging around him all the time, he would have to talk to them. He telephoned the laundry.

"Al?"

"Yeah?"

"Send one of the *picciotti* to meet me in front of the Russian Tea Room in New York—West Fifty-seventh Street—at ten to one."

"What kind of a specialist?"

"Get him there. I need him to park my car."

He drove from South Brooklyn to the Tunnel, up the West Side Highway, east on Fifty-seventh Street. He got to the restaurant at five to one. Vinnie Le Pore was waiting for him on the sidewalk in front of the restaurant.

"Park it, Vinnie," Charley said. "And if you can't park it keep driving around the block till I come out."

"How long you gonna be, Boss?"

"I don't know. Maybe two hours."

"Jesus, I better get gas."

Charley went into the Russian Tea Room. Claire Coolidge had beat him to it, which was all right, he told himself; it made him look cooler. What flashed across his mind was the movie guy who told him that he always got laid an hour before he had a date with the woman he loved because then she could sense his aloofness. Charley marveled.

Claire Coolidge was divine in the real sense of the word, he thought, like a goddess. Red-gold hair, green eyes, a beautiful *sweet* face, and the most gorgeous legs he had ever seen, but she held her feet pointing in different directions like a gin drinker. It was a lucky thing he hadn't remembered her as being this beautiful because he never would have made it here today—his legs wouldn't have held him.

They had a large booth, up front, for six people, just the two of them.

"I want to get one thing straight, Mr. Partanna," Claire said before they could even order a drink. "I don't want you to get any wrong ideas about me. I was working for Mr. Gibson because I had to eat and

I had to somehow get together enough money so that I would be able to wait through the season until something opened for me in ballet. That's it entirely. And you'd better believe it."

"You must like that kind of dancing," Charley said.

"Since I was six years old—" A waiter appeared. "I'll have a *jugo de piña con Bacardi*," she said.

The sentence went through Charley like a knife. The only other woman in his life who had ordered that drink had been his late wife, Corinna. No, that wasn't her name. Phyllis? Faith? It would come to him, but even if he didn't have her name on the tip of his tongue— Mardell! Mardell Dupont!—he remembered the drink. "Same for me," he said.

"Since I was six years old I have dreamed of being a dancer," Claire said. "When I was sixteen I appeared in my hometown ballet company in Winsted, Connecticut. When I was eighteen I danced for the Dallas Ballet. I am now twenty-two. Since then I have appeared with the Minneapolis, Los Angeles, and Boston companies, although I have never danced in opera. And, despairingly for me, I have never danced in New York."

Charley felt stronger. He knew a little something about opera, but he had not known that they danced there because he had only heard opera on the don's phonograph records. "Would you like to dance in an opera?"

"My God, Mr. Partanna, if you could get me a place with a New York opera company, I—I just don't know what I'd do. Thank you," she said to the waiter.

"Menus?" the waiter said, extending the cards.

"Later!" Charley said, hitting him with a piece of fear that turned his spine to water.

He had one thing on his mind. He had to get a book on ballet, memorize it, then come on strong.

"Call me Charley," he said to Claire. The waiter had fled.

"Please call me Claire."

"Did you know that St. Claire was the patron saint of television?"

"I am a Unitarian."

"Claire—lissena me—I gotta say this. When I saw you, I went. I am in love with you. I am outta my head about you."

"Does that mean you can place me with a ballet company?"

"Opera or straight?"

"Opera, I think—because I never did opera."

"Where do you live?"

"I'm at the YWCA right now."

Charley took a deep breath and a tremendous chance. "Would you like a nice apartment—say near the opera—if I could do that for you?"

She looked at him quite directly, not even blinking her beautiful green eyes. "If you could place me with the opera, I think that would be absolutely wonderful, Charley."

The crowded, sweaty past thawed and resolved itself into a dew. The present took on a fifth dimension of sensation. The future shone so brightly that, surreptitiously, Charley had to adjust his clothing.

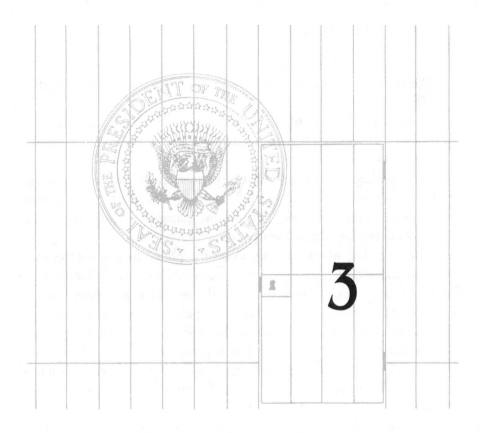

3

Four months later, in May 1986, while Charley was wildly in love with an absolutely lovely black woman named Ellen Beauwater, whom he met while she was selling him some socks over-the-counter at Bloomingdale's, Maerose, his fiancée, finally found the time to admit that she knew that Charley was seeing another woman.

"Charley, lissena me," she said after destroying dishes and furniture noisily. "You have another woman, I know it. And I'm not gonna hold still for it, you understand?"

"Mae! Fahcrissake! Whatta you want from me?"

"We're gonna get married."

"Married?"

"Nineteen years, Charley. You know who you need to shack up with? A psychiatrist."

"Married?"

"Yeah. We're gonna get married and live at my place in New York."

"Jesus, Mae—"

"I was busy day and night planning a future for us, and you took advantage. Did I sneak off with other men? Did I?"

"How do I know?"

"You're almost fifty years old, fahcrissake. How long can you keep on sniffing around? Don't answer! It's all over, Charley. A nineteen-year engagement is too long. People are gonna start laughing soon. We're gonna get married, Charley."

The next day, when he was told on the phone by Amalia Sestero, the don's daughter/hostess/cook, that he would be having lunch with the don in three hours, he realized two things: (1) it was lucky that all he had had for breakfast was a glass of grapefruit juice and a couple of leftover *pagnoccati;* and (2) he was absolutely sure that Mae had turned the don loose on him because it was too much of a coincidence, her talking about getting married last night and the don giving him absolutely no notice to get over there today. It was a slow process, but once Charley understood something he hung on to it.

He marveled how Maerose could twist her grandfather, the don, around her finger whenever she wanted to. He had never known anyone else who could do that, nobody, not even Pop, who had been close to the don for over fifty years.

There had been a lot of times when Charley had tried to figure out how come he was always changing women. He knew in his heart that he had always been happy with only two women—Maerose, and whoever else happened to be there when he rolled over in bed. In the beginning, a long time ago, he had thought it kept happening because he was (basically) your typical hot-blooded Latin. He had read a lot in magazines about Latins being passionate and how they needed more action than other people, but he knew a lot of Latins in Brooklyn and there were plenty of them who first figured out what it would cost to take a woman to dinner and maybe a movie, then decided to shoot some pool with the guys instead.

Charley had had money coming in from overall points in the street operation ever since he had been Underboss. He had been Boss for seven years with even more points. He had almost enough money in Swiss banks and here and there to redo Brooklyn along the lines of Paris, France. He could have bought anything for women. Take Claire Coolidge. She was grateful when he offered her a season pass to the Mets that his assemblyman had given him, on the day they parted two months after he had set her up with the opera ballet, and she knew he was giving her to another man, but she wouldn't take it. She liked him because part of the mystery that surrounded Charley's responses to women was that somehow he picked women who were going to turn out to like him, and no matter how often it happened, he never got tired of it. But Mae had put her finger on it: he was forty-nine years old, practically a middle-aged man if he lived to be a hundred, and the time had come for him to stop fooling around. It came to him why he was always changing his mind about women, crazy about them for a while, then not able to remember their names or their faces.

Gradually, he realized that he did it because he was exhausted with the monotony of his life. The same problems, the same solutions: stupid guys would get outta line and Vincent, or the don, or Pop would tell him to zotz them. The same thing over and over. He realized that it had probably been a mistake to get a high school education because more and more as time went on he realized he had nobody to talk to except the women—educated women, cultured women, interested women—not the lumps of muscle he had to try to talk to all day long like Al Melvini. Other people in the world couldn't have this problem, he thought. Maybe I have too much money or something, but I don't spend it because the IRS could find out, so how could I know? He kept changing women because it was the change away from the monotonous life he lived from the beach to the laundry. He wanted to change and, instinctively, he knew Maerose knew how to get that for him so (basically) he stuck to her.

Charley nodded to Calorino at the front door, kissed Amalia on the cheek, and asked her if she felt good, and they went up the two flights of stairs to the don's huge room. As they reached the top, Charley could hear the tenor herniating in the role of Avito, a former prince of Altura, in Italo Montemezzi's *The Love of Three Kings*. Charley entered the don's room.

"My boy, my boy!" the don sang. "How good of you to come. We are about to sit down to lunch." Don Corrado stood up abruptly and moved with eagerness to the dining table. He gestured to Charley to take a place at his right hand.

Amalia came in with steaming bowls of *zuppa d'accia,* a Calabrese specialty, which was a celery broth holding large pieces of sausage with cheese and hard-boiled egg that she served with grated cheese and pieces of toast. The don attacked the soup without a word. Charley, because of past experience, ate as sparingly as he could. The don asked for a second bowl of soup; Charley begged off. Next they attacked mountains of *risotto alla Siciliana.* Then, with great gusto, the don brought his gargantuan appetite to an enormous platter of beet salad, turned bright, blood red by its pigment, betacyanin, which, because the slight, little man had inherited two recessive genes, passed out through his urine the same color as he had swallowed it, truly symbolizing his meaning as a *capo di mafia.*

Amalia tottered in, trying bravely to support a *testa di puorco,* a pig's head, which had been boiled with celery, carrots, onions, and herbs and set in a jelly made from the stock, flavored with Marsala and some vinegar. Because it was a cold dish it signified to the don that he was having a light lunch. Charley had one helping. The don returned for a third helping, drinking Albanello di Siracusa, a dry white wine that had a dry and appetizing finish and eighteen degrees of alcohol. The light lunch was topped with a *cassata,* alternating layers of sponge cake and cream made with ricotta cheese flavored with chocolate and candied fruits, topped with a frosting perfumed with almonds and lemon.

Charley nearly went under. The drowsiness dropped heavy weights into his head and upon his eyelids. His head lolled. His eyes rolled and closed, but he fought to keep awake. He counted on the jolt of a strong cigar to counteract the coma that always happened after he had lunched with the don.

At Don Corrado's bidding, he made it to the easy chair that was placed beside, and three-quarters facing, the don's chair.

"Please," the don said, "you must have a cigar and a grappa."

Charley lit a Mexican cigar and poured himself a jelly glass of grappa but did not drink it.

"I want to tell you I am pleased that the tests of the orgy opportunities have gone so well," the don said in the dialect of Agrigento.

"It fills a need," Charley said.

"In September I want to proceed with the nationalizing. Will you have your people write the operating manuals?"

"Yes, *padrino.*"

"By the end of the year the salesmen must be ready to take it into their territories."

"Yes, *padrino.* And, it is necessary to say this, because Girolama Picuzza has done such a really great job on the test operation, I recommend that we give him three-quarters of a point in the national and let him run it."

"That is perfectly all right with me."

There was a considerable pause. Charley felt a need to sip the grappa.

"Charley, you are like a son to me. No—I want to change that— you are more than a son, you are part of the Prizzi meaning which Vincent, God rest his soul, never achieved."

"Thank you, *padrino.*"

"You are nearly fifty years old, and for nineteen years I have seen you with my granddaughter and I have wished, with all my heart, that one day soon you would come to this old man who has so few days left upon this earth which God, in his kindness, created for us and ask me for my granddaughter's hand in marriage." He stared at Charley with his most implacable stare, hastening Charley to answer lest the ancient, tiny man reach out and strike him down.

"It is settled, *padrino.* I went to Maerose last night and I pleaded with her to marry me. I am deeply moved to be able to tell you that she has accepted."

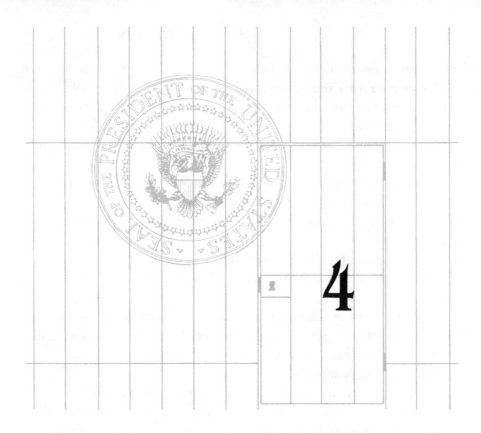

4

Maerose Prizzi and Charley Partanna were married on August 9, 1986. Their courtship had begun in 1967, but there had been complications. It had picked up again in 1979, just before Charley's marriage, and after his wife's tragic death it continued in fits and starts because Charley's attentions wandered whenever a woman of his dreams happened into his life and because Maerose had begun her serious work as executive assistant to her uncle at the top of Barker's Hill. She worked until she dropped every day to make herself indispensable to her uncle and to learn everything he knew about the operation of Barker's Hill, mother lode of all the great American El Dorados and her birthright.

While Mae applied sweat to oil the grindstone, Charley was dormant romantically, with the exception, after the first six months of his

18

widowerhood, of a reasonably short but wild infatuation with a parking meter officer named Babe Matzger.

The marriage to Mae, when it finally happened, had enveloped Charley as unexpectedly as any normal disastrous earthquake. Maerose had been relentless about setting the whole thing up. Not that there weren't small complications. Nineteen years before, in 1967, Maerose Prizzi had gone to her grandfather's house to tell him that she was going to marry Charley Partanna. But that intention was not to be realized. So in 1986, the second time around, she felt she would lack credibility if she made the announcement without Charley at her side, even though she knew that Charley had been summoned by her grandfather and given his orders to marry her.

This essence of credibility had not been easy to arrange. Charley had been reluctant. It was an organizational matter to him. "Look," he told her, "I already seen the don on this. I'm involved here, I admit, but it's a family thing between you and your grandfather. You wanna talk to him, talk to him. He wants to talk to me about it, he'll send for me. I don't go walking into the don's house unless he says he wants to see me."

"Charley! Come on! Do this right! I'm forty-one years old, fah-crissake, and I coulda been married a couple dozen times if it wasn't for you."

"Ah, shit!"

"Anyway, what's the big deal? He's a sweet little old man."

Charley shuddered. He took a deep breath and spoke on the heavy exhale. "All right. I'll do it. But you gotta do the talking."

They arrived at the don's house in Charley's black Chevy van. Calorino Barbaccia was on the door, cradling the sawed-off shotgun in his arms as a matter of ceremony, not necessity, because too much international business and industry as well as the political health of the country through its PACs depended on the don staying well and strong for anyone to want to try to break in and zotz him. Calo showed Charley the respect, and, after Charley had asked for his kids by name, for his wife by name, and for his mother, they were shown upstairs to the don's space, which had started out as a room, then had extended into two rooms, and now took over the entire top floor.

19

The don sat reposefully, dreaming his terrible dreams, listening to the record player deliver the prologue to Arrigo Boito's *Mefistofele,* not because he was so crazy about it but because it had been a favorite of Arturo Toscanini's, who had chosen it, with the third act of that opera, for his only postwar performance at La Scala, in 1948, when the don and his wife, now long with the angels, had been there on the only trip back to the old country they ever made.

"Ah," he said as they came in, "the young people." Maerose knelt beside his chair and kissed his hand. Charley bowed stiffly. "Sit, please," the don said. "Have a cookie."

They arranged themselves in small straight-back chairs facing him.

"As it was meant in heaven, Grandfather," Maerose said tremulously, "Charley and I are going to be married."

The don sat straighter. Seriousness replaced the arch gaiety. He looked from Maerose to Charley. It was a look of consequence. Charley had hosed out a lot of fear himself in his time, but what he knew about giving fear compared to what the don knew was at the Cabbage Patch doll level.

"You're gonna have kids?" the don demanded.

Charley nodded automatically. Maerose said, "We want children very much, Grandfather."

"There is something I want you to do for me, Charley," the don said, staring at them.

"Whatever you say, Grandfather," Maerose said shyly.

Charley nodded.

"It is something that will only be between us and the lawyers. Nothing will change. To us, you will always be Charley Partanna."

"What do you want Charley to do, Grandfather?" Maerose asked anxiously.

"I want him to change his name. The way you changed your name to Mary Price twenty years ago so you could be a society decorator. And Eduardo."

Maerose was thrilled and renewed by those words. They meant that her grandfather was getting hooked on respectability, just as she had been steadily guiding him toward it, and the don's hunger for respectability was the trigger that would fire her ambitions and that would allow her to help him forward in shaping and solidifying his goals until, when he died, which had to be sooner rather than later, she would control everything.

Attorneys of a Barker's Hill affiliate firm filed a petition for the Partanna name change two days later in the courthouse of the town of College, Alaska. The petition was granted.

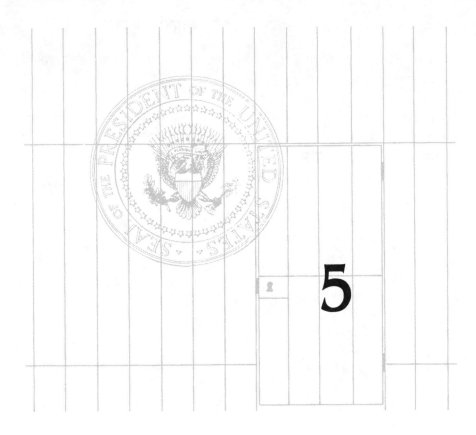

In July 1987, eleven months after Maerose's wedding, her Aunt Amalia, the don's daughter, led the way up the stairs. As they reached the door they could hear the overture from Rossini's *William Tell*, with its beautiful passage for violoncellos, through the heavy door. Amalia knocked lightly and they heard Don Corrado's voice calling out faintly for them to enter. As she went into the huge room, Maerose, once more, was inundated by its decoration. There was hardly a space on any of the three walls that was not covered with heavy gold picture frames in many sizes, which contained such a variety of painted subjects as had not been seen, except in Sicily, where they had multiplied on the walls of aristocrats in the decades before Garibaldi came and the Honored Society had entered its modern phase.

Her grandfather beamed most kindly, not showing any teeth,

working hard to make his eyes simulate feeling. "What a wonderful time," the tiny old man sang, "because it has brought you to me." Maerose knelt before him and kissed his hand.

"Sit down. Sit down," he said gently. "Where are the cookies? You must have a cookie, my dear." Amalia moved the huge plate of cookies from the table at the don's side to the table that stood between them. She kissed Maerose on the cheek and left the room.

Maerose sat primly on a chair at his side, her feet held together, her hands correctly in her lap. She was dressed in dark, simple clothing. Her only jewelry was an old-fashioned brooch that had been her mother's, pinned to her dress at her throat. She was a striking woman, as beautiful as a condor.

He held on desperately to his smile, allowing her to get used to its implied threat, staring at her with what he hoped to be benevolence. "How is your marriage?" he asked in the dialect of Agrigento.

"Rewarding, Grandfather."

"No complaints?"

"Not one."

"I have a complaint."

"A complaint?"

"When are you and Charley gonna have kids?"

"Why shouldn't we have kids?"

"You are married for a whole year! Where are the kids?" he shrilled.

"Of course we're gonna have kids. Why shouldn't we have kids?"

"When you have kids you wanna be somebody for them and you and Charley are somebody."

"Maerose looked away.

"Whatsamatter?"

She took a deep breath as if forcing herself to say something that she had been rehearsing for a long, long time. "In the old country, Grandfather, to be a *mafioso* was to be a man of honor and respect. You were an important part of the life of the country—the people looked up to you, the government and the aristocracy understood that they had to respect you, and you made the history of Sicily."

"Yes?" He was perplexed by her use of the obvious.

"Here we are criminals."

"*Criminals?*" His tiny jaw dropped with disbelief.

She shrugged. "Read the papers."

"What are you trying to tell me?"

Tears welled up in her eyes. "I am saying that I don't want to create children who will be seen as criminals with a father who is the Boss of a *fratellanza* family."

"What else should they be? Your father, my son Vincent, was the Boss before your husband. I, your grandfather, was Boss before that. Your children will be Sicilians who will be born into the Honored Society. That is their good fortune. What else did you think they could be?"

"Do you want your grandchildren to be outcasts?"

"Outcasts? With the other families owning all the legit businesses and industries they own, we control the country."

"You think money is everything?"

"Gimme an example where it ain't."

"Yeah? Do you remember when the Lindbergh baby was kidnapped and Al Capone offered, from the can, to intercede to get the baby back—what did the Lone Eagle say? He said, 'I wouldn't ask for Capone's release if it would save a life,' that's what he said, and I am telling you that because you're always saying what a nice man Capone was."

"Lindy said that?"

"Grandfather—thirty years ago you invented franchising—before McDonald's, before Pizza Hut, before Colonel Sanders. That let you expand your business nationally and internationally, while sharing in the profits with the franchisees. You had operating manuals written on every franchise operation, no matter what it was: labor racketeering, recycled postage stamps, dope, loan sharking. The one on the shit business alone, at 504 pages, is thicker and better than the manual for Burger King. You made it possible for dummies who couldn't find their noses with both hands to put big, tricky operations on a businesslike basis in hundreds of cities everywhere, extending our influence, tripling our income from the royalties, but letting the franchisees take the heat."

"So?"

"Grandfather, lissena me! The family's street operation—Charley's operation—it's too labor intensive! Everybody along the line takes a piece of the action before what is left gets to you. Who needs that?"

24

"Whatta you mean?"

"I mean if you franchise the entire New York East Coast street operation to the Blacks, the Hispanics, and the Orientals, and you take the same high net royalty that you take from the franchise operations around the country, the profits will be absolutely *net* profit—the franchisees will have to live with the cuts their soldiers and capos take and be stuck with handling all the political payoffs. It could deliver a net that is bigger than Charley's street operation delivers to you now."

"How come you know so much?"

"My father was your Boss! My husband is your Boss! I am a certified public accountant and a lawyer! I am in charge of the Cray XMP 48 super computer that Barker's Hill has in Omaha!"

"The computer says this is the way to go?"

"Grandfather—I can show you the printouts—it cannot miss."

"What does this have to do with you and Charley not having kids?"

"You said—I didn't say it—when you have kids you wanna be somebody for them."

"So?"

"So—by franchising Charley's street operation, we take the family out of all the areas which the media and the politicians keep calling the organized crime area. In America, which is not Sicily, that is something that kids are supposed to be ashamed of. So, right away, when I have kids, they don't have to grow up ashamed of their father and their *family*."

"Who's gonna enforce it with these franchises? Who's gonna collect?"

"Just like now on the national basis. Charley sets up a unit."

"If we lease out the street operation, what happens to Charley?"

"Charley moves up to take over Barker's Hill Enterprises."

"You mean after Eduardo retires?"

"Now."

"If Charley takes over Eduardo's spot now, then what happens to Eduardo?"

"You run Eduardo for president in 'ninety-two. He'll have to campaign for two years just like the other twenty-six candidates."

"President of the United *States?*"

25

"Eduardo is the leading financier and industrialist in this country, among other things, and his public relations department, the biggest in the world since the Office of War Information in World War Two, has been reminding the country of that for over twenty years. Eduardo is sixty-nine years old. After two years of campaigning he'll be seventy-one, which most of the American people consider young for a candidate. Even if he doesn't get elected, it can be arranged so that he's appointed attorney general, a profitable spot for us."

"I see what you mean."

"That'll give Charley a year to set up the East Coast franchises and organize the enforcement, and it'll give Eduardo time to break Charley in with my help."

"Mae, lissena me, Charley ain't no Eduardo. Eduardo is a Harvard man, a lawyer, a business school graduate, a leader of the community, or else how could we be talking about running him for president? Charley is—well Charley is not only the Boss on the street but, after all, he had a lot of years as the *vindicatore* of this family."

"How did you get Eduardo started? You gave him a new name, a new nose, and, even before he began Harvard, you got somebody to teach him how to speak funny. That's what you'll do for Charley, and he'll be as respectable in the eyes of the world and in the eyes of his own children as Eduardo. The family will be out of street operations, the net profit on all operations will go way up, and you will make the Prizzi family as respectable as money has insisted that all very rich families be since the dawn of history."

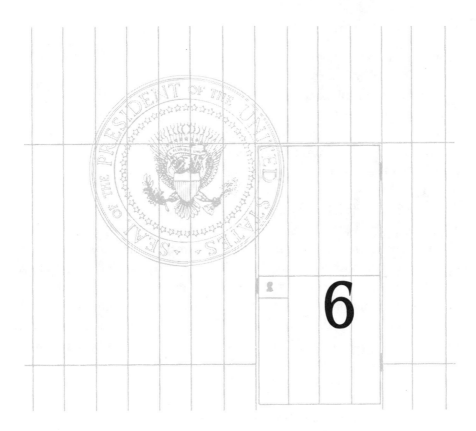

6

Outwardly, Corrado Prizzi was an American because he had the papers to prove it and because he had never failed to go for a buck. But, internally and eternally, he was a Sicilian who kept an open countenance and a closed mind. When he thought of the old country, more and more often in the past few years, he remembered the part he had never really known, the great house of the Duke of Camardi. He remembered the almost suffocating pleasure of not more than eighteen minutes alone in the great rooms of that house one afternoon in a distant summertime.

After years of routine Sicilian suffering, he had earned the privileges that came with being made a member of the Honored Society, but time had taught him that it was not in any way the same as having been born into the nobility or the aristocracy or even as being seen by the world as a *galantuomo*.

He had consolidated his position as a member of the *fratellanza* from the day he had landed in New York with his little family because that was his destiny as much as if he had been born an American. He moved with determination from that day. He had more money sewn into his clothes than any other Sicilian immigrant who landed before him or with him.

Before he left the isolation of Sicilian rocks and wasteland, he had earned and saved $885, more than most Sicilians ever saw in a lifetime. He had earned the money dangerously. From the time he was fourteen until he was almost eighteen, he had voluntarily become a *cancia*, a usually doomed occupation because it meant acting as a middleman between the *contadinos*, who wanted their wheat ground into flour, and the flour mills, owned by the Mafia, which were placed at distant and inaccessible points along the northern coast, fifty to seventy miles away from the sources of the wheat, so that the Mafia who owned the mills could hijack the flour from any peasant who was foolish enough to make his own deliveries.

The *cancia* had to guarantee the safe return of the flour to its owner after undertaking the long journey with the wheat to the flour mill, then to repeat the journey with the milled product back to the client. It was a violent profession, a very tricky one considering the ferocity of the mill owners and the relatively small profit each journey produced.

Corrado had considered all sides of the opportunity, deciding that it would be greedy to hope to keep the *cancia*'s entire fee, so he had laid the proposition out before his mother's brother, the most successful bandit operating out of the adjacent Cammarata mountains. The arrangements were made for the protection his uncle would sell him, so that all deliveries of grain and of flour were made without incident (although Corrado had to accept 80 percent less as his share).

When Corrado married, at seventeen, his father-in-law, Cusomano Pianelli, was a *gabellotto*, a man of respect, who had "leased" the estate of the Duke of Camardi. *Gabellotto* meant tax collector, but that was a euphemism. As a *mafioso* he did not work the land himself but parceled it out among sharecroppers on extortionate terms. The sharecroppers passed down as much of their own misery as they could to the day laborers, the greatest percentage of the population, who were at the bottom of the pile.

Anyone who could learn to read or write could escape all this by joining the Church. Corrado, who could read and write, escaped by succeeding so well as a *cancia* that he was invited to join the Honored Society while he was still seventeen. From the moment he became a *mafioso*, he and his wife began to plan to emigrate to New York to seek their fortune. Corrado had his $865, after paying for the steamship tickets, and the *gabellotto* had endowed his eleventh daughter with a dowry of $100.

In New York in 1914, they moved into the Sicilian community along the easterly side of Flushing Avenue in Brooklyn, not far from the Navy Yard. He had just turned nineteen years old. He had enough to start a storefront bank and, in eight months, enough to start a neighborhood lottery. Both made money, and by 1922 he was in the booze business in a big way, he had the old Palermo Gardens going, and a lot of people who had come over from Sicily looked to him for help and friendship. He had two families that were the same family: he had his wife and two sons, Vincent and Eduardo; his daughter, Amalia; and his orphaned sister, Birdie; plus the Sicilians of Brooklyn; and he had such manliness and humility that he became the natural leader among the *capi di famiglia* of the city.

He had taken his ideal from Baldassare Castiglione: behave with decorum; win the favor of one's superiors and the friendship of one's equals; defend one's honor and make oneself respected without being hated; inspire admiration but not envy; maintain a certain splendor; know the arts of living; be in one's proper place in war, in a salon, in a lady's boudoir, and in a council chamber; live in the world and, at the same time, have a private and withdrawn life.

Through various associations that extended beyond Brooklyn, he was recognized by the Irish and Jewish gangs that operated over the bridge in New York as a factor who could enhance their business.

Corrado Prizzi's art was in controlling individual people. His qualities appealed to man's whimpering need for leadership: the warm/cold combination of affection/fear that he projected, his massive dignity, which was so unexpected from a man who was barely five feet, two inches tall, and the total reflection, mirrored by every attitude of his life, such as of the preposterousness of anything he did being considered criminal, reassured everyone who met him—senators, judges, and police—that he had the power to help them to make an extra buck. All this was possible because deep within himself he saw himself and carried himself both as an aristocrat and as a continuing family service whose organization was ready to provide goods and assistance to all the people to whom such goods and services were denied by law. In that sense he felt as concerned with the welfare of America as his father and uncles before him had been concerned with the welfare of the Sicilian people.

Never one to leap into the abyss, Don Corrado, for almost a year, mulled over his granddaughter's plan to break into what had always seemed to him to be the impregnable fortress of respectability, reading copies of the computer printouts at the end of every week and talking through every part of such a drastic change in course with his *consigliere*, Angelo Partanna, who was the great technician of all street operations. Now, in June 1988, he sat listening to the music, weighing his decision, and thinking of many things.

His granddaughter, Maerose Prizzi, he thought, was effectively his own self-portrait. She thought as he thought despite her college education and her gender. At forty-three, although the don did not know this, she was carrying out the basic plan she had held since she was twelve years old. It was a simple-enough plan, considering that it was intended to control between nine and eleven billion dollars. She had obeyed the wishes of her grandfather by getting high honors from a university education. She had excelled from the beginning when she had started her own interior decorating business, which she had allowed her grandfather to finance so that she could have reason to report to him and keep him involved. She had built the business into an international success with branches in London, Paris, Rome, Beverly Hills, Washington, D.C., and Palm Beach; then, with the help of her grandfather, she had sold the business to her uncle, Edward S. Price, financier, banker, philanthropist, and industrialist, to become his executive assistant within the family's international holding company, Barker's Hill Enterprises, which administered the legitimate businesses that had been bought with money that had been laundered from street operations. She had never taken a wrong step where business was concerned.

Maerose Prizzi's basic plan was to outwait the senior men of her family, and, when they were all dead, or too old to be useful, she would succeed to their various portfolios because she would have made herself the only one qualified to handle such complex and entirely special operations. Once she had gained the total power, she would remain in the background, pulling the strings to drag the ever-accruing power to herself.

The family's income was divided into two parts: the street operation and the legitimate operation. Until she was twenty-two her grandfather had run the street operations. Then her father, Vincent Prizzi, was made *capofamiglia* by her grandfather, who retired to his house in Brooklyn Heights to oversee and expand both operations. The street side handled what the media obediently termed the "organized crime" side of the operations, even though the transactions involved almost two-thirds of the American population: gambling, narcotics, vice, loansharking, labor racketeering, prostitution, pornography, and extortion were only a few of the money-spinners. It also ran the family's casinos in Nevada, Atlantic City, Florida, the Bahamas, Aruba, and London, as well as all numbers and policy. She could hardly believe it but, in the year just reporting, 1987, the American people had bet $198 billion on dog races, horse races, bingo, numbers, poker, casinos, lotteries, and team and individual sports, and that didn't even include bets on elections and the stock market. It had generated $3,938,000,000 worth of gross profits for the Prizzi family alone, plus the bonanza from the popularity of cocaine, marijuana, heroin, and the other divisions, bringing up the gross and net sharply since the early '70s—all of it tax free.

Nonetheless, as Maerose had reasoned, the street operation was extremely labor intensive. Everyone took a piece of the action. The soldiers who did the heavy work took their piece; then the *capos* took theirs, passing what was left up to the Boss to take his end; then the rest went to the Family.

On top of that, about 12 percent of the gross every year had to be held out for federal, state, and local politicians and police as well as a big *puntura* going to judges, prosecutors, cops, and prison officials.

When what was left of the gross was in the Family's hands, it was transferred out of the country to family-owned banks in Switzerland, Panama, the Bahamas, Hong Kong, and the Caribbean, then reinvested in legitimate businesses in the United States by Barker's Hill Enterprises, which owned institutions and organizations in such areas as banking and investment banking; insurance; aerospace, oil, electronics, construction; and long distance telephone and transportation systems. It owned real estate (2,231 downtown and midtown office buildings from coast to coast, as well as 1,612 shopping centers and malls) and took enormous profits from merciless residential rental and condominium sales in cities with a population of over five hundred thousand. It was heavy in cable television, brokerage and underwriting firms; department store and specialty chains; wineries, junk bonds, giant buyouts/takeovers, soft drink companies; all professional sports; high-tech consumer credit; fast-food chains; theatrical and television motion picture production, financing, and distribution; the food industry from agriculture to restaurants to supermarkets; undertaking and cemeteries; heavy media concentrations in television and radio stations, newspapers and magazines, phonograph records, videocassette and book publishing companies; 734 stretch limousine car rental services; racetracks and blood stock breeding farms; parking lots; 32 law firms; 19 certified public accounting firms; 381 hospitals, 1 flower farm, 137 hotels and 3 laundries, which, taken all together, produced an annual gross income of $16,900,000,000 each year.

As CEO of Barker's Hill Enterprises, Edward S. Price was the sole client and in full control (on behalf of the Prizzi Family and the twenty-three other Families of the United States) of Salvatore Penrose, whose Washington, D.C. firm, Brooke, Penrose, & Watt, was the registered lobbyist for the *fratellanza* with the American government, handling all adjudications with the executive, legislative, and judicial branches of each succeeding administration with tact and money. Ed Price also maintained parallel organizations in the state capitals of those states in which *fratellanza* families operated and, in extreme emergencies, was available to intercede at the local, big-city level.

Barker's Hill maintained a public relations department, the Community Affairs Division, which had been working for the past three years to press home the reassuring fact that the Mafia (per se) was living on borrowed time. Don Corrado's counsel had persuaded the *capofamiglias* of most of the larger families to work with the Blacks, Hispanics, and Orientals to lower their profiles while they advanced their legiti-

mate enterprises. The Community Affairs Division also established as-
siduously in the public mind that the true reason the Mafia was finished
was that it was unable to recruit any new blood while, in practice,
Barker's Hill, for one, had the prime pick of the new MBAs who emerged
every year from the universities.

The Prizzis' legitimate acquisitions had been started by Don Corrado in the early 1920s, following his first great successes in supplying
liquor, light wines, and beers as Prohibition got under way. As the
acquisitions merged with each other, elevating the value of each company each time it was bought and sold, the list of Barker's Hill holdings
grew every month until it was impossible to define them and evaluate
them in listing form except by on-line, main-frame computers.

Maerose had anticipated the problem of controlling the street side
of the family business by marrying Charley Partanna, successor to her
slain father, Vincent, and Boss of the family, and, after years of having
cross-examined her father while he was alive, she knew as much about
the street operation as Vincent had. After eight years of working directly at the side of her uncle Edward S. Price, attending night classes
at NYU in accounting, until she was certified, and business law, she
knew everything there was to know about the operation of the colossus,
Barker's Hill Enterprises.

She was consolidating her position with Charley and with her uncle while she waited for her grandfather to die. Her grandfather was a
very, very old man. Even he couldn't last forever. That would leave
only Eduardo to be handled. Charley was no problem. Charley had no
more ambition because, as far as he was concerned, when the don made
him the Boss, he had reached the top of the heap. After long, difficult
study she decided what had to be done with Eduardo. She would lay
the whole thing—well, most of the whole thing—out for her grandfather and let him set Eduardo up.

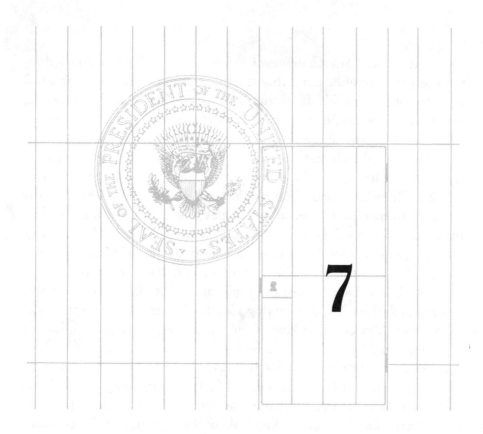

7

The three-story sixteen-room brick house (owned by the Little Sisters of Pain and Pity, a spinoff of the Blessed Decima Manovale Foundation), had been built sixty-one years before at the top of a Brooklyn slope that rolled through a large garden to the riverfront. The holy order rented the house to Don Corrado for ninety-six dollars a month, which took a bite out of his Social Security benefits. The tenant was allowed to rent the furniture and furnishings of the house: bibelots, rugs, exotic chandeliers, and heavy lamps, and all the overstuffed furniture. There were gold fringes everywhere, on everything, hundreds of pictures in gilded frames, a fine phonograph record collection, the dark 1980 Buick automobile in which he rarely rode; all of the suits, shirts, underwear, cravats, shoes, and shoelaces he wore. And he got all this for an additional eleven dollars a month because compassion had shown the gentle nuns that he was an old man with little time left and they planned to use the house as the bingo center for western and southern Brooklyn after his death.

The back of the house faced the river and the jagged teeth of lower Manhattan, a sight that never failed to stimulate the tenant, who saw the island as the lower jaw of a gargantuan alligator whose widely opened mouth had poised an invisible upper jaw far above, which would one day chomp down upon the guilty. He hoped he would never witness this terrible event because some of his best friends were New Yorkers. He was a tiny man, white-haired and seamed, who resembled a chalk-white stalk of dwarf asparagus, having a multi-indented top and no shoulder definition. It was a question whether the eyes in that overused face or the terrible, terrible smile was the more terrifying. Taken all in all, Don Corrado, at least on his exterior, was as lovable as a dropped load of napalm.

Almost one year had gone by after his granddaughter had planted the idea of respectability—her message still hung like incense in the great room that the don inhabited—before he reached its resolution in the summer of 1988. On a July day he sat alone at the dining table, because he could not bear to share food, and made his decision. Very few men, never women, had sat at his table. To be invited to join him for food was a measure of the don's admiration, which few had enjoyed. He dined in the room that had been made off the upstairs kitchen, which had been installed because his daughter, Amalia, was getting too old to carry so many dishes up two flights of stairs. In a lifetime of gluttony he had never known such a cook as Amalia, and sometimes he grew frightened when he tried to imagine what he would eat after she died.

Amalia was a widow. She had two sons: Rocco, who was one of the three *caporegimes* of the Prizzi family, and Pasquale, also known as Arthur Shuland, the name his grandfather had persuaded him to adopt legally, twenty-four years before he had become the lieutenant governor of California. Arthur was the elder son, but more remote, although he was in constant touch with his uncle, Amalia's brother, Edward S. Price, the financier, arbitrageur, philanthropist, arts patron, and CEO of Barker's Hill Enterprises.

Don Corrado ate slowly, which was uncharacteristic, but he was thinking. Whenever he was awake he was plotting, a concentrated form of thinking. The process resembled a *mattanza del tonno* that he had witnessed off the coast at Trapani when he was eleven years old when the tuna, as always, had entered the many-chambered nets to be slaughtered. Some of the fish had been nine feet long and had weighed almost a thousand pounds, like some of the ideas he had when he had done his best and most concentrated thinking.

He finished the second bowl of the inspiring *zuppa di pesce alla Siciliana* with zest, savoring the lingering taste of fennel and thyme. At once he began to eat Amalia's delicious *cavatoni incannati* with its rich sauce that held up chunks of zucchini and fried eggplant, nourishing his thoughts. His thinking as he chewed became more like that of a fisherman who is trawling a line behind a moving boat: each catch of new thought was random and different.

As he started to eat the beet salad on the platter Amalia placed before him, he thought for the two hundredth time of what his grand-daughter had said to him about respectability. He had admired respectability since he had been eleven years old and, one summer, while the family of the Duke of Camardi had been on holiday in Paris, while his father did his business with the *gabellotto*, he had found himself allowed to wander through the main rooms, sitting on the chairs and the sofas, admiring the hundreds of paintings on the walls. It had been the greatest eighteen minutes of his life. That day, and its associations with respectability, had remained with him always.

It had been his duty to get the power, then the money, to insure his continuing influence in a new country. He had known many respectable people, including Pope Pius XII, Arturo Toscanini, Enrico Caruso, and Richard M. Nixon, over his years of power, and they had made indelible impressions upon his susceptibility toward the respectable. He was a student of the nobility and aristocracy of Sicily, keeping his records of them as carefully as any good philatelist might keep a stamp album. Researchers in universities in the old country were retained by him to send information, history, and background from every leaf and branch of Sicilian nobility. The hobby had taken up an important part of the last ten years.

All in all, his favorite granddaughter's appeal to him was, in a sense, a strong and deep appeal to his pariah complex, so ingrained since he had been allowed to wander through the duke's country house. He saw at once, as Maerose had spoken to him, that what she had foretold must be made to happen. Nonetheless, if he agreed with her too quickly he would lose a more important point. She would have to agree to give him great-grandchildren, plus his street operations in New York would have to show a proven capability of yielding a sharply increased net profit.

He marveled at the Sicilian essence of his granddaughter. She had set her trap and made it impossible for him to avoid it. If he wanted great-grandchildren from her, and a sharply increased net profit, he had to give in to her while insuring that his blood and his line would be accepted everywhere in the years ahead, allowed to become leaders of the most respectable people in the United States of America. Besides, it could all bring about his only surviving son's becoming the attorney general of the United States—which could be very good for business.

His thoughts changed to this son, Eduardo, whose name and nose had been changed to Edward S. Price before he had entered Harvard. Eduardo was a great mountain of respectability who sat on the boards of the great museums, opera companies, libraries, two great universities, twenty-three banks, and more than sixty-seven American corporations. Eduardo held more honorary degrees and titles than any American in history excepting Herbert Hoover. His listing in *Who's Who in America* ran on for almost three pages.

The don considered the past and the future carefully. He listened to the plea of history, to the immutable law that stated that great amounts of money and property demand respectability, and he bowed his head to the inevitable. It had been slightly different in the old country. There, as here, the people who had been able to enforce sudden ownership of large tracts of property—if they also had the arms to persuade the locals to work the property for them—became dukes and princes. There, however, the *mafiosi* were also men of respect, even if untitled: lawgivers, an honorable society that merely chose to take a different path to power and riches. What could be the objection to exploiting one's power over other men? Here, in America, it was a way of life except that it was done differently.

In the past few months, Don Corrado had aided his digestion by thinking about that law of nature that demanded inexorably that respect be delivered unto money and property. He thought of his descendants, all Americans, and how he could make certain that they would take their places among the *acknowledged* leaders of the United States—a marked difference from the unacknowledged—as he had already arranged to happen for his son Eduardo.

Thinking of Eduardo and of his place among the mighty suddenly clarified for the don what he had been slow to realize: that he had been looking at the problem from his own narrow perspective, that of the old Sicilian, still enamored of the local duke. His granddaughter had seen it from the other, wider side, Eduardo's side, and to her it had become vividly clear. His organization, the Prizzi Family and its international branches, had functioned as part of the vast marketplace that was the world, offering goods and services to its customers, the consumers. The laws of supply and demand, which defined any national marketplace, had ruled the relationship. Supermarkets did not sell cocaine. Department stores did not make book on the National Football League.

Nonetheless, he reasoned with himself as he chewed and swallowed the delicious red beets, trying to anticipate the next course Amalia would lay before him, a certain mystique had come to surround all the transactions of his family, which was due, without doubt, to the old-time Warner Brothers movies; the television about Capone, a Neapolitan; the occasional congressional investigation; the ever-cooperative media; and many paperback novels, which gave his organization a certain glamorized aura but which barred the way to respectability within the national community.

Instinctively, he had been on the right path when he had remade his son's name, nose, and speech before Eduardo had entered Harvard. With total clarity he saw that, if his blood line were to realize its greatest meaning so that full use of Prizzi wealth and power could be developed, he must *extend* the method he had used to legitimize Eduardo. He would insure that generation after generation of his seed would embrace the total potential of their power by becoming wholly acceptable, even socially desirable, to all of the voters and consumers who were the rest of the North American population. When he had laid down the rules defining the actual marriage of his granddaughter to Charley Partanna, he had done the right thing by repeating the first step of Eduardo's program—telling Charley that he must change his name.

Maerose's way of allowing Eduardo to step down gracefully, without loss of dignity or honor, by running for the American presidency, while at the same time she was providing for Eduardo's successor was the most brilliant stroke. Not that Eduardo could get elected—he was tainted by being an Eastern establishment banker. But it would keep him busy campaigning for two years and after that, Maerose had been right again, they would see that he became attorney general.

But there still was one big problem.

Maerose's husband, Charley, didn't have any of her instant respectability. He was a *sicario*. When the family of Ciccio Saporita, in Cincinnati, had tried to cheat on the royalties they owed for the fake credit card operation in their territory, Charley had gone out there and had iced the grandmothers of the heads of the Saporita family: Ciccio Saporita's own grandmother, his *consigliere*'s, and the grandmothers of his two *caporegimes*. The cheating had not only stopped right away, it had given the lesson to everyone else they did business with.

But, and it could be a big but, Charley had done the job on so many people in the course of the years of his work that there might be big mouths who would say, if he put Charley in Eduardo's slot, that Charley had in fact done the job on too many people ever to be entirely respectable. But Don Corrado refused to believe that the power of rumor was greater than the power of money. Surely rumor could not hinder the inexorable command that a man be respectable if he was told to be respectable.

Twenty-six of the don's descendants had achieved respectability on their own, without help or hindrance from him, but, excepting his son, Eduardo, and his grandson Arthur Shuland, the lieutenant governor of California, they were only people, not the kind anyone would expect to carry on a line. They had married legitimate people and had had two generations of children without a single police record among them. But only his granddaughter Maerose had the cunning, the ferocity, the singleminded ruthlessness, and the desire to insure a real Prizzi ascendancy. Eduardo had it, of course, but Eduardo was too old, and not only a widower but childless, for consideration in carrying on the Prizzi line.

Don Corrado built upon that promise of respectability that great wealth made to all of its owners. He could see that it could be a wonderful thing. Look at Eduardo: square people would practically lay down in front of him so that he could have a softer something to walk upon and not get his shoes dirty. Look at his grandson Arthur Shuland, a lieutenant governor of one of the biggest states, who was absolutely sure to be swept into the U.S. Senate whenever he decided he was ready.

Amalia removed the empty plate in front of him.

"How old am I now, Amalia?" he asked her.

"You are ninety-two, Poppa. And you never looked better."

He nodded at that and at the large plate of his second pasta of the day, the *chi vruoccolu arriminata,* a beautiful assembly of twisted *maccheroncelli* with broccoli, anchovies, tomato sauce, pine nuts, onions, and raisins, all of it entirely the most delicious part of every Sicilian's heritage, which achieved the heights of heaven because of the sauce—garnished with eggplant and sweet red peppers—made from very ripe tomatoes with basil, anchovy, olive oil, and garlic. How could they say Sicilians were Italians, he wondered? Italians would never think of making a tomato sauce like this. Sicily had been Italian for only a hundred and thirty years, fahcrissake, he thought. It had been Phoenician, Carthaginian, Greek, Roman, Vandal, Ostrogoth, Arabic, Norman, German, French, and Spanish for fourteen hundred years before that. And what would have happened to Sicilian food if it hadn't been for the Arabs? he asked himself.

His son Vincent was dead so nothing could make Vincent respectable. That would have been an impossible job anyhow, he agreed with himself. It was impossible to make his daughter, Amalia, more respectable, in the same way that it would be to make a cathedral more respectable. Amalia's son Rocco had decided to become a hoodlum so there was not much to work with there. Amalia's daughter was married to a chiropractor in Iowa and her children had scaled heights in the 4-H Clubs, God bless them. Twenty-six members of the family were lawyers, managers, accountants, technicians, or publicity people at Barker's Hill, and no one could get more respectable than that.

That left his two granddaughters: Maerose and Teresa. Teresa was respectable in London, Ontario, where he had set up her husband in a solid dental prosthetics business. But the sister, Maerose, who on the outside looked like she was the most respectable of all of them, had too much of his own character. Of all of them, she was *mafiosa;* there was something so perpetually devious and eternally patient about the woman that he felt, in a rush, if respectability for the family were to be accomplished in the few moments of time left to him, because it stood to reason that he couldn't live forever, he had to begin now to pave the avenues to make it accessible.

"Amalia, my dearest child," he said after swallowing dreamily, "ask Angelo to come to see me."

"Yes, Poppa."

Angelo Partanna, seventy-seven years old, had been his friend and adviser for sixty years. Angelo did not need a mantle of respectability. He was immensely dignified, beautifully put together, and pitiless. Angelo was *mafiusu*, the heartless Sicilian *omo di onore*, when it came to business. His son, Charley Partanna, Mae's husband, had all his life tried to better himself, to be more American than the president of the United States. But he wasn't sure Charley had any feelings about respectability. Chances were he thought he was already respectable because he had a high school education. Charley was a slow thinker, but if everything was explained to him clearly, if all the pioneering thinking was laid out in front of him and he was told that this was his duty to the family to carry out what was required, there was no man alive who could or would deliver the results the way Charley would do it. And most certainly after Charley had the future explained to him by his wife, after he and Angelo had laid down the major line to Charley, there was no other way for Charley to go except the right way.

Four things had to be done, the don decided with a feeling of release, to accomplish a meaningful plan: 1) he must make those of his people respectable who wanted it; 2) Eduardo, who was certainly ready to be retired, had to be kicked up the stairs so that Charley could succeed him; 3) Charley's past work had to be cleaned up; and 4) Charley and Maerose had to have some children so that they could succeed Charley and so that their children could succeed them. What else was respectability for?

Amalia took the bare plate away and placed before him the platter of *coniglio in agrodolce*, the dish from his home province of Agrigento, rabbit in a sweet-sour sauce that was so different from the *agrodolce* found in Italy. The magnificent sauce had pieces of eggplant, celery, olives, capers, roasted almonds, honey, lemon, and vinegar. The Arabs

41

hadn't wasted their two hundred years in Sicily for nothing, the don salivated proudly as he attacked the plate.

"I called Angelo, Poppa." Amalia, a *buffona*, a woman with a not unpleasing moustache, said.

The don nodded.

"He'll be here at half past four, right after your nap."

"Good," the don said. "No telephones, dear child. Not even the White House."

8

Calorino Barbaccia, a short, dark man of abnormal physical strength, tripled as a front doorman and *lupara* specialist as well as acting as the don's valet. He was a retired shtarker who had made the occasional hit as a standby replacement during the annual summer holidays of the regular workers. He was a handy fellow with a garrote or a pillow when close quiet work was demanded.

Calo removed the old man's bed socks tenderly, rubbed his feet either pink or until feeling returned to them, whichever was first, and gradually dressed the upper half of him while he was still in bed. Then, with a series of practiced, quick movements, he slid off the don's pajama bottoms and slid on, in succession, his long woolen underwear and his trousers. He swung the short, frail legs off the bed and pulled on the woolen socks, then the tiny, soft shoes made of vici kid.

43

"How is your boy?" Don Corrado asked.

"He's still in solitary, *padrino.*"

"How can we help him, Calo? The most important thing to him is beating up on policemen, now prison guards. Every time we have it set to have him transferred to the farm, he sneaks up on a guard."

"That is *smorzando, padrone.*"

"More like *spiegando.* Why don't we have somebody dope him for a couple of weeks? At least until we can get him out of the constant solitary and on to the farm if he's too doped to wanna beat up on a guard."

"That's wonderful, *padrino.* That's terrific! Can you do that for my boy?"

"Starting tomorrow. Get me to my chair."

Calorino lifted the don as if he were a bag of toy balloons and carried him across the room to the chair, which half-faced the river and the great up-thrusting teeth of lower Manhattan. "What time is it?" the don asked.

"Half past four, Excellenza."

"Send Angelo Partanna in."

Angelo sat in a comfortable chair facing the don, not speaking because he had not initiated the meeting.

"Have a cookie?" the don asked, indicating the several large dishes of cookies and confections on the table at his right.

"I think a cigar."

"You got one on you?"

"No."

"Calo!"

Calorino appeared in the doorway. "Yes, boss?"

"Bring cigars." He turned to Angelo. "You want some grappa?"

"To tell you the truth, Corrado, I'd like a nice glass of iced tea."

Calorino offered the opened box of Mexican cigars to Angelo, who selected one from the center, where it had been exchanging aromas with the cigars on either side, bit off the end, spat it into Calorino's palm, and accepted a light.

"I'll get the tea," Calorino said and left the room.

The don spoke generally about the hot weather and the traffic on the river, so Angelo knew he was waiting for the tea to come and for Calo to go before he would say what was on his mind. "How's Charley?" the don asked.

"Fine."

"Is Mae pregnant yet?"

"He didn't say nothing."

"He woulda said?"

"Yeah. Anyways, Amalia woulda heard from Mae herself."

"What are they doing when they go to bed? They are married two years! I had two kids when I was married two years."

"It's in God's hands, Corrado."

"Lissena me, Angelo. No more hanging around. She's gotta go to a couple of specialists and find out what they're doing wrong."

Calorino brought the iced tea: a tall glass, a tub of ice, and a pitcher of tea and ice cubes with lemon slices floating on top. He prepared the tea elaborately and served it to Angelo. He bowed to both men and left the room.

"So?" Angelo said.

"We gotta do a lot of thinking, Angelo."

"Just give me your general direction, Corrado."

"We all gotta take our chances, okay? But I spent my whole life figuring out how to beat the odds. The future keeps crowding us, Angelo; then all of a sudden there is no floor to walk on—we're not even here anymore—so while we're here, we gotta concentrate on beating the odds."

"Just give me an idea of what you got in mind, Corrado."

"I'm gonna make a will. Not actually a will, with a lawyer and all the tax problems, but a statement that you and Amalia and maybe the Papal Nuncio will witness, that tells what has to happen when I'm not here to make sure."

Angelo nodded. Angelo did not deny the don's possible death.

"I'm gonna put in the will I don't want no big funeral. Not even a small one. Just you and Charley and Mae and Amalia and Eduardo."

"Whatta you wanna do a thing like that?"

"I wanna be in the ground before the papers get it. I wanna keep the TV and the FBI away. We gotta protect Eduardo and Charley. *Capeesh?*"

"Whatta you mean—protect?"

"I don't want Eduardo standing in front of no television cameras at a funeral where all the families in the country are there. I got some big ideas for Eduardo. And Charley is gonna be the next Eduardo after that, don't forget it."

Angelo shrugged.

"If you can figure out how to do it," Don Corrado said as if he hadn't already figured out the whole thing, "I'm gonna say in the will that Charley is the one who is gonna run Eduardo's thing."

"Figure out how to do it? Like whatta you mean?"

"For starters how do we get Eduardo out?"

"Out?"

"I already figured that part. That part is easy—we run him for president in 'ninety-two."

"*President?*" Angelo blinked. "Eduardo?"

"It will take up every minute of his time."

"The election's four years away."

"We need a year for Charley to do some work that I'm gonna tell you about and for Eduardo to break him in on the quiet. Then we need the three years for Eduardo to campaign all over the country."

"But, Jesus—"

"Don't be so nervous. He ain't gonna get it. He'll be one of the nineteen candidates they run for president to keep the people's mind off the real issues. In the old country they have nineteen parties each with two candidates; here we have nineteen candidates and two parties. Go figure it. We'll let Eduardo run like third. He'll have the honor."

"But what platform does he run on? Eduardo has had to work every side of the street."

"So he'll run on the platform that if he's elected, he's gonna resign in favor of Ron and Nancy, fahcrissake!" the don snarled. "Who cares what platform he runs on?"

"Listen—there's nothing wrong with that platform. It's a great platform. Jesus, what a sign-off for Eduardo. He'll cream."

"Then we will make him attorney general."

"A key job in law enforcement no matter how you look at it." He

46

understood at last what he had just said. "Holy shit, Corrado! Sensational!"

"The problem is Charley taking over," the don said. "After thirty-five years, Eduardo is a pillar of this country."

"Wait a minute. If Charley takes over from Eduardo, who takes over from Charley?"

"Nobody. That's the beauty part. We won't need the street operation. We're gonna franchise all the action to whoever bids highest, division by division."

"Corrado, lissena me. It won't work. Franchising things like the recycled postage stamps and credit cards, or race horses or shopping malls, even the orgy opportunities, is one thing, but that ain't gonna work in New York."

"Why not?"

"New York ain't the Big Apple for nothing. This is where it is. New York turns over more than alla the rest of them together. You tell the New York families you wanna franchise here and they'll think you're through and they'll move in on you."

"No."

"Why not?"

"Because I'm gonna have Charley set up a regime of collectors—enforcers—a coupla hundred soldiers, all workers—under Santo Calandra so the franchisees are gonna know, if they think they can fuck around, that they got a real war. They are gonna see that—why fight for it when you can buy it? Everybody's rich. We got the biggest territories—Brooklyn, Queens, Long Island, and Staten Island. We franchise it and let the other guy knock himself out. The real problem is Charley taking over from Eduardo."

"Why is that a problem?"

"Eduardo's an elder of three religions, an industrialist, a philanthropist, a leading banker. He's a patron of the arts, a lawyer, a college man, a Mercedes owner, a society leader—and everything else that a great front man has to be. But Charley is the problem."

"How do you mean?"

"But he's your son and he's married to my granddaughter. Eduardo has gotta be over sixty-five, maybe seventy," the don said, thinking it

47

all through seconds before he said it. "Who else am I gonna have run the ownership of about thirty-two percent of this country—only five points down on the Japanese—except my granddaughter and Charley—some stranger?"

"But how do you mean Charley is a problem to take over Eduardo's spot?"

"Fahcrissake, Angelo, Charley is a Boss. Charley was the *vindicatore* of the family for twenty years. Those things could carry over."

"But if we tell Charley to do it, he does it."

"You remember Eduardo when he was in high school?"

"Sure."

"The big nose, the way he talked only Brooklyn? That doesn't seem possible now, does it?"

"Well—no."

"We changed him into a Mayflower American, and we changed his name to Edward S. Price. We found him that speech teacher. He was a natural learner. We told him where to buy his suits. It was no miracle, Angelo, it was just good planning. It was cutting the odds on the future."

"You mean—"

"Look, Henry Garrone, my nephew, handles our business in Zurich. Charley goes there and Henry sets him with a good face doctor, then a top dentist, and we bring a speech teacher in. I never told you, but before him and Mae got married, I had him change his name."

"Charley changed his *name?*"

"Yeah. Listen, it was good thinking."

"So what is his new name?"

"It ain't Sicilian, Angelo."

"So what is Charley's new name?"

"Charles Macy Barton."

"Jesus!"

"I'm not talking about a new face, just a face changed here and there maybe, like the name, and maybe his prints, so none of the media people or some cop can make him if they see him. Maybe a little bald or he'll wear glasses or something. Charley knows how to run people, so when we put him in Eduardo's slot all he'll be doing is running a couple of hundred managers, nothing for Charley. When it comes to the new stuff that's gotta come up and has to be decided, he'll have Maerose to talk it over with. She's had nine years with Eduardo. How can he miss?"

"I can figure out the Barton part—that's like Partanna—but where did you get the Macy?"

"It was Mae's idea. And a very sweet thought. Your wife's name was Macellaro—right?"

"Yeah."

"So that's where the Macy part comes from."

"That really is a sweet thought."

"But I ain't making a move till they have a kid."

"The whole move depends on that?"

"What are you gonna do? It's the name of the game. What is immortality if people don't keep having kids? Lissena me, Angelo—"

"Yeah?"

"The will I made, the letter—"

"Yeah?"

"I want you to swear the one very important thing so you can do what I want after—if—I go down the tube."

Angelo crossed himself. "Corrado, please—"

"I want you to make sure that there is no big public funeral. Just the close family. Nobody else. *Capeesh?*"

"Sure. Absolutely."

"Swear it. Take an oath on your only son's head."

"I swear it. No big funeral."

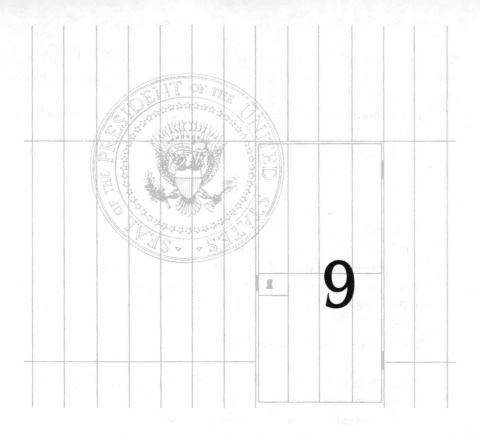

9

Charley and Maerose Partanna had had a long and stormy courtship of nineteen years, but no matter what had happened to them, and plenty had happened, no matter how long the separations, they always found their way back together again. Charley was aware of her, as Vincent's daughter, by the time she was five years old and he was in his teens. They had come together formally at a birthday party for Mae's sister, Teresa, at the old Palermo Gardens, in 1967. They had had a fairly involved affair then, but, due to circumstances which were (probably) unfair, Maerose had been exiled from Brooklyn by her father for nearly ten years, because she got drunk at the party for her engagement to Charley and ran off with some guy to Mexico. She was barred until her father happened to get zotzed. It was toward the end of the exile that she and Charley had seen each other again, but, what with one thing and another—like Charley getting married to a California woman, then the woman dying tragically on him—they didn't get a chance to spend much time together. But, throughout the exile, they had seen each other at family weddings, christenings, and funerals.

Really finding each other had been a slow, even excruciating, process. Charley had tended to "lose himself" with a flock of other women, undoubtedly trying to forget the wife whom death had torn out of his arms, meeting and seeming to become infatuated with either eight or ten, or thirty or forty, young women in such a succession that their names and faces had become a blur, even to him. Through all of this, perhaps from the day she met him, Maerose seemed to have been in love with her own sense of who and what Charley was. By force of will, by a stamina that far exceeded his stamina, and keeping in mind whatever it was she needed to keep in mind about what Charley Partanna could provide for her special needs, Maerose gradually surrounded him, as the Sioux had surrounded General Custer at Little Big Horn. When they finally married, to the utter satisfaction of Don Corrado, Maerose was forty-one years old, and perhaps somewhat rigid in the pelvis to deliver children, and Charley was forty-nine, perhaps somewhat rigid in the head for adjustment to marriage, but despite the flight of their youth and the drawbacks of long familiarity, it was a marriage that had been made in heaven.

Maerose was a woman who had matured with style. At twenty-two she had resembled a Tuareg queen in the deep Sahara at the time of the Crusades, surrounded by an ardency of knights who had wandered from their crusade to find her, deep in the desert, to seek her out and join her mystery. Now, at forty-three, after ten years of exile in Manhattan, after twenty-one years of flinging herself at the rock of Charley Partanna, and a certain amount of secret champagne, she resembled rather a hunting falcon dressed by Balenciaga, causing that great man to weep with gratification wherever he was, as he looked down and wondered where he had taken the right turning. She was elegantly predatory. She was singleminded, and she hunted only for the food for her power.

Maerose had a magnificent nose, passionate, yet merciless; eyes so glorious in their brightness and liquidity, in the fish-shaped, caramelesque calm of their implacable stare that surely they had been re-

51

touched, repolished, and replaced before the final gift of life had been bestowed upon her. She wore clothes as a work of art by Caravaggio wears paint. Her fingers were of such length and her hands of such slenderness and lightness of touch that Charley told her, adoringly, that she could have been one of the great cannons of all time and he meant it from the heart.

With all this external perfection, Maerose Partanna had an inner life that combined the objectivity of Albert Einstein with the brisk efficiency of Attila the Hun. Most of the time, which is to say between the ages of eighteen months and the present, she was less than straightforward because not only did she admire her grandfather, Don Corrado Prizzi, but indirection, subtlety, and labyrinthian deviousness were to her as if they were parts of the oath of the Girl Scouts of Sicily, and, deep within her spirit, Mae wanted to prove with her life that she was more Sicilian than her grandfather had ever been.

People who live with each other are seen by outsiders to be coping with each other's immutable traits when, all the time, they are merely intent upon developing their own unchangeable foibles. Any outsider would have thought that the union of Maerose Prizzi and Charley Partanna would fall short of any possibility of success, but, because they were so different, it was a perfect marriage: each supplied what the other lacked.

Maerose was quick and informed. Charley was slow-thinking and had a suspicion of information because, in the practice of his business, people had seldom proved to operate the way the instructions on their package said they would. Charley was chary of commitment. Maerose was its agent. They had approached their marriage with considerable circumspection, perhaps needing to insure themselves that their judgment was correct, but more likely needing to get any number of other things done before they settled down to domestic life. The fact that they had overdone this caution was characteristic of both of them because Maerose found it almost impossible to make any decision that did not immediately advance her in terms of power, and Charley was just as indecisive unless something happened, anything at all, that could release him from the chores of his daily existence into one or another (and yet another) steamy Eden of romance. Charley was a ruthless romantic. Maerose was a devout realist. Maerose was brutal in conception, Charley in execution, and he had done a lot of those.

When they were both sure that, by marrying each other, they would get what they had to have, they entered into holy matrimony at a high Anglican Church of England service, in Manhattan—a happenstance that the groom hoped his parish priest, Father Passanante, never found out about, entirely because his don had ordered it—in which the bride had exulted because of the presence of her uncle, Edward S. Price, at his father's bidding, giving the bride away, with the preeminent Washington lawyer, S. L. Penrose, standing as best man, and, somehow by some miracle, the lady general of the Salvation Army at Mae's side as her maid of honor, all resulting in the formation of the true Prizzi dynasty, an all-reaching reality to house and legitimatize the Prizzi billions. At the benign intonation of an Episcopal dominie, she had been transformed from Mary S. Price to Mrs. Charles Macy Barton. The announcement on the *New York Times* society page stated that the groom, chief executive officer of Lavery, Mendelson, the great Wall Street investment banking house, was a descendant of Clara Barton, founder of the Red Cross, and Captain Richard H. Macy, founder of the great department store that bore his name. Lavery, Mendelson was a wholly-owned subsidiary of Barker's Hill Enterprises, which was a wholly-owned subsidiary of Corrado Prizzi.

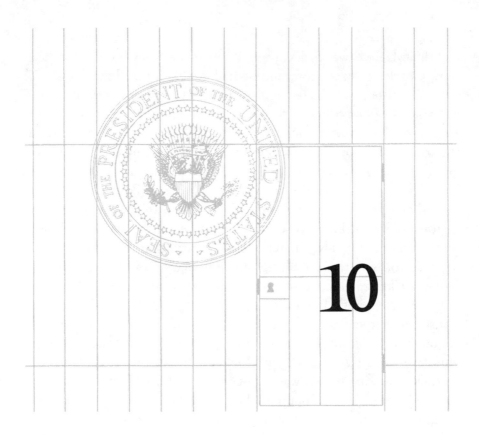

10

Charley Partanna had not, in fact, iced the grandmothers of the Saporita family in Cincinnati. Almost the entire muscle of that family—the contractors, the arm twisters, and the leg breakers—came from a family that had served the Saporitas since 1923. Their family name was Nonna. Beppino Nonna was the Saporitas' first enforcer. He had twelve sons, nine of whom followed in their father's style. It happened to be that the word *nonna* meant grandmother in Italian so, when the news came back to Don Corrado through Angelo Partanna that Charley had scored the four top Nonnas of the Saporita family, thereby easing the whole franchise-royalty problem, the don, either because he had gone temporarily ga-ga, or because the idea had appealed to him, always remembered the story to Charley's disadvantage.

This embarrassed Charley, but he had made it a rule decades before never to contradict the don. If anybody else figured they could make a joke out of the thing, Charley broke his elbow. Charley Partanna was 100 percent a rule book player.

He was a large man, built like a moving van, with a face like a slab of concrete on which the company retained to draw the graffiti on New York subway cars had drawn heavy eyebrows, small eyes, a fleshy nose, and a straight line for a mouth. His teeth were undistinguished, even shabby, as if he had a mouthful of Roquefort. The overall effect made him look as if he were on the hard side, but that was strictly an acquired characteristic. Charley had practiced looking hard and throwing out fear ever since he was ten years old. He had worked with the mirror in his father's bedroom, which used to be his mother's mirror. His mother was with the angels.

Charley wasn't hard, at least not hard in the sense that hard meant unfeeling. He was an organization man who ran his life by an unwritten book of rules that had been handed to him by his father. Charley obeyed orders to the letter. As he rose in the family's command structure from the day he had made his bones on Gun Hill Road in the Bronx when he was thirteen (and using him to do the job was the only way the Prizzis could get anybody close to Little Phil Terrone), he grew more and more doctrinaire. He had become a made man in the *fratellanza* when he was seventeen. From the day his mother died, Charley lived and ate with his father, listened to his father, spoke like his father, and, because the only thing his father was interested in was the environment, that became Charley's life.

Charley learned numbers from his father. Both the Partannas could read a balance sheet like it was a McGuffey's Reader, or like Leopold Stokowski lying in a hammock and browsing through a Paganini score.

He had learned to cook and keep a clean house from his mother. When the don retired, his son Vincent became Boss and Charley was made Underboss and was invested as the family's *vindicatore*.

His devotion to duty had made him Boss when Vincent, a ruffian's ruffian, had inevitably been zotzed. Charley was firm but fair, as the rule book states for leaders everywhere. Also, his acquired bearing, to say nothing of his past performance, scared the shit out of every *capo* and soldier in the family.

If Charley was a slow thinker, he was a tenacious one. Not anyone's typical man-of-action, he was thinking all the time. Within the American culture, which was itself studded with Sicilian mores, he had found a philosophy in the pages of women's magazines, which he had started to read for household hints, then had continued to read for their wisdom. Not an originator, he could carry out orders with the dedication and mindlessness of a lieutenant colonel of the U.S. Marine Corps. It could have been that his reputation for having delivered some sixty-seven hits for the family in his time, probably an exaggeration, alone made him attractive to women, but whoever thought that way was wrong. Women, by and large, wanted what other women wanted. Because he was a tender romantic, and possibly combined with the implied mastery that comes with a reputation as a top zotzer, women wanted him. It was probably because Charley was a romantically tender man who, until he had passed the first great energies of his youth, had been so taken with, and so serviceable to, the women who had reached out for his heart that Maerose had taken so long to marry him. She had lost him to eight other women (known to her) during their nineteen-year engagement, something that could have broken the heart of a less resilient woman, but now that Charley was relatively exhausted from romancing so many other women, and because he was preoccupied with the administrative problems that came with running the street operations of a family as complex as the Prizzis, and because her grandfather looked as if he were ready to make the big decision when she put it to him, Maerose entered into the sanctity of marriage.

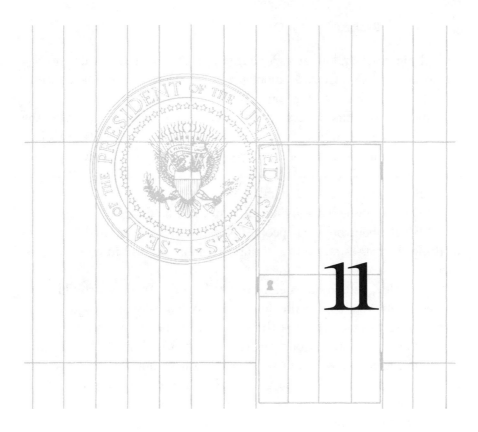

11

At 8:30 A.M. on July 11, 1988, which Amalia Sestero explained to them was St. Gomer's Day, the saint invoked against hernias, the patron saint of glovemakers, Angelo and Charley Partanna were summoned to Don Corrado's house. She led them up the two flights of stairs to the don's enormous room, knocked at the door, opened it, then left them. The don waved them absentmindedly into the room as, simultaneously, he pursued his hobby, the lineages of the nobility of Sicily from the Arab invasion to the arrival of the American troops in the western end of the island in World War II, which had so vigorously reestablished the Honored Society after it had been almost wiped out by the Italian government.

"Come in, come in," the don called out gaily, then ignored them for the next twenty minutes. Angelo Partanna lighted a cigar. Charley looked out the window at two youths mugging an old woman on the esplanade until Don Corrado announced his readiness to open the meet.

"I got two big jobs for you, Charley," he said. "First, we're gonna franchise all the East Coast operations either to our own people, the other New York families, or to the Blacks, Hispanics, and the Orientals, which means, deal for deal, you gotta scare them shitless so we can be sure of collections."

"Blacks, Hispanics, Orientals?"

"What's wrong with giving the other guy a chance?"

"What about our own people? We got eleven hundred out there working their asses off and nine hundred more around in case we need them."

"Charley, lissena me. Before you talk to the Blacks or the Hispanics, certainly you'll offer the franchises to our people and, if they're ready to put up more money than the Blacks or Hispanics, then they get it. I don't needa tell you, loyalty comes first with me. The big thing is—whoever gets it we gotta be sure we collect our end so out of the people we got out there, you gotta hold out a couple of hundred soldiers—from the rest who'll be absorbed by the new guys—for enforcement and collections."

"Don't worry about the collections, *padrino.* Anybody takes a franchise from us, I make the collections."

"That's the second thing I want from you, Charley. After you set the franchises with solid people and after you set up the special enforcement to make the collections—you don't make any more collections yourself—I want you to move up into Eduardo's job."

"*Me?*" Charley's jaw dropped. "What about Eduardo?"

"We're gonna run him for president."

"But—*whaaat?*"

"Don't worry. In the end he'll settle for attorney general. But what you gotta do is get us outta the street operation. I want strong franchise deals for every piece of action we got going for us—not like the national franchises, where we were choosy about what we let them have—but franchises for everything we got going on the East Coast and maybe Colombia, Turkey, and Asia. All we're gonna have left is the enforcement organization you're gonna set up."

"The operating manuals for every racket we operate outta New

58

York are all mimeographed and ready, Charley," Angelo Partanna said. "They run more than five hundred pages each, and they make it just like the franchisee has signed on to run a Taco Bueno. Anybody can run a franchise if they follow the manual. You just gotta sign up the franchisees and put the fear into them, then line up the *picciotti* you want to do the enforcing and collecting."

"And a solid worker to run it," the don said.

"Run it? I'll run it." Charley wasn't the quickest guy in the world to catch on.

"After you set it all up," the don said patiently, "you are off the street."

"Off the street? I won't be Boss no more?"

"Boss of what? There won't be no street operation. You wanna be Boss of enforcement and collection? You're an executive. Execute. No pun intended."

"Charley, lissena me what the don is saying to you," his father tried to explain. "You are going up to the top, to where the big money is, you're gonna run Eduardo's operation. You're gonna triple your money." Charley was already banking 6 percent of the street operation and 2 percent of the national franchise operation in eleven safe banks overseas. He had no idea of how much money he had.

"What do I know about Eduardo's operation?"

"You know how to run the people who run everything Eduardo runs," the don snarled. "And whatta you needa know about the inside over there? Your wife can tell you anything you needa know. She's been Eduardo's assistant for nine years."

"She's smart, Charley, we don't needa tell you that," Angelo said.

"What you needa tell me is how we're gonna get away with this. Eduardo is a big man in every department. The media and the cops know me. What are they gonna say when I take over an operation the size of Eduardo's?"

"Charley, on paper you are already CEO of Lavery, Mendelson in Wall Street."

"I never been on Wall Street in my life. They'd make me the first day."

"That's the third thing," the don said.

"There's a third thing?"

"After you set the franchises up, you and Mae are going to Europe. Harry Garrone is lining up a good face doctor, maybe also a dentist, and Mae is looking now for somebody to show you how to talk like Eduardo talks."

"Jesus, *padrino!*"

"A couple of tailors will come over to Switzerland from London, and in eight months, a year, you'll be ready to come back to New York to take over Eduardo's spot."

"What happens to the real me?"

"The papers will run it that you got pneumonia or something and that it put you under. We'll give you a big sendoff and everybody will forget all about you. No offense meant."

Charley gave a little shrug. "Well, if that's what you want, that's what I'm gonna do, but no wonder today is the saint's day for the patron saint of hernias."

As they drove away from the don's house in Charley's van, Pop said, "Whatta you think of this franchise idea for New York?"

"It's hard to say."

"It can't work. They'll go along with it. They'll pay the advance because Corrado is who he is, but it ain't gonna work. They'll run with it and they'll laugh at us when we come for the royalties."

"But why would the don make a mistake like that?"

"Because he's hung up on this respectability thing. I can't do nothing with him. That's all he wants. He's through with the street operation, throwing away all that money just so that everybody can look up to his descendants. Well, what the hell. He made the biggest score of alla them in his time. I tried, but I can't change his mind; there ain't nothing I can do about it. So we gotta go with it."

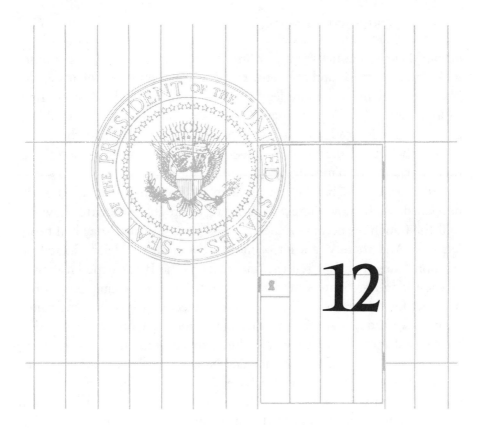

12

To clear his thinking, Charley scrubbed the kitchen floor at the Matsonia on East Thirty-seventh Street, in New York, where Maerose had had an apartment for over twenty years and where he and Mae lived. While he scrubbed, Maerose watched "The Wodehouse Playhouse" on PBS in the living room to keep them current on perfect speech.

Charley wasn't exactly confused, because the don had never told him to do something that he knew Charley couldn't do, but he was having trouble imagining himself at the head of Barker's Hill Enterprises. It was bigger than Exxon and more complex than AT&T and, Maerose had told him, it had 9,208 senior executives, lawyers, and accountants. The number of middle managers, she said, was bigger than the population of Staten Island. He felt it in his bones that he was going to have to subscribe to *Forbes* magazine, and probably *The Wash-*

ington Monthly. He had a lot of things to get straight. He was going to look different and sound different, but that figured because what he was going to be doing was more legitimate than running a bank so he had to look more like a banker than any banker looked. What he couldn't get through his head was that he wouldn't be Boss because the Prizzi family, the biggest mob ever put together in history, wasn't going to be there anymore so, naturally, they wouldn't need a Boss.

He decided to handle the problem by thinking about it when it happened. Right now there was going to be trouble no matter how he sold the franchises because somebody was going to think they had been left out. And there was a lot of money going on it. He shuddered at the don's idea that they sell the franchises to the Blacks, the Hispanics or the Orientals. Santo Calandra, his *vindicatore,* for example, was his manager for the extortion division, a nice piece of whose income came from shaking down the automobile companies, for one example, domestic and foreign, for every car they brought into the metropolitan area, a pretty big area, which included New Jersey, lower Connecticut, Long Island, and the five boroughs of New York—about fifty million people, which was a lot of cars. It had turned out to be such a good business that the don had franchised it out to families right across the country, and, all together, it produced about $60 million a year. The operation took down eighty cents for every new car that came in and forty cents for every used car that was sold by a legitimate dealer. Santo had also made a solid arrangement with all the food chains operating in the city and was knocking them off for three cents a shopping item, and he took down 3 percent of the gross on each one of his projects before passing the rest up to his *caporegime.* Maerose had said once that it was the constant population increase that caused inflation, but just looking at the range of Santo's projects, Charley wasn't so sure.

He knew that if he sold Santo's division as a franchise to anybody else, whether Black, Hispanic, Oriental, or even Santo's own uncle, there would be trouble. Multiply that by the about nineteen divisions that had to be franchised and the Prizzis could have a war on their hands.

He knew he had to sell the franchises inside the family and figure out how to explain it to the don afterward. Let one dollar be moved outside the family and there would be a war. They would have to go to the mattresses and that was rotten public relations. The media would get all excited, the cops would want more money, the politicians would start investigations, and it would all be bad for business. Still, he had to be proud of Mae. She had thought the whole thing up, and when you looked at it, no matter how much of a *collevazione* it caused, it was going to bring in a bigger net profit and wipe out almost the entire overhead, so, if a couple of dozen soldiers had to get mussed up, no matter how you looked at it, it was worth it.

He finished scrubbing the floor. Thinking about his own wife dreaming up a thing like this made him horny. He got to his feet. "Hey, Mae," he yelled.

"What?"

"Come on. We're going on the bed and get some real work done."

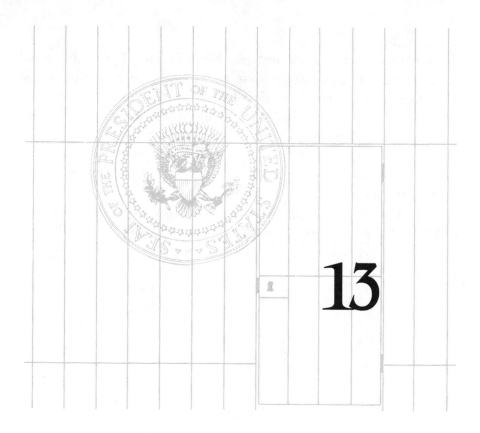

13

The don invited his son, Edward S. Price, to lunch with him on the same day he received the Partannas. Eduardo was a man so carefully and impressively dressed that, as he completed the daily wearing of each of the sixty suits in his rotation, his people then air-shipped each one to Huntsman, his tailor in London, to be pressed. He was a short, bony man, slightly taller than his father, but there were nine-year-olds who were taller than his father. His hairstyle was engineered and executed by Henry Desmond Purvis, the man responsible for the adventurous hair of the senior politicians in the Congress, the man whose work had startled more television viewers than the introduction of hard rock music.

Eduardo had an aggressive, not to say hostile, personality, in imperial opposition to everyone excepting his father. He seemed to return to his boyhood when he was with the don. As a boy he had been quiet and studious, on the shy side, perhaps rather too reserved. He had been all business, slaving long hours at his homework, ignoring distractions, and seeming to model himself upon the Mickey Rooney performance as young Tom Edison. His ambition from the cradle had been to be different in every known way from his brother, Vincent.

He had earned his earliest degree at Harvard University in three years instead of four, by going without summer vacations. He had been Law Review at Harvard Law School. He had excelled at the Harvard Business School, finishing as number three in his class when he was awarded an MBA. When his father thought that his education should have been completed, he continued it by enrolling himself in the Dale Carnegie Institute. His mastery of the Carnegie system marked his parting with shyness. Shyness was never to be a problem for Edward S. Price again.

He developed into a lordly man. Except when he visited Brooklyn, he traveled with an entourage that included hard-eyed men who murmured into hand mikes. His DC-10, called the "company plane" but whose use was restricted to Edward S. Price and his invitees, had been acquired from his late, great friend, the Shah of Iran. Within it, his public relations people had persuaded him to accent austerity rather than luxury to contrast with the universally known extent of his riches; the interior design was a replica of a Vermont country store at the turn of the twentieth century, with a cracker barrel, a brass double bed, horsehair furniture and spittoons in the main cabin, and a large rolltop desk that had dozens of pigeonholes in the office area, to which Eduardo went upon boarding and where he sat, belted up, on landing, dictating to Miss Blue, fiddling with a computer, barking orders into satellite telephones, and expanding his manifold businesses.

Heaven knows Eduardo had dignity, but the don estimated that, in any measurement of wisdom, Eduardo could be considered a smart man only when compared with his late brother, Vincent. Both of his boys had been shrewd with even more than average Sicilian deviousness; their cunning was a tribute to their heritage, but, for the rest of it, vanity had crowded out the smarts in both of them, in the don's secret judgment, which must have, somehow, conveyed itself, because Eduardo was (almost) humble in his father's presence.

65

•   •   •

When Eduardo had been firmly packed with one of his father's cruel lunches, a Mexican cigar shoved into his dentures and a glass of grappa wedged into his right hand, the don broke the news.

Eduardo was horrified. "*President?*" he cried out in bewilderment. "Poppa, I am sixty-nine years old! I'll be seventy-three when I'm elected. I'll be seventy-seven at the end of my first term. I simply don't have the energy for a job like that."

"So?" his father said. "You'll take naps. You'll learn to wave. You'll delegate. You'll let the other guy handle details. You'll make jokes about what you do wrong. You'll take a lotta vacations. The people expect that."

"But I have commitments! The museums and the charities and the opera of this city, not to say the nation, depend, to a large extent, on me. I am *deeply* into ballet!"

Eduardo was panicking because he was completely, even madly, devoted to his protégée, a Miss Claire Coolidge, who called him Woofy and whom he called Baby; he could not see how he could bring her with him to the White House. He had been able to arrange her transfer from the corps de ballet of the Metropolitan Opera Company and to place her in a few strong secondary parts with the New York City Ballet, winning her heart utterly when he had been able to enroll her in the advanced classes of the School of the American Ballet in exchange for a mere $100,000 endowment.

"I've been working hard at it all my life," Eduardo ran on, "and finally I am a member of the old guard of New York's nouvelle society. I have a right to retire when the time comes to consolidate that position. I am considered as being second in line to the arbiter." By a miracle of applied phonetics, his speech patterns, if not his vocabulary, could not have been differentiated from those of William F. Buckley, Jr.

"Lissena me, Eduardo," the don said harshly. "You have earned the honor of running for president. You are a great man in our country. Whatta you think running for the highest office in the land is gonna do for you in New York society? Your country owes this to you and I am talking about Air Force One as your personal plane."

"I already have a plane that is bigger than Air Force One."

66

"You'll have Camp David. There is no hideaway like it. You'll have the CIA to square anyone that ever crossed you. You'll be getting inside information that will make you a fortune!"

Eduardo snorted. "Hilarious," he drawled.

"You have worked and you must be rewarded with the honor beyond all honors, the recognition that comes with running for president."

Eduardo stared at his father, a different look suffusing his face. "Well," he said slowly, "I have a lot of friends around this country. If I did campaign out there for two years with the rest of the pack, I think I could count on a great deal of statewide and local support form American business and cultural leaders."

"What else?" the don said. "And every family we work with in this country, and all the people they do business with, is gonna have such a quota of political action committees that you are gonna have the biggest campaign fund of anybody that ever ran for that sacred office."

He rose to his feet with some difficulty and opened his little arms wide to his son. Eduardo stood, stepped forward, and entered the tiny arc. "I am proud of you, my son," Corrado Prizzi said brokenly. "This is the proudest day of my life." They broke the embrace and returned to their seats.

"If you don't mind my asking—who is going to take my place at the top of Barker's Hill?"

"Charley."

"Charley?"

"Charley Partanna."

"Charley Partanna!" Eduardo regurgitated his loathing. "As head of Barker's Hill? Why he's nothing but a hoodlum!"

"Some of your best friends are hoodlums, Eduardo."

"He'll be exposed for what he is on the first day in that office."

"Trust me."

Eduardo loathed hoodlums, the *fratellanza*, all immigrants, and Brooklyn-Italian speech patterns, and he had almost been able to live with the idea that the continuing cash flow and capitalization of Barker's Hill Enterprises depended upon other enterprises that were so loathsome to him that he would not allow meetings with the money-movers who brought the cash into Barker's Hill accounts. It was not a moral thing. It was that everything the family's business stood for represented the *lumpen* murderer, sweater, and bath-free meaning of his brother, Vincent, who had spent his boyhood humiliating Eduardo with his utterly ineffable vulgarities. Six times in his life Eduardo had gone to his father with statistics as to the family's wealth and influence and had pleaded with him to disband the family's unsavory activities, but the don had laughed at him. "You're just hanging out with the wrong people," he said. "You think they ain't gonna like you if they find out where the money comes from. Lissena me, Eduardo, we got more than any of them. They are gonna kiss your ass."

"There are several things you may have overlooked here, Pater," Eduardo said, strangling diphthongs, "and one thing in particular."

"Yeah? What?"

"What does Charley know about finance or international networking or interlocking philanthropies or the intricacies of corporate takeovers, or the art of the arbitrageur? Most of all, what can he possibly know about public relations? His life, necessarily, has been lived in the shadows. The entire thing, like everything else in this country, balances on an almost lapidary control of public relations. And have you forgotten what Charley's profession has been for the past God knows how many years?"

"Eduardo, lissena me—nobody is indispensable, right? And nobody outside the Prizzi family is gonna take over if you got hit by a taxi, right? The way I look at it, this is strictly a management proposition. You have built an organization of experts and if there is one thing Charley knows how to do it's how to run an organization."

"Poppa, believe me, I appreciate everything you say. But thinking about it, campaigning for the presidency all over the country for two years is not something I really think I want to do at my age. I am sure you understand that."

The don spoke softly but his words had sharp dentures built into them. "Eduardo, lissena me—you are gonna run for president is the way I look at it. But if you decide you don't wanna run, then you are out anyway and Charley goes in your job. And even if you went back this afternoon and tried to transfer money from the company into your Swiss bank accounts, you would find out you can't get at it. Also, it's natural, you might be thinking that you can fix everything legally so that if and when I die, you got the stock proxies to vote you in and vote Charley out. Don't believe it. I wrote a letter to the family. It has fourteen witnesses, all healthy. The letter says that as recognition of your running for president you will get twenty percent of the business. But if you don't run for president—too bad—you don't get a nickel. And I got people who will enforce that."

"Who gets it?" Eduardo asked bleakly because as far as he was concerned he had always believed that when his father died he would automatically become the owner of Barker's Hill Enterprises; after all, he had created it and built it from nothing to the colossus it was today, a $16 billion company with subsidiaries in every country of the world plus a firm footing in outer space. Twenty percent! The bitterness of the injustice nauseated him.

"Hang around for the reading when they read it."

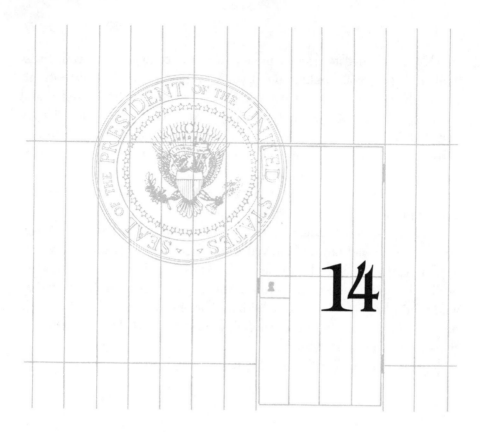

14

Charley, in an apron, was stirring a pot of *riso chi cacuocciuli*, boiled rice with cut-up eggplant, turnips, artichokes, and peas, in olive oil, flavored with onions. Maerose was frying some tiny *sciabacheddu*, working twelve of the little fish in the pan. They had that wonderful relaxed look of people who had been completely satisfied with each other's work on the bed.

"Did you know that there are about twenty-five hundred different varieties of rice, some of which is red, blue, and purple?" Charley said.

"Is that so?"

"Yeah. And I read in a magazine that eggplant looks like it drinks up all the oil in the pan, no matter how much you put in," Charley said, "due to very spongy tissue which is almost all air pockets."

"No kidding?"

"Yeah. But when the heat and the oil begin to collapse the air pockets, it's like squeezing a sponge—the eggplant gives most of the oil back to the pan."

"Thank you, Fanny Farmer, junior. Charley, don't tell me from cooking. Tell me from franchising! You are worried about it."

"It could cause a lot of unemployment."

"They're all specialists, so when you sell the franchises, who's gonna know how to run them except the specialists who have been running them for us? Whoever buys the franchise is gonna need them."

Charley brightened. "Yeah. Maybe. But the guys we have who run the specialists, they gotta figure they are losing a lotta cash."

"Like who?"

"Like the *caporegimes*. Like Matteo Cianciani who runs the shit operation for us."

"So you sell them the franchises and they'll make double. Besides, the *capos* are mostly old guys. It's time to retire. With a bonus."

Charley dumped the *riso* into a serving dish. "There could be a war," he said. "This could split the family to pieces."

"What family? That's the whole pernt. The don is getting us all outta the family."

"It's all Greek to me."

She arranged the tiny fish on two plates. Charley opened a bottle of Akragas, the Greek name for Agrigento, the Prizzi family's home base. It was strong, dry, and white. They sat down and began to eat.

"The day the franchises are sold and you move out and up, we are gonna go to work to make a baby," Maerose said.

"You been holding out, Mae?"

"Charley, lissena me. You want your kids to grow up in the environment?"

"What wrong with that?"

"They'd be outcasts—that's what's wrong with that."

"Outcasts? I'm an outcast?"

"Charley, are you ever invited to the Academy Awards? Eduardo is."

"I never thought about it."

"Well, I thought about it. And the don thought about it. Whatta you think he's gonna run Eduardo for president for, he's gonna send you upstairs to take Eduardo's place in the business for if he don't want our kids to be respectable?"

"I always figured you had set him up for that, Mae," Charley said cautiously.

"The thing is he *wants* it. You think anybody can sell the don anything, he doesn't want it?"

"You want it, too."

"Why not? My father threw me out of Brooklyn, Charley, and I found a new world. I like it there."

"The thing is—your grandfather gonna like it there?"

"I'll explain it to you as we go along. You ever been to Switzerland?"

"No."

"It's the best. As soon as you get the franchises settled we just sit in two of those first class Swissair seats, and from then on everything works. The food, the hotels, the face doctor—even the climate is right— no smoke, no smog, no soot, no slums."

"How come you know about it?"

"I went to school in Switzerland for a year after Manhattanville. The nuns said I was too young for college. Jesus, Charley, your rice is delicious."

"My mother. Also your fish."

"I hate to say this," she lied, "but I think you're a better cook than I am."

"There's gonna be a war. I can smell it."

"Charley, fahcrissake. You're talking small money."

"Small money?"

"You're going up to where the big money is. You think my grandfather is dumb? Barker's Hill has a Cray 3 computer in Omaha. Before I talked to my grandfather, I had the Cray work out the vigorish. No matter who you sell the franchises to, they have to net a bottom of thirteen point seven percent more than they are making now for the family, and—if they are operated as efficiently as you are operating them now—then they'll bring in a net of up to twenty-two point eight percent more, even allowing for inflation."

"How come?"

"Because everybody won't be taking a split all the way up and down the line! Because everything will be pure profit."

"We gotta pay the team who's gonna collect and enforce."

"Not if you set it up right. The franchisees gotta pay a handling charge. The service charge covers the enforcers plus a little profit. And as fast as that money comes in, we'll be reinvesting it at Barker's Hill until we gradually buy up thirty-seven percent of the whole country. That's the Cray 3 talking, not me."

"I called a meet for tomorrow."

"Sunday?"

"People feel more peaceful on a Sunday."

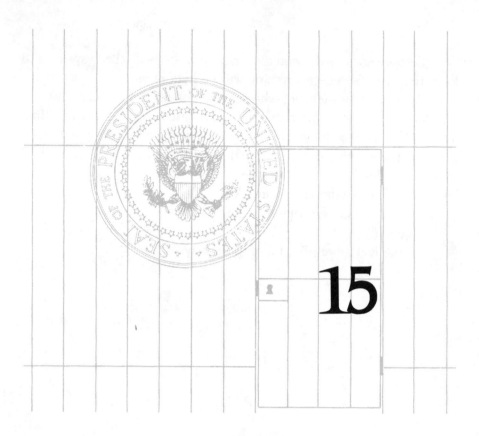

15

Everything wasn't exactly open-and-shut about setting up the metropolitan area franchises. Six hundred and nine soldiers decided to retire to Miami or Atlantic City, where there was still a good dollar. One hundred and eighty-nine began to think about setting up chicken farms in New Jersey. The three *caporegimes* felt that since the Prizzis were going to get out, they should inherit the whole Prizzi business without having to buy franchises, that they were entitled to divide up the whole operation among themselves. The heads of each operating division under the *capos*, particularly Matteo Cianciana, who ran the shit, coke, crack and boo operation, and Vanni Aprile, who handled gambling—the national sports book; the numbers and the lottery; the Sport of Kings; the blood stock importing business; the boxing industry; the jai alai frontons; the international tennis book; the relationships with two football league owners, coaches, referees, and linesmen; the three Prizzi hotel casinos in Vegas and the three in Atlantic City—got very agitated at the idea of anyone else being able to outbid them for what they had come to consider as their own thing because they were already skimming the split with the *capos*, Charley, and the Prizzis by almost 1 percent, a lot of money.

Charley called a meeting of all administrators at the board room of the Dorsetshire Bank & Trust Company in downtown Brooklyn immediately after ten o'clock Mass got out on the first Sunday of August 1988. It was in a big cork-lined, sound- and bugproof room, about forty feet by twenty-eight feet with a twenty-seven-foot-long table set at its middle. There was a pad, a ballpoint pen, an ashtray, and a sixpack of Mexican cigars at each place. These could have been Havana cigars, because contacts at the CIA had offered to bring them in, but Corrado Prizzi had never forgiven Castro for closing down the family's two casinos in Cuba.

Angelo Partanna, the three *capos*: Rocco Sestero, Amalia's son, who was Maerose's first cousin; Salvatore Prizzi, Vincent's son by a first marriage and Maerose's half-brother; and Pinocchiaro Li Causi, who had gotten the job on merit. Under them were the people who headed up the principal divisions: the shit operation, which was the big operation for profits; gambling, which ran second; labor racketeering, loansharking, extortion, prostitution/pornography/orgies; recycled postage stamps and credit card fraud; and Santo Calandra, the family's *vindicatore* and chief dispatcher of the shtarkers, who did the heavy muscle work and made the hits, as required. Santo was a resolutely stupid man who had an ego that convinced him that he was smarter than the men who had invented the computer and the self-winding watch, kinder than St. Francis d'Assisi, and more long-suffering than Abraham Lincoln. Angelo Partanna, who measured such things, had had to send to Sicily for Santo's birth certificate because he had told Charley that Santo couldn't be a Sicilian, he was too stupid. Also, and it figured, he tooted coke.

Charley came into the meeting, after everyone had assembled and was seated around the table, with Calandra and three sidemen. Vanni Aprile, who was as slippery as home-made ice, went over to Charley with a big smile, his hand extended.

"Fuck you, Vanni," Charley said, brushing past him. Charley took his seat at the head of the long table; Santo stood behind him and the three helpers leaned against the wall around the room. Angelo sat at Charley's right hand. The *capos* were in chairs on either side at the top of the table. The rest of them found seats wherever they could.

"All right," Charley said. "Now lemme tell you something." He hosed fear down each side of the table, soaking everyone in the room with it, including, for the first time, his own father. Angelo had to marvel at the increasing power and intensity Charley had been able to pack into his stare over the years. He decided Charley did it partly with the eyes, the nostrils, partly with that "unconscious" quiver in the muscles of his right cheek and the terrifying way he held his mouth. He had never thought he would ever see Corrado Prizzi's equal at fear-spraying, but Charley had done it.

"What the fuck do you think the Prizzis are, a fucking charity?" Charley said to them. "The don built this business when most of youse still had your ass hanging out of your pants. He watched what you could do and he took you out of a fucking soldier's job where you had to break your balls to make more money than you ever thought you'd see in your life and made you what you are, making more money than you ever thought existed. What are you? A bunch of *cafoni* who were too fucking lazy to be peasants so you worked the street as hoodlums. How long do you think you'd stay in your jobs, making the kind of loot you're walking with, if the don don't want you there?" He hosed the fear on them again.

"All right—the don is going to franchise the New York operation. That's it. Whoever gets the franchise in each division carries his own overhead, delivers a gross percentage to us, and we take care of the cops, the courts, and the politicians. Nowhere could you get a better deal. We're giving you first shot. You don't want it, then there are four other families in the area plus the Blacks, the Hispanics, and the Orientals are waiting in line. You get my pernt? You get first crack. You make us an offer. Then we let the people on the outside make their offer. Then we give you the right of topping their offer which is what nobody else outside this family will ever get. If you can't top it, then they get it. *Capeesh?*"

There was a low rumble from the room. Nobody looked at anybody else.

"We are witchew one hunnert percent, Boss," Jerry Picuzza, who ran the hookers, gay bars, and lost child placement, said loudly.

"Lemme second the notion," Rocco Sestero said loudly.

"Any questions?" Charley asked.

After a silence that seemed to brick up every member of the meeting into a separate room, Matteo Cianciana, the shit and coke manager, stood up slowly. "You know what, Charley? You can shove your fucking franchise right up your ass. That is my question." He sat down.

"Anybody else?"

Vanni Aprile got up. "I got the same question," he said. He sat down.

Charley became still, but more pleasant-looking.

Angelo Partanna said, "Let's have a show of hands. Everybody who buys the franchise idea, put up your hands."

Everybody's hand went up except Cianciana's, Aprile's, and Sal Prizzi's.

"Well," Angelo said, "majority rules."

"Majority, my ass," Charley said. "Don Corrado Prizzi, who decided to make the rich get richer, made the rules."

There was a nervous laugh. People were edging away from the three partypoopers.

Charley said, "I appreciate you guys coming here on a Sunday. I'll be at the laundry tomorrow. Write down how much you wanna bid, sign your name, and bring it in by Wednesday. And don't worry—we're gonna help you with the credit arrangements but no shylocking." The men left their chairs and filed past Charley to shake his hand. Charley, as customary for a Boss, took the handshakes sitting down.

Matteo Cianciani, Vanni Aprile, and Sal Prizzi were still in their seats when the rest of the meeting had been cleared. Angelo and the muscle kept their places.

"You don't needa hang around, Sal," Charley said to Sal Prizzi.

Sal stayed where he was, staring sullenly at Charley. Sal was a Prizzi through his father. Rocco Sestero was a Prizzi through his mother. It had made a big difference because each one had a totally different point of view on the advantages of being a Prizzi. Sal, like Iago, felt that he had been passed over for promotion. His father had been Boss so he believed he should have been made Boss when his father had been zotzed, not Charley Partanna. That had burned a few holes in his mind. Rocco didn't care who was Boss. Nobody in the world was closer to the don than Amalia Sestero, his mother. The don was a very, very old man. When he went, Amalia would come into a pile, which was the same as saying that he, Rocco, would come into the pile. "Let the other guy knock himself out" was Rocco's slogan.

Charley looked contemptuously at the three rebellious men. "Whatta you waiting for?" he asked them pleasantly enough. "There is nothing to talk about. You are out."

"Out?" Vanni Aprile said.

"You are not only outta jobs, but you better get outta town," Charley said.

"You are telling *me* I am out of a job and *I* should get outta town?" Sal Prizzi shrilled with concussed outrage. "Did you freak out, Charley? I am a Prizzi."

"You most of all, Sal. Them two is just hustlers."

"I'll tell you what I'm gonna do, Charley," Matteo Cianciani said. "I got the connections in Miami; I got my organization up and down the coast. Go ahead and sell the shit franchise. The thing is, whoever buys it is gonna have one tough fucking time meeting my prices."

"You going in business for yourself, too, Vanni?" Charley inquired softly.

"I ain't getting out if that's what you wanna know, Charley."

"Okay. You got a perna view." He got up. Angelo got up. They left the room with the three muscles. Santo Calandra stood at the head of the table just looking at the three seated men, shaking his head gently to express his compassion, then left.

"You guys must be crazy," Sal Prizzi said to the two other holdouts. "You tryna get whacked?"

"What about you?" Matty asked him.

"I got insurance. I'm a Prizzi."

"That hit shit is a golden oldie," Vanni Aprile said. "They ain't gonna zotz anybody. They'll negotiate and it all has to come out as a better deal."

Sal left first, then Vanni. Matty lit a cigar from the sixpack and considered his options.

Charley and his father were in Charley's van. Santo leaned in the window.

"Hit Matteo when he comes out of the bank," Charley said. "He goes first because he smells like the most trouble. Then, tonight, or whenever, hit Vanni."

"What about Sal?"

"I gotta clear that with the don." Charley started the van and it rolled away.

"Whatta you think, Pop?"

"It looks like problems."

"But if we nail Matteo and Vanni right away, then it's settled."

"Maybe."

"Whatta you mean?"

"Matteo and Vanni are just a couple of businessmen. What they want is to talk it over and maybe work out a sweetheart deal. Sal is something else. He doesn't give a shit about franchises one way or another. He wants to get even because you're Boss and he thinks, because he's Vincent's son, that he should be Boss. And he's just as dangerous as Vincent ever was."

"Matty is the live one."

"That's not the thing. If you don't contact him to set up a private meet, he's gonna try to hit you before you hit him. All three of them are. But Sal is breathing the hardest."

"First, we get an okay to hit Sal," Charley said. "If the don okays it, I'll handle Sal myself."

Calorino was at the door of the don's house when Charley and Pop arrived at 11:20 A.M. Charley said, "Lissena me, Calo. I'm putting a man on the back door and a man on the don's floor for a coupla days. Who do you like?"

"Placido and Pino Salvaggio. They are stand-up. But make sure they know I'm gonna run them."

"I'll talk to them."

"Tell them to bring tools."

Pop led the way upstairs. He knocked lightly at the don's door. They waited for the faint response from the other side, then they went in.

"Today was the meeting?" the don asked.

"Matteo and Vanni don't want it, Corrado," Pop said.

"Who else?"

"Sal Prizzi."

"I thought so. He's like Vincent, a dumb ox. How're you gonna handle it, Charley?"

"Santo Calandra is gonna try for a zotz on Matty and Van when they come outta the bank."

"What about Sal?"

"I hadda clear it with you."

"Charley, that is very nice. I appreciate it. I don't have to think about it because I knew how it would go. He's like Vincent. They go *pazzo* under pressure. You won't believe it but he drinks gin. A Sicilian, what does he know about gin? But he knows he does a thing like this, he's gotta take his chances. What kind of loyalty is it when out of all those people, Sal, my own grandson, betrays me openly? I got no choice."

"Then I better get moving."

"Charley—"

"Yes, *padrino*—"

"Let your people handle it. It's better if you're not the one. This is a Prizzi thing. He's Maerose's brother, you know what I'm saying?"

Sal Prizzi, from the day his father had been hit, had bitterly resented Charley being made Boss. He was a Prizzi, his father had been Boss, so when his father got iced, he should have gotten the job. He was a Prizzi. Nobody could change that. He was the top *capo* in the *famiglia*. Charley was just another plugger whose only experience in the family's business had been doing the job on people. It was his fucking sister, that Maerose with her fucking college education, who had set it up, he thought. She was always in and out of his grandfather's house. His grandfather never asked him over to the house. He was going to get a bottle of gin, go home, and figure the whole thing so that Charley Partanna would be out on his ass.

Sal Prizzi was a short, dumpy, unpleasant-looking man of fifty-two with a blue-black underbeard and mean eyes. He treated people just as badly sober as when he was drunk, the way a peasant treats his animals. Dr. Adler would have diagnosed a superiority complex with Sal, a notion as old-fashioned as Sal's belief that being born a Prizzi could solve everything.

He sat in his shirt-sleeves at the kitchen table in the house his father had lived in and left to him in Bensonhurst and broke the seal on the bottle of English gin. His wife, Asunta, was at her father's in New Jersey, getting ready for Columbus Day. If she knew he was going to hit the gin, she would have hit him with a chair. Sal was a bad drunk because two drinks and he was peeing in his pants and because on the best day of his life he was short on empathy and long on resentment, which had begun when his mother had died and his father had not only married again but had knocked out two children who, right away because they were girls, became the focus of his grandfather's eye. His father had been as crafty and brutal as Sal had become.

A wave of disgust rolled over him. He knocked back a half-tumbler of gin, wishing he could have slit open his father's belly because Vincent could have set it up any time he wanted, but Sal wasn't even made until he was twenty-nine years old, even though he had knocked and beaten and slugged and hounded more union people than anybody else in the family. He had dominated the hospital and the city employees' union, particularly the cleaning women who worked in federal and municipal buildings. He had established the Prizzis in those areas. Charley Partanna was made when he was seventeen years old, the little prick, just because he made a lucky hit when he was a kid. He, Sal Prizzi, could have done that work. His father could have gotten him that work. In fact, it was his father's own work, fahcrissake, he was the *vindicatore* then, but it was too tricky, he lost his nerve, so they sent a dumb kid in to do the job, and that had made Charley with the don.

Now this crazy fucking franchise operation. His grandfather must be ga-ga to think up such a crazy fucking thing. Sal Prizzi, a *caporegime*, a man who was more responsible for the family's success than anybody else, was now supposed to dig down and pay good money for what he had built up with his own fucking hands. He gulped down another half-tumbler of gin. They wanted him to buy what was, by rights, already his. He couldn't get it through his head that out of everybody at that meeting, only he and two other guys had told Charley what he could do with his franchises. He sat brooding and drinking.

Almost an hour went by. He thought he smelled smoke. He tried to stand up, but he fell back into the chair. He got a good grip on the table and pulled himself to his feet. Jesus, he did smell smoke. What the hell was this—he could hear like the sound of fire, a sound like distant trains running. He moved unsteadily to the door to the dining room, which they never used. When he opened it, a roaring fire leaped at him. He was dazed by the shock of it, and the gin, which had widened all the blood vessels on the surface of his body, doubled the searing force of the heat. He slammed the door. He ran as well as he could to the back door, which led out into the yard. He fumbled with the lock, put on the outside light, and stepped out on the back porch. The porch and the back of the house were on fire. A bullet hit the frame of the door. Another bullet smashed into the door beside his head. He pulled back into the kitchen, slamming and locking the door. It was that fucking Charley. They were trying to zotz him. The fucking ceiling was on fire. Where was his piece? He ran to the door that opened into the living room. The piece was in his harness on the sofa in the living room, which was ablaze. What the hell kind of a thing was this? Were they outta their heads? He was a Prizzi. He was a Prizzi, fahcrissake.

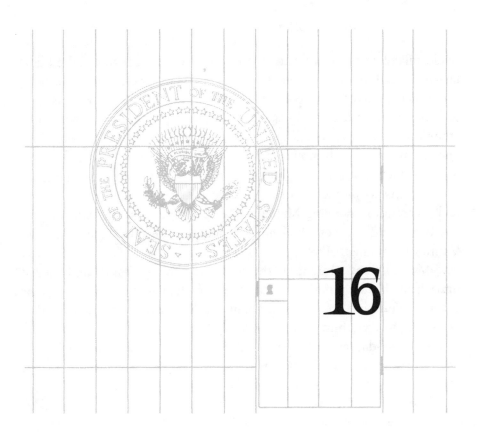

16

Vanni Aprile was even more arrogant than on the day he was born because the Prizzis had made him so much money. He thought life was a proposition whose odds were controllable. It wasn't that he was a gambler—he had been a sure-thing bettor all his life and he had it in his head that it was a sure thing that Charley would negotiate a better deal because the other way was old-time stuff. That kind of thinking could be the only reason why he left the bank building by the front door and got whacked by Santo's people before he could make it half-way to his car.

Matty Cianciani had more humility. He knew he was just a field hand as far as the Prizzis were concerned, so he took precautions before he went to the meeting at the bank. He sent his second man, Lucio Tasca, to the bank on Saturday afternoon when the relief shift was on.

Lucio talked to the head watchman and gave him fifteen hundred dollars to spread around his Sunday staff; then he arranged for the head watchman to take Matteo out of the meeting—Matteo was the last one to leave the meeting room—and to take him upstairs to the bank president's office on the ninth floor, where Matteo could make some telephone calls and get himself picked up at the back door of the bank at seven o'clock that night by four of his own men, but by that time there was nothing to protect Matteo from because Santo Calandra's people had given up on popping Matteo as he strolled out of the front door of the bank, and the cops had finished making the chalk marks around Vanni's body long before.

Matteo went straight to the airport, flew to Miami, and locked himself in. He sat quietly in a comfortable chair in the apartment that was his safe house and thought about the best way to set Charley Partanna up; to have him blown away.

On Tuesday morning he called Charley at the laundry in Brooklyn. Charley gave the high sign to Al Melvini to put a trace on the call; then he let 220 seconds go by before he picked up.

"Yeah?" Charley said.

"Too bad about Vanni and Sal."

"Whatta you want me to tell you?"

"Charley, I wanna make a truce. I want peace."

"Why not?"

"Listen, we can settle everything. I musta been crazy. I got hot and now I regret it. I wanna put in a bid for the franchise."

"You got till tomorrow like everybody else. Send in your bid."

"I wanna have a meet."

"Where?"

"Someplace neutral. Not Brooklyn."

"Where?"

"How about Miami?"

"Where in Miami?"

"Wherever you say."

"After I get your bid."

"How come?"

"Because there is nothing to talk about except if you put in the top bid. We can talk then about terms—nobody has that kind of cash—about collections and whatever."

"Okay. I'll send in my bid tomorrow."

Al appeared in the doorway. He nodded and made a copacetic sign like he was the beer endorser in a TV commercial.

"Good, Matty," Charley said into the telephone. "I'm glad you cooled down." He hung up. He raised his eyebrows at Melvini.

"Up the coast from Miami a little," Melvini said. "Hollywood, Florida. In an apartment on Forty-sixth Avenue, I wrote down the address, under the name of Fred Goldberg."

"Gimme the address." Melvini handed it over. "Santo out there?"

"Sure."

"Send him in."

Santo came into the office, closing the door behind him.

Charley said. "We found Matty."

Santo grinned. When he was around bosses he was Captain Amiable.

"You got backup in Miami?"

"Sure."

Charley passed the piece of paper across the desk. "Tell them to see Matty tonight."

"I'll handle it myself," Santo said.

"Have somebody tip off the local papers after you see Matty. I wanna let people know we are serious about these franchises."

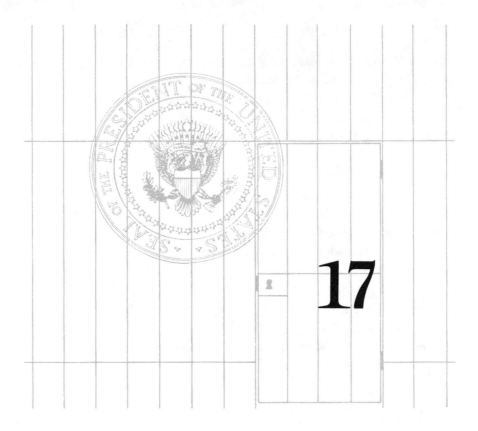

17

At 5:00 P.M. on March 10, 1990, at the don's house in Brooklyn Heights, Charley had his final meeting with his father and Don Corrado, grateful that he had been spared an invitation to lunch. It was five hours before his departure from Kennedy for Zurich with Maerose. Charley was ready and stable when he went into the meeting but kind of disoriented when he came out.

He had had a general idea of what they wanted him to do, but now it hit him that he was probably seeing Brooklyn, from the inside, for the last time in his life. Flashes of stickball games and the little broads, Coney Island, and the welcome feeling he had every time he drove over the bridge lit up a scene with people he thought he had forgotten. The don and his father had asked him to do some pretty whacked-out things in their time, but this one he felt like it had never hit him before.

86

"Everything is set at this end, Charley," the don said. "All you gotta do is work hard at your end beginning tomorrow in Europe. Harry found a nice house for you and the doctors they got is the best."

"I'm not so sure what I'm supposed to do," Charley said.

"All you do is listen to Maerose," the don told him. "She knows both operations, she can talk like Eduardo sounds, and she knows what you should wear and how you should sound. She's been running the PR people at Eduardo's for eleven years besides a lotta other things, so she'll also handle that end of the operation. By the time you get back, you'll be well-known here."

"That's the whole thing," Charley said. "To certain people I am already well-known."

"Charley, lissena me," his father said. "You're not gonna be around to be known to anybody anymore. Mae and the don got it all figured. You leave tonight and you are what it says on your new passport—Charles Macy Barton. Meanwhile, next week back in Brooklyn Charley Partanna gets sick, goes inna hospital, then he goes with the angels. We got a funeral organized that is gonna convince all those people you are talking about that you ain't around no more."

"*Before* the funeral even," the don said, "nobody is gonna connect you with Charley Partanna. You won't be here. You'll be in Switzerland where you're gonna get a new face, new prints, new clothes, and a whole new life."

"But who is gonna be buried?"

"Just the casket. There won't be nothing in it."

"It is gonna be a terrific funeral, Charley," Pop assured him. "I'll send you all the coverage on it. You'll be knocked out."

"I was gonna have them make a video of it," the don said, "but they got a different kinda current over there."

"So make one anyways," Charley said. "I'll play it when I get back."

Charles Macy Barton, as he rode in the forward cabin of a Swissair flight from New York to Zurich that night, said to his wife, Mary, "Don't ever tell the Prizzis how to rob a train."

"It will be beautiful," his wife said. "Absolutely beautiful."

"Well, it'll getta lotta people out in the fresh air." He thought for a while. "Mae?"

"Yeah?"

"How'm I suppose to run a business as big as Eduardo's? I read in a magazine it was the biggest business in the world."

"So?"

"So how do I run it?"

"Charley, lissena me. You are gonna have PR people telling the country how smart you are, you are gonna have economists, cost accountants, trained executives with high batting averages in sales, production, marketing, buying, personnel, all around you, giving you the answers."

"That figures, but how does it work?"

"We set up a schedule of meetings with people—the home office people plus we bring them in from all over the country. You lissena them. You don't say yes you don't say no. You put a little fear in them. They go out and do it."

"Suppose they are wrong what they tell me. How would I know? What then?"

"Every week the computer brings you a list of what the companies won or lost. These are compared to last month, six months ago, and last year. Statistics back it up. They say how much money the public has, will have, used to have, how they are spending it and where. You'll know which companies are winning and which are losing."

"Like a form sheet."

"Yeah. So if some companies are winning, you tell them they are doing good. If they are losing, you bring them into New York and you put the fear in them. It's no different from running a division for the family."

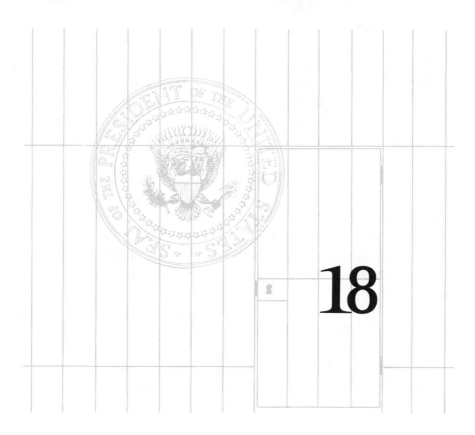

18

It had taken seventeen months, until February 1990, for Charley and an insistent sales force to place all of the franchises with the right buyers on acceptable terms, which involved cash down payments and secured credit arrangements of slightly more than $30 million and assured continuing royalties of 11.2 percent on the gross earnings of each franchise, all net profit. Thirty-one people had to be taken out during the negotiations but, surprisingly, only a few of these were discontented Prizzi soldiers. Mostly it was people from the other families and a couple of greedy Orientals. Finally, it had to go to the Commission to get straightened out.

Two-thirds of the eighteen active franchises went to organizations outside the family: three of the five families in New York took over the shit business and the gambling except in Spanish Harlem; the flesh operations went to United Bamboo, a Taiwan-based organization founded by Chiang Kai-shek (the leadership of which, in a statement to the Business Day section of *The New York Times*, said that they had been drawn to set up operations in New York out of admiration for Corrado Prizzi's concept of controlling available "air space" in the city for use by his building construction operations, so they paid $7,382,010 for the air space franchise for New York, Long Island, and Jersey, then were attracted by the food and automobile operations and bought the franchise for the extortion business, which called for making a tremendous settlement with Santo Calandra because he was very possessive about that). The Black syndicate acquired the numbers and lottery franchise, two large savings banks, the jai alai holdings, and a national brokerage operation.

Many Sicilian competitors interpreted the Prizzi withdrawal into franchising as a sign of weakness and did their best to wrest control of various divisions, mainly the shit business, and, to an extent, the national football book, but Charley Partanna's management skills defeated these attempts. Nine killings and it was all over because Charley also made a case before the Commission.

More than 700 former Prizzi workers were absorbed into the new franchises. For the remainder, compulsory retirement plans were activated by bribes, threats, and a minimum number of payoffs, the net cost to the Prizzis in pensions and bonuses being $4,821,649.07, a miracle of persuasion. A staff of 117 enforcer/collectors was held out of the old labor pool. Santo Calandra was in charge of running this operation, supervising a team of tested people who "had done the work," as Santo explained as he laid out his table of organization. The unit reported directly to Angelo Partanna, who was the link to Don Corrado Prizzi.

On March 18, 1990, Charley Partanna died of infectious meningitis at the family-owned hospital, Santa Grazia di Traghetto. Due to the nature of the illness, the body was not laid out for open casket viewing. Charley had been a popular leader and an established figure throughout the environment. The mourning for the loss was extensive throughout the Sicilian, police, judiciary, media, Hollywood, and political communities; therefore, his death, coming upon the heels of the Prizzi family withdrawal from street operations, created confusions. But the Prizzis were off the street by then, so it didn't matter to them.

The funeral was a colossal event even for a city the size of New York. The media worked it for all it was worth for three full days prior to the funeral. Every family in the country sent delegations. Don Pietro Spina personally sent a representative, "Mi nuncio," from the old country. The five TV networks utilized twenty-six cameras and crews to provide the kind of coverage that had been equaled only by presidential inaugurals, working out the details from each setup with the PR people of the Prizzi family, who were on loan from Barker's Hill.

Movie stars, sports champions, and *capos* from rival families put in pleading bids to be made pallbearers. As a token, as opposed to a real, gesture, the mayor of the City of New York offered to proclaim a "Charley Partanna Day." The New York *Post's* coverage of the funeral, led by a copyright story by Abner Stein, biographer of the famous, which would appear in his forthcoming book on celebrity funerals, perhaps said it best, leading out of the headlines, which took the entire front page, to a page three story with a carryover to a page and a half of pictures.

GANG BOSS PLANTING
THRONGED BY THOUSANDS
BY ABNER STEIN

NEW YORK—Charles "Charley" Partanna, the feared and fearful "boss" of the powerful Prizzi crime family, was buried today, attended by tens of thousands of mourners, at the cemetery of Santa Grazia di Traghetto, the "lucky" parish church of the Prizzi crime family.

The sealed bronze casket had solid silver and bronze double walls. The body lay upon a couch of white satin with a tufted extra cushion for his left hand to rest on. At the corners of the casket were solid silver posts carved in intricate, but dignified, designs. The casket itself was modest in a hushed silver gray, wholly content with the austere glory of the carving and the simple scroll set into the casket top, which read: *Charles Partanna, 1937–1990.* Silver angels stood at the head and foot of the casket with their heads bowed in the light of the ten candles that burned in the golden candlesticks they held in their hands. On a marble slab beneath the casket was the inscription *"Suffer the little children to come unto me."* Over all this lay the soft mantle of the perfume of flowers whose total retail value was estimated to be $88,900 in the form of wreaths, blankets, lyres, hearts, and placards made by woven orchids, lilies, chrysanthemums, carnations, and roses. The *Unione Siciliane*, trade association and lobbying force of the Honored Society, sent a 9 foot by 12 foot placard of lilies of the valley which read "Goodbye, Pal" in giant letters of superimposed forest violets.

Softly treading, deftly changing places in the Guard of Honor were Charles Partanna's friends and co-workers in their well-tailored dark suits. To show their grief in the traditional manner, none of them had shaved in the past three days, revealing their blue-steel jaws in sharp relief. Three were weeping.

In the soft light of the candles at the head of the $38,590 casket sat Angelo Partanna, a senior executive of the Prizzi family, father of the deceased, a picture of parental sorrow. A highly placed source in the Prizzi family said that Corrado Prizzi, aged 95, was too overcome by grief to attend the obsequies, that his medical and security advisers had pressed him to remain at home.

The eulogy, spoken by the deceased's pastor, Father William Passanante, after a requiem mass, delivered a blessing from the Vatican and the White House, then spoke of Mr. Partanna's many kindnesses and his generosity.

The dense congregation of mourners overflowed the church, out into the street and filled both sides of the Doris Spriggs Freeway.

To the Dead March from *Saul* close friends and associates of the departed—*caporegimes*, or family soldiers all—bore the casket to the hearse. Close behind, with solemn tread, numb with sorrow, followed Angelo Partanna and close members of the Prizzi family. Plainclothesmen circulated quietly among the funeral party on guard against any unwarranted attacks.

For many blocks in every direction, from the street, from the windows of buildings and rooftops, thousands of people watched the cortege forming. Three miles long, it included thirty-one cars and trucks to carry the flowers, three bands, and a police escort. Police Commissioner Herbert Mitgang had forbidden the New York Police Department to join the mourners, but when the great procession had crossed the Verrazano Bridge to reach the Santa Grazia de Traghetto cemetery on Staten Island, an Honor Guard of NYPD officers had formed, led by Lieutenant David Hanly (ret.), former head of the Brooklyn Borough Squad.

As the cortege started for the cemetery, more than 10,000 people fell in before and behind it. Mounted police had to clear a path through the dense crowds so that the mournful motorcade could advance. Mrs. Angelina Fambia, 22, gave birth to a baby daughter in a telephone booth at the first intersection crossed by the procession, although this was not discovered until 47 minutes later, after the cortege had passed.

At the cemetery about 8,000 more people waited to watch the kneeling mourners as the thousands following the cortege poured into the cemetery, some people needing to stand bare-headed in the rain as far as three hundred yards from the grave site. Father Passanante led the mourners in reciting a litany, three Hail Marys, and the Lord's Prayer, his face obscured by the hedge of television network and radio microphones.

PRICE PLANS TRIPS TO FIVE STATES
EARLY THIS YEAR, WITH MORE LATER
BY DICK ADLER
Special to The New York Times

NEW YORK, March 19—Edward S. Price, international business leader and philanthropist, widely regarded as a possible Presidential candidate in 1992, said today that he would travel to Iowa, Florida, North Carolina, Texas, and California and that "there will be more" national trips by the mid-year.

The widely admired big business executive, whose company, Barkers' Hill Enterprises, may be the largest in the world, has repeatedly said he is not running for President, denied that the trips were linked to a race for the White House. But many national political figures, who have told Mr. Price he must signal his intentions by early 1990 if he is to have any chance of winning the Presidential nomination, said they view his travel plans as the early stage of a White House campaign.

"There is no basis to saying I'm being coy about running for President," Mr. Price said in an interview. "If I chose to explore the Presidency, I wouldn't do it in a backward way. I'd say I'm exploring the Presidency."

But when asked outright if he was running, he did not completely rub out the possibility of a race. "It's what I always said: I have no plans," he said.

He added that in the past he had frequently turned down speaking engagements elsewhere in the country for fear of generating speculation about the Presidency and that, as a result, "I have forfeited the opportunity to say good things."

The five states he will visit include ones considered crucial to any Presidential race. Florida, North Carolina, and Texas in the South, an area where many strategists have said Mr. Price needs to spend time to soften an image as "a Northeastern liberal." Many national strategists say the South could be the key in the 1992 race for the Presidency.

"I would suspect that for Edward S. Price this is the first stage of something," said Gov. Gordon G. Manning of Connecticut. "This is the first I have known of any concrete evidence that he might really be an interested candidate. The fact that, although he has traveled to individual cities in the past, he disclosed five trips at one time is viewed by national strategists as an intention to send a signal."

Later in the interview, however, Mr. Price sounded a theme that he has been talking about more and more and that many expect would be the thrust of a Presidential campaign. He talked about the failure of the Heller Administration and by Washington generally to recognize that economic problems—unemployment, the Federal deficit, the imbalance in trade, third-world debt—are interconnected and require a broad, unified solution. "With this wonderful opportunity the Party has fought to win comes a very heavy burden of responsibility because you now have to produce."

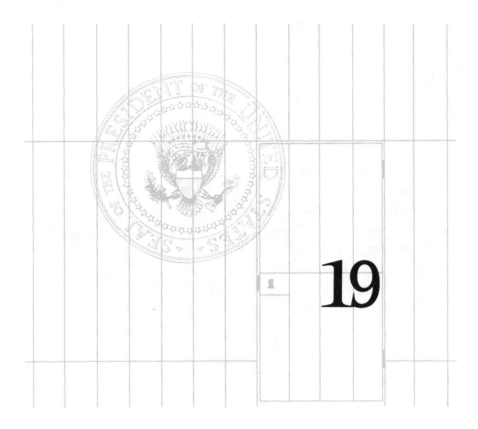

19

They sat comfortably in the *stube* of Harry Garrone's villa overlooking Zurich and its lake in Switzerland, reading the media reportage of Charley's funeral in New York.

"This is sensational coverage!" Harry Garrone said. "What a turn-out!"

"Where does he get that 'feared and fearful' crap?" Charley asked, staring at the newspaper.

"Seventeen PR people worked nine hundred and sixty-two man-hours to set it up and to turn out the crowd," Maerose said. "The woman having the kid in the phone booth was a good touch. My people tell me that something happened with the normal circuits to the Vatican so they had to bring the blessing in by satellite."

"That's good," Harry Garrone said. "Like a verce from the sky."

Harry was Maerose's second cousin, whom Charley had known all his life, and the family's prime money-mover. "Jesus, you sure know how to make a *cuddiruni* pizza, Mae," Harry said. "I love Swiss food, but, you know, I miss the old-fashioned stuff."

"Charley made it," Maerose said.

"He can cook?"

"Wait'll you taste his *sfasciatelle* and his *nipitiddata.*"

"Come on, fahcrissake!" Charley said. "Tell me what's gonna be."

"Tomorrow morning we drive to Lucerne and you go inna clinic there," Harry told him. "I got the very best face man inna world, Dr. Abe Weiler, an artist."

"*Face* man?" Charley said.

"A surgeon, Charley," Maerose said. "He does nose jobs."

"What's he gonna do on me?"

"He's gonna sort of resculpt your face."

"How long is it gonna take?"

"He does it in easy stages, Charley," Harry said. "The whole thing will run about a month, six weeks."

"That long?"

"Don't worry. He's the best."

"Will he handle my prints?"

"That's later. After the face. And after the dentist. We are flying in a specialist for prints from Hong Kong."

"How long?"

Mae shrugged. "Another eight, ten days. But you'll be moving around, don't worry. In the whole time you'll be maybe three days onna bed."

"Moving around where?"

"Harry got us a villa on the Burgenstock, which don't open for the season till the end of May," Mary Barton said. "You never saw such a beautiful place, nine hundred feet up on a private Alp looking down on that fabulous lake."

"Jesus, Mae—I dunno—I hate the idea of going under the knife."

"And while you still have the bandages on, the tailors will come over from London—I already picked the materials—and measure you up for thirty-one suits, a coupla tuxes, and a set of tails."

"Thirty-one?"

"One for every day of the month, silly. You'll never have to buy another suit again."

"Sports jackets?"

"Seven."

"Then what?"

"When the suits are ready—and the shirts and shoes and socks and hats—"

"Hats?"

"Four hats, three caps, and a deerstalker—we'll go to England to work out with the speech teacher."

"I gotta make a *speech?*"

"She's gonna teach you how to talk like Eduardo. Starting after the operations, while we're still at the Burgenstock, we don't talk Brooklyn any more. We talk English to each other so you can learn how. *Capeesh?*"

"Yeah."

"Then after you have the speech part down pat, we work in London with a guy who used to be CIA, very Sicilian, a doctor, on the biofeedback so you can learn where Charles Macy Barton came from, who he is, and et cetera."

"Jesus."

"It sounds like a lot when I just say it, but, believe me, this time next year you'll forget it ever happened."

"Yeah?"

"Not that it's gonna be easy, Charley, but we got terrific teachers. The face man, Weiler, is like the Gutzon Borglum of his business."

"What's that?"

"An artist. Like a Michelangelo. The dentist has done the teeth of more movie stars—international stars—than any other living dentist. He'll give you teeth that could get you on television. They are terrific, but the really tremendous teacher is the one who is gonna teach you how to talk. I can't wait."

"Yeah?"

Maerose stood in awe as the hospital nurse unwound the last bandage from Charley's head. She gasped, "Jesus, Charley, you are gorgeous. I'd follow you anywhere."

97

"Gimme a mirror."

Dr. Weiler, a shortish, gray-to-white-haired man with a Perlmutter moustache, handed him a large rectangular mirror. Charley gazed into it. Mae watched Charley's eyes. He did not speak for a long time but studied the face in the mirror with the concentration a good witness puts into a set of police mugshots. His formerly somewhat simian nose had been narrowed and lengthened. He touched it gently.

"I never saw such a nose," Mae said breathily. "I could fall in love with that nose alone."

His mouth was wider with narrower lips, and the teeth that could be seen behind them were as beautiful as any Hollywood agent's, the dentist's criterion. Distinguished work-and-worry bags had been placed under each eye, giving him the striking appearance of a giant raccoon. His brow had been heightened, and (he had really needed eyeglasses for over eight years, since he had been forty-five) he wore important, high-fashion, large frame, black, thin-shell eyeglasses. His hair, formerly rounded on his forehead in the fashion affected by arrested juvenile personalities, was now parted on the left and combed straight back. It was no longer straight, but undulated in soft, black, shiny waves. It was rather fluffy, at least rumpled looking, in the Wendell L. Willkie manner, and it had a nice body to it.

"The hair is nice," Charley said.

"The hair?" Dr. Weiler said.

"You are terrific with that long face, Charley. I can't tell you what the new long face does for you."

"That's me?" he said at last, his voice ringing with awe, his surgically widened eyes staring at what he knew surely could not be his likeness in the mirror.

"I humbly believe it is one of the best jobs I have ever done," Dr. Weiler said, "but I don't take all the credit. You've got a beautiful integument there."

As if altered internally, Charley rose in his chair with the majestic importance of a significant man. He took Dr. Weiler's hand and shook it warmly, doing something he had never done before, holding the handshake with both hands. The meaning of the new face had blazed a path within him, deep into his soul, taking him straight to where he had always wanted to go but had never had the chance because of the handicap of his former face. His new face gave him a Lincolnesque sense of destiny. He had become, truly, Charles Macy Barton, leader of men. No one would ever figure him for a wiseguy again.

Standing, Charley picked up the mirror and stared into it. "I think everything's going to be aaallll right," he said. The force of American mythology had turned him. He felt legit. He knew in his heart that he deserved to walk among the mighty and control the prices to be charged for everything to tens of millions of his countrymen.

Maerose rejoiced in her heart. The first and most vital phase of the transformation, the place where Maerose feared they might find trauma that could have the effect of destroying all of the plans she had been setting down since she was twelve years old, had been conquered. Charley Partanna had died before his own eyes. He was Charles Macy Barton, American tycoon, at last. Sobbing with the joy of her so-precisely-realized ambitions, she rushed into her husband's arms. She would be the first woman don the Honored Society had ever known. She was able to convince herself that the reason for her utter happiness was only a matter of how Charley's new façade would affect the dimensions of her power. She tried to stifle the more natural response—her reaction as a woman. She tried to tell herself that the rather average-looking man she had acquired to be used and whom she could take for granted if she chose had been repackaged into something that would be even more useful in the new environment in which she would require him to perform.

But her heart had almost stopped as the surgical nurse had unwrapped the bandages and displayed a face that contained separate memory responses—snapshots from her childhood, her adolescence, and her fantasies, composite paragons whose features her imagination had formed, now all combined in one face, Charley's face, responses that warmed her—thrilled her—the peaceful, resolute, meaningful face of a man who had understood his life as it had happened to him, forming the character of a *grand seigneur*, creating the compassion of noblesse oblige, the face of a man who would reach out in empathy to dedicate what he felt, and would feel, to her well-being and fulfillment.

She hadn't been in love with Charley for many years, not since the few months after he had come back from the West Coast with the news that his wife had died. They had had a perfect three months and eleven days until Charley had fallen head over heels in love with the first of almost countless women, an organizer for the Delicatessen Workers Local 159 named Tootsie Lodz. Mae would never forget her even if Charley had, long ago. She had spent the next few years seeing him in and out of dozens of useless romances until all the meaning had gone out of what she felt for him.

Now that man was gone from her life forever. A new, entirely different man had emerged from under the bandages. She looked on that magnificent head that seemed to have been carved out of rose quartz by Praxiteles, a head like *Apollo Sauroctonus*, a head that belonged in a niche in the Vatican beside other works of art, and she knew that she had found the husband and partner for the rest of her life: Charles Macy Barton. She was a woman in love who was also locking up the powerlines that led to establishing her as the first woman *capa di tutti capi* in the history of the world.

Charley was astonished as he looked into the mirror that Weiler held up to him. He felt as if he had been stashed in the perfect hideout. He had beaten the system. He was in a place where no one could possibly find him, wearing a cloak of respectability so complete that, at last, he had done something of which Maerose could approve. It had worked just as she had said it would work. He was ready for whatever the next steps to absolute respectability would be.

But the calm majesty of his new face also made him begin to worry about his place in natural time. Before he left New York, he had read a magazine article on quarks and, although it had been interesting, it hadn't really bothered him until now—the moment of his rebirth as a totally different man. The life span of a quark, he had read in the magazine, an energy flash within an atom, was so short that it had taken science a couple of thousand years just to find one, even after they knew the quarks had to be there. What made Charley brood, at the moment he looked at his new face, was that a quark's life span was so short, in terms of the way people measured time, that to a human's idea of time, it was what the physical measurements of an atom were to the universe.

He had been able to get a hold on the size of an atom when the magazine had said that the structure of wood atoms in a pipe bowl was almost identical with the structure of the planetary system. Protons re-

volved around a nucleus the way the planets revolved around the sun.
What bothered him was that this universe he and Mae were standing
in could be an atom in the structure of a briar pipe somebody was
smoking someplace outside the envelope. If that was how it had been
set up, he thought anxiously, if the time span of a quark could be
parallel, within a hugely expanded time period of some dude who was
smoking a pipe that contained this universe, then his survival time
would be relatively equal to the life span of a quark. Worse still, the
whole thing had to work in reverse. A quark could be a universe to
some kind of a thing that was a planet in a system that was a quark to
our universe. It was very depressing. It all made him feel that he didn't
have a lot of time left if one man's eternity was just another man's
quark.

"Jesus, let's go out to dinner, Mae," he said.

They had dinner in Lucerne and talked about the future. "The clothes
are gonna be so right," Mae told him, "that you could make Prince
Charles look lower class. So you don't have to worry about the clothes.
Or the teeth, or the face, or the prints."

"But you are saying there is something I am gonna have to worry
about?"

"Not worry. There is nothing to worry. But you are gonna have to
work, Charley."

"On what?"

"On how you talk. People know, when they hear, where other
people come from. They can tell if they are slobs or rich people, if you
know what I mean. We are gonna teach you how you'll talk like super-
rich, like tremendously high-level people. Believe me, Charley, the way
you talk is more important than the clothes or even the face. It is even
more important than the background, which will be an easy fill-in for
you when we get to London. Six weeks and you'll have the background
down pat."

Fifty-eight days later they were settled in a pretty, white house with a
breathtaking view of a quiet English valley, a house called St. Bartho-
lomew's in Semley, near Shaftesbury, England, which to Charley had
an oddly familiar ring, on the Wiltshire-Dorset frontier, to work with

Lady Verena Smollett, a phoneticist and grammarian, who lived nearby in Mere. Maerose had reasoned correctly that a female teacher would gain a better response from Charley, but the first meetings were almost a disaster. Charley went bananas over Lady Verena, agonized with guilt and frustration because his wife was always in the room whenever he and Lady Verena worked, but he was drawn to her as he felt he had never been drawn to a woman before. Maerose read the symptoms: the light sweats, the lower lip clenched between his teeth, the rocking motion with hands held under his arms crossed on his chest, the inability to sit still combined with the inability to stand because of the bulges in his clothing.

She discussed the problem with Lady Verena.

"I wonder if you've noticed anything odd about my husband," Mae asked casually one evening after a long session that had so exhausted Charley that he had stumbled off to bed.

"Yes, actually. I get the distinct impression that he has fallen in love with me."

"Precisely."

"He must be an awfully susceptible chap. Considering his age. I mean to say, he's not a callow youth."

"It's his nature," Mae said reasonably. "Are you married, Lady Verena?"

"Oh, yes."

"I've been wondering if it would be asking too much if we were to invite your husband to dinner here. Or lunch if he prefers."

"Well—"

"It is also my husband's nature to be unable to continue any infatuation with a married woman. Please don't ask me to explain it. I can't."

Lord Smollett came to lunch. He was a large uncommunicative Ulsterman who was impatient to leave on a business trip. He was unable to understand anything Charley said because all of his vowel sounds and diphthongs were suspended between Brooklyn and Oxford. Nonetheless, Charley absorbed the knowledge that the man was Lady Verena's lawful, wedded husband, which ended his aching love for the man's wife as if she had been exposed as a member of the federal prosecuting attorney's staff. Charley's creed, which was that happily married

102

women were inviolate, saved him. After that, the three of them—Maerose, Lady Verena, and Charley—worked uneventfully on Charley's speech formation for 201 days, ten hours a day.

At first he unconsciously resisted the new sounds they were trying to insert into his larynx, but a breakthrough came in four days when Maerose thought to have a wall-sized mirror installed opposite Charley's chair in the room. He was unable to fit Brooklyn sounds with his new face and the swanning naval officer posture that had been drilled into him. All at once, he came to accept the combination of sounds that the phoneticist was forging for him: a combination of a Boston accent with Locust Valley lockjaw, blended with the vitally necessary overtones of the speech of William F. Buckley, Jr., which had carried Edward S. Price so far.

Working glottal stops and vowel changes with clenched teeth and outthrust jaw while mastering all the historical, regional, and character phrase variations; then making the unstressed syllables and dropped syllables, and mastering the consonant changes and a compendium of typical words and phrases, mainly from the New England area, using Harvard as its capital; using correct exclamations such as "Blow my shirt," "What in tunket," and "Godfrey!" as if they were his ingrained second-nature responses to stress—it was all extremely difficult for Charley as it would be to any foreigner. But the two women beat on his concentration. They spent their days in that small house yelling at Charley despairing. Gradually, he mastered the new speech forms. There would be flashes when newcomers might have thought that they were listening to one of the new aristocrats that the continually burgeoning American gross national product had produced; then he would have severe lapses into the gullah of Italian-American Brooklyn and the indignant women would beat on him again.

There was one terrible result inflicted by the new face and the new speech: Charley discovered that he had lost the gift of putting the fear into people with a glance. "It's gone, Mae. It's just gone," he said.

"How can it be gone? You need it, Charley. That is what is going to make the whole Barker's Hill thing work."

"I can't do it."

"Do it, let me see."

He made a pathetic attempt to throw the fear out at her, but it was almost a comical failure. It came across his face like an upperclassman's sneer at an elementary school but, in actual factual fact, wasn't that effective.

"Charley, lissena me. When you first knew you could do it with a look, did it just come to you or was it an acquired characteristic?"

"What do you mean?"

"I mean did you have to practice it!"

"I saw the don give the fear and—" He seemed reluctant to continue.

"Yes—what?"

"I went home and every afternoon I practiced in front of the mirror until I got it. Then I practiced more until I perfected it. Then after a coupla years I could scare anybody."

"That's it, then! That must be it! Dr. Weiler shifted your face muscles. The *levator labii superioris* muscles and the *aguli oris* and the *zygomatucus major,* those great pulleys of the face, have been modified! That just means you'll have to work harder with the superficial surface of the subcutaneous adipose tissue around the malar bone and the masseter and Buccinator muscles. Weiler has lightened the weight of your eyelids. You've got to start again—at the beginning. You've got to retrain your entire face."

"How?"

"You'll practice! In front of a mirror! I'll shift the speech lessons to only afternoons and nights, and you'll practice the look all morning every morning."

In seven weeks Charley had the look back. They went out to dinner, and he tried it out on a waiter. The waiter fainted. Lady Verena couldn't understand what had made the waiter faint. Coaxed to demonstrate, Charley hosed fear over her. She fainted.

On August 9, 1991, the vocal transformation was complete; the Savile Row clothing and new luggage were delivered; and an enormous Rolls-Royce, a Design PV22 touring limousine built on a Phantom V chassis whose extra seventeen inches of wheelbase made possible the car's steeply raked back, sweeping lines, and enlarged luggage space, arrived at St. Bart's to take them to London, although the Barton luggage followed in another vehicle.

At the Berkeley Hotel in London, where they would stay for a few days until the staff got the Mount Street flat stocked with food and ready for them, they occupied a four-room apartment on the mews side. Over a bottle of room service Krug '59, Maerose told Charley that she was pregnant.

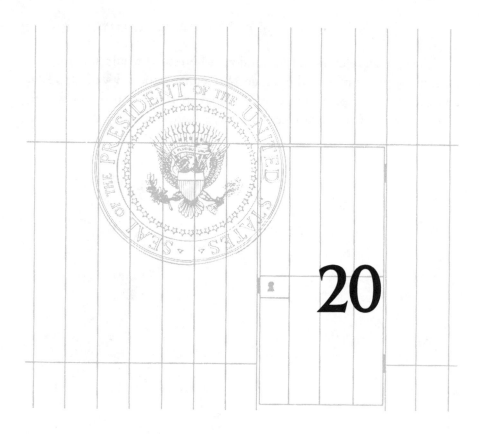

20

While he flew in the company DC-10, the *Ronald Reagan,* or rode in the limousine between campaign appearances, or stretched out, exhausted, on some motel room bed after he had finished a day's endless campaigning, for as long as he could stay awake, Eduardo thought about his father's letter of intent that would allow him to inherit only 20 percent of the Prizzi fortune, as represented by the capital assets of Barker's Hill, $14 billion (and 20 percent of $14 billion was only $2.8 billion), after he had spent his life, from the day he had left Harvard, building Barker's Hill from a paper Delaware corporation into one of the great industrial colossi of modern times. He thought about it when he showered in the morning and during the two deep massages he got during the day between campaign appearances. He thought about it immediately after the time he had alloted to thinking about Claire

Coolidge. It was deeply resentful thinking, which corroded his soul and violated his well-being.

He could hardly believe that Charley Partanna, the son of a sweaty immigrant (which could have been true because Angelo Partanna had landed in New York from Sicily in late July and could not have escaped perspiring), would—for doing absolutely nothing—inherit the helm of Barker's Hill Enterprises, while he, the man who had built all of it, had been cut down to a 20 percent share. He thought it all through carefully, considering what he would need to do to win some fraction more than the 20 percent, if only a token amount to prove that he cared.

Because he was conditioned by his lifetime of training under his father, part of the problem was winning back some token amount of that money tax-free. The depression that had fallen upon him after being told he would be cheated out of his own money stayed with him for so long that he was simply unable to receive Charley Partanna for as much as a lip-service interview in advance of handing over the direction of Barker's Hill Enterprises. Instead, after the Macy Bartons had moved overseas, when Eduardo announced his candidacy for the presidency after he had been running for seven months and had spent $5.25 million of campaign funds to establish that he hadn't decided whether he would run or not, pressed by his father, almost as an afterthought, he named Charley as his successor.

Eduardo had always patronized Charley, naturally feeling the contempt that a law-abiding citizen has to feel for a fellow of Charley's sordid origins, but, on the other hand, he felt enormous gratitude to Charley for having given him Miss Claire Coolidge almost at the instant Charley had perceived how important Claire was to him. He knew that Charley had not sacrificed himself because of his indifference to her—no one could be indifferent to Claire. Charley had done it for the greater good of the family, Eduardo was certain of that. Charley had not hesitated. It had been an incomparably generous thing to do, but all of that gallantry notwithstanding, Eduardo was not going to receive Charley Partanna at Barker's Hill headquarters until the complete physical overhaul had transformed him into Charles Macy Barton and he was able to enunciate like a human being and not like a Brooklyn Italian wop.

Anyway, he knew it wasn't Charley sticking in his craw and it

certainly couldn't be his nephews, Conrad Price Barton and Angier
Macy Barton, on whom he had never set eyes. It was the injustice of
that 20 percent that his father had thrown to him as feed is thrown
before chickens. He would not go against his own father, dead or alive,
but he knew that if he thought about it long enough he would find a
way to better the odds.

It was a prerequisite of presidential campaigning, despite the attention
span of the voters, to spend as much money as the candidate could lay
his hands on before the January of the election year so that whatever
was expended could receive matching funds from the government. He
was almost at the bottom of the money barrel because he didn't intend
to use any of Barker's Hill money. The early money had been readily
forthcoming from leaders of business and from various associations of
his father's, but he was facing the final year of the campaign with only
the financial support of the forthcoming matching funds from the government. Nonetheless, he was more confident than he had been when
he started. "I am certain of my candidacy now," he said to the *Los
Angeles Times*. "I am reasonably confident of victory next year."

When he campaigned in California, there was a special bonus,
utterly unexpected by press and public alike. During a layover weekend,
he spent a considerable amount of time with Arthur Shuland, the lieutenant governor of the state, his nephew, the son of Amalia Sestero.
He set Arthur right on the basics. "Charles Macy Barton, who has
succeeded me at Barker's Hill, is a friend and a friend of the friends."

"That figures."

"If he calls on you, consider it a part of the general plan, your
grandfather's plan."

"I am at his orders, Uncle."

"While you're at it, do you think you can do anything for my
campaign in the state?"

"I'll think of a way."

Three days before the Republican presidential primaries, the popular Democratic lieutenant governor of California backed into a safe
endorsement of Edward S. Price. He said, "Although, as a loyal Democrat, I am one hundred percent behind our great president, Franklin
M. Heller, because as God knows there is no more staunch member of

the Democratic party than I, I have to say that Edward S. Price is just as stalwart a Republican who deserves every vote of every real Republican at the polls on primary day." Shuland's support for Ned Price was put down to the fact that he was, after all, a Californian, a crossover politician in a crossover state and that he must have some local reason that only a Californian could figure out, because he had certainly delivered over $400,000 in PACs to the Heller campaign funds.

Edward S. Price was a maniacally persistent man who, aside from his father's constant counsel and the most extraordinarily tax-free cash flow in the history of capitalism, had successfully established a complexity of interwoven businesses and industries that represented an enormous empire. His experience and knowledge of inner politics and administration, as well as his arrogance, were profound. Also, he had complete access to the secret files of S. L. Penrose, famed Washington lawyer who was the Washington lobbyist for the *fratellanza*, a fellow Sicilian whose family name had been Scriverosa. Sal's files would have enough on the necessary majority of members of the House and Senate to assure his success as president. For almost fifty years he had grown addicted to his own continually expanding ripples of power until, in terms of absolute power, the presidency would have been the only way to go if only it were possible for him to take Claire Coolidge along with him.

He would put his mind to solving that problem after he had been elected, he thought. Claire was so lissomely beautiful, so effortlessly and poetically sexual, that despite the fact that he was in his seventies and despite his deplorable affliction, Peyronie's Plaque, which, when in erection, caused his penis to bend at the middle, then curve drastically downward, which would have rendered it useless to any other woman, Claire was still able to engineer practical responses to what had been an utterly impossible situation for him for the past ten years. Somehow, miraculously, she had designed and then had attained what would have been an impossible position, except for a ballerina in training, and had actually contrived to place him within her, somehow bring it all off in an upside-down backward placement that was so much more like pyramiding than the old-fashioned missionary position. How had she ever learned the sexual eccentricities she understood, he had wondered over and over again. She was so *learned* about sex—so *caring*.

109

He worried about losing her every moment he was on the campaign trail. He had thought of marrying her, but the media would make short work of the candidacy of a man in his seventies marrying a ballerina who was almost forty-five years his junior.

He had received Charley briefly, on Charley's return from Europe, in his tower at Barker's Hill headquarters, wearing his statesmanlike, visionary Woodrow Wilson dentures. Eduardo had had several sets of variously shaped dentures designed for wearing at the right place at the right time. To dominate board meetings he always wore either his Von Hindenburg dentures, which gave him heavy authority and served up the sounds from his larynx as if they had been placed on large Chincoteague oyster shells, or, if the assembly were a hostile one, his Sicilian dentures, which narrowed his face threateningly, having narrow high teeth and deadly incisors. For meetings with his father, to indicate his total submission, he wore a copy of George Bush's teeth, made from photographs taken on the day the Iran-contra scandal had broken.

He wiped from his mind any idea of Charley Partanna, a vulgar street boss and professional executioner, having any connection whatsoever with this elegant, extremely well-spoken, indefectibly tailored gentleman now before him. Charley Partanna was dead and in his grave, but, were it even figuratively possible to stand the two men face to face, he knew that Charles Macy Barton would have turned away in distaste, if not dismay. Being able to think like that proved that Eduardo would make a great president, the first Sicilian president the nation had ever had.

He counseled Charley at the two-hour meeting. "Never give an answer to a direct question. Tell whoever it is who asks that you will get back to him, then seek a consensus within the professional density of vice-presidents in the Office of the President. They are capable men in their fields who know, when you ask them a direct question, not to answer immediately but to seek a consensus from the trained people under them. Within a short enough time you will have a good idea of the answer to give to the man who asked you the question in the first place."

"Doesn't that eventually put a terrific burden on the office boy?" Charley asked.

"How do you mean?"

"I mean, I ask the vice-presidents, then they cull through the options of whoever is under them, who naturally ask the more broadly experienced people under *them*. Eventually, doesn't the whole burden fall upon the office boy?"

Eduardo ignored that, thinking Charley wasn't capable of listening to what he was saying. "If you aren't sure," he said, "go over the whole matter with Maerose. She has been with me for over ten years and she knows every procedure. Most CEOs I know well go over these things with their wives anyway."

He did his best to dominate Charley with his heavy, penetrating gaze and his wavy, blue-white hair. "Our policy decisions have a fail-safe factor built into them so that even if, despite all the consensuses, you have made the wrong decision, the PR people and the accounting department will get signals almost immediately and you will know automatically to reverse your course and cut your losses, shift the blame to an underling, and no matter what happens, look good under any circumstances."

"I'll ask Mae," Charley said.

No one in the media would admit to never having heard of Charles Macy Barton because Edward S. Price and the Barker's Hill board, who were the leaders of America, had chosen him and because the fact sheet on him that accompanied the handout was one of the most distinguished business biographies any of them had ever read. The newspaper stories referred to Barton as "a private person" who "preferred the background," saying that he was known as "the Lone Ranger of international finance" who "worked out of his mansion on East Sixty-fourth Street to avoid the traffic congestion that a daily trip to Wall Street would entail" but who was "the personification of the American dream": success without effort.

The New York Times wrote: "Indeed, Mr. Barton is best known as a defensive specialist. When corporate America became paranoid about takeover raids, Mr. Barton built up a monumental business protecting his clients from unwanted acquisitions. Over a period of a few years, Mr. Barton, who has a reputation for doggedness, had signed up more than 140 corporate clients who did not want to be taken over, each of

111

whom paid him a fee of $110,000 a year for the service and each of whom was successfully defended from raids through quiet strategies devised by Mr. Barton."

"He is a bona fide star," said one lawyer who specialized in take-over business. "I don't think there is an investment banker who wouldn't talk to Charley Barton if he wanted a job."

The *Wall Street Journal* marveled that Charles Macy Barton had never been even remotely involved in insider trading. He was one of the three living people working in the financial center who had never been so named (the other two, however, had been charged and convicted of gross embezzlement). And the *Journal* went on to say that he was "perfectly cast" as the CEO of Barker's Hill Enterprises. "There is a strong rumor," the newspaper wrote, "that Mr. Barton has just returned after personally having closed for the purchase of the Republic of Ireland whose stock and bond issue he will underwrite on world exchanges."

Mary Barton had worked hard with Charley, drilling the biographical information into his memory. It had been the technical absorption of Charley's overall background story that had kept them in London for more than four months.

When the announcement story broke, Charles and Mary Barton were at sea on the maiden transatlantic voyage of the new luxury motorship, *Thuringia*. Mary Barton said to her husband, "When we land, it is really going to hit the fan. They're going to ask you a lot of questions. All you have to do is remember that you are our Democrat and Eduardo is our Republican. You admire and support him, but you oppose with all your might what he stands for politically."

"Will that work?"

"Of course it'll work. It's been working for over two hundred years."

"But, ginger! Suppose they ask me some posers? How will I know what to say?"

"You'll be wearing this miniaturized radio receiver in your ear. It's almost invisible. I will pick up the questions they ask in the bedroom and, if I see you are stuck for an answer, I'll tell you what to say and you'll say it."

"Godfrey! Isn't modern science the Dad-blamedest?"

"It was developed by CIA scientists for Ronald Reagan's press conferences so you know it is state-of-the-art."

When the ship landed in New York, it was overrun with reporters, photographers, and the network TV cameras that showed up everywhere. Charles Barton granted a formal media audience in the living room of his suite aboard the liner.

"What can I tell you?" he said in part when the photo opportunity period was over. "Ed Price is a Republican, I am a Democrat. I wish him well and urge him to recall the great presidents the Republican Party has given to the people of the United States—every one of them an outstanding manager, a tried veteran of the complexities of corporate administration—Warren Harding, a handsome man; the great waver, Ronald Reagan; and the others, such as Calvin Coolidge, who knew what it was to work a two-hour day. National politics aside, I shall carry on Edward S. Price's tradition at the helm of Barker's Hill as a simple surrogate for the man who is being called by his people to make his attempt at achieving the highest office in our land."

Mrs. Barton entered the room to end the interview and surreptitiously distributed metal-point roller pens inscribed with her uncle's campaign slogan: "Price is RIGHT!" after her husband had retired to a salon across the companionway to accommodate the television people.

After Semley and Switzerland, the Bartons had stayed on in London for four months in a flat overlooking the Mount Street Gardens to give Charley time to get used to wearing hats and neckties while he was briefed and reprogrammed by Dr. Ciccio Ciaculli, a Sicilian neuropsychiatrist who had formerly been in the employ of the Central Intelligence Agency. Professor Ciaculli used hypnosis, biofeedback, and state-of-the-art brainwashing techniques.

Dr. Ciaculli was assisted by Mary Barton and, indeed, in a semiconscious way, by Charles Macy Barton himself, who wandered around the flat under the heavy influence of various grades and selections of psychotropic drugs wearing an electronic headset during the months the prepared tapes were continually being played back to him on an endless loop. The purpose of the tapes and the drugs was to impress upon his psyche, for automatic response to any casual or formal future inquiries, the elaborate cover story that Mary Barton had fabricated in the form of a 237-page, 75,200-word biography of her husband's illusory past: where he was born, the highly placed and distinguished records of his forebears, names of boyhood friends (now deceased); schools, colleges, and graduate schools attended (Rosay, Yale, Harvard, Stanford, and the London School of Economics); the various high Episcopal churches at which he had worshipped and the history of his militant support for universal ecumenism; honors (including the equivalent of a Thai knighthood and an eternal place as an honorary lama in Lhasa, Tibet; athletic achievements (Olympic archery championship; discovery of Pele, the soccer great); experiences and anecdotes relative to his successes as a lawyer, as an arbitrageur and investment banker; war record (high in the councils of Combined Allied Intelligence Services and credited with cracking the code that led to the Eskimo revolt from German weather-tracking services in the high Arctic); illnesses (a severe cold in 1978 that confined him to bed for two days and a full night; his slow recovery from amnesia after an automobile accident in 1976, which left him with an irregularly recalled memory of his life before the accident, but which had impaired him in no functional way . . .

Before the Bartons left England for America, this biographical *precis* had been distributed among three publishing houses in New York discreetly owned by Barker's Hill Enterprises. On the day the Bartons sailed for the United States, an "auction" of the publication rights was in progress, and the first two bids had exceeded $700,000, excluding world serial rights and translation rights. There were published reports that Warner Brothers and Metro-Goldwyn-Mayer had been maneuvering to acquire the film rights to the Barton story, but Charles Barton's innate modesty had precluded any such deal. He had brushed the possibility aside with the comment to *The New York Times* bureau in London, "Sylvester Stallone is a magnificent actor, but to me, as a bone-bred Yankee, he is too Italian-looking."

No one had the time or energy to check out *all* of the details of the Barton story, but, if some nosey Parker did rumble around among the accepted facts, he would soon discover that Charles Macy Barton (or a stand-in) had indeed run the course, but that the invisible stand-in had soon afterward passed away at Corrado Prizzi's suggestion.

Charles Barton had been exhaustively documented with birth and marriage certificates, Social Security registration, tax receipts going back for twenty-five years, driver's licenses, club memberships, and a subscription to W magazine that had been predated back to the founding issue, together with all of the other scraps of proof-of-being litter that any sensible community requires.

The headset he wore day and night also fed Charley the jargon of his milieu, imbedding into his memory such doctrinaire acronyms of big business as TIA, CPM, AQL, PERT, ROI, and ZBB, which stood for trend impact analysis, critical path method, acceptable quality level, performance evaluation and review technique, return on investment, and zero-based budgeting. Charley and Mary Barton breakfasted each morning while exchanging those and other buzzwords that businessmen used to bring mystery to the art of buying cheap and selling dear. After two months of it, Charley could use key buzzwords and phrases effortlessly, in easy-flowing sentences—mobicentric management, adhocracy, horizontal integration, zero-sum game, change agent, futurists, Delphi technique, break-even analysis, span of control, interface, and suboptimization—at will, without seeming to need to think about it. He acquired equal conversational authority on the arts, where his vocabulary and imagery-within-tradition were prodigious. Conceptions such as *enchainement de grand jetes en tournant* while discussing ballet, and punching out melodic lines, or Diz jamming, were a part of the new language to Charles Macy Barton. He knew album-oriented rock from mainstream pop, but it was his mastery of the jargon of the high, modern, and pop graphic arts that took the breath away, and his conversational prejudices for opera and the concert hall were equally impeccable. Verbal responses to modern painting were the most difficult for Charley to master. He felt, with considerable justification, what can one say about a Motherwell or a Warhol that has not already been said?

These expanding successes impressed upon him day and night the need to remain au courant with all argots related to the most remote of his interests as winespeak and dressmakerspeak. For seven hours every weekend, when other people were dawdling in McDonald's or looking at television or exploring sex, Charles Macy Barton sat quietly in the biofeedback position with the headset strapped on and the tapes containing the last trendinesses of American speech being absorbed by his relentlessly retentive mind.

115

Charley liked being respectable. The written record of his never-never life struck deep chords within him. Their repetitions through the feedback had the chords growing into something more complexly logical than J. S. Bach's "Goldberg Variations." The very sonorities of respectability, so various, so new to Charley, filled his central ego with new aromas as if, at Thanksgiving time, a deep-breasted turkey had been roasted, then stuffed with an exotic dressing that was redolent of new, exotic flavors.

Since he had graduated from high school, he had yearned for recognition for himself, not just for his work (as legendary as it had become throughout the Honored Society), which, by social insistence, had to be shrouded in anonymity. A *vindicatore* could be recognized in song and story by his peers, but where was the vigorish when that could be incriminating among the straights? He wanted recognition from the world at large: a *W* interview, a *Rolling Stone* cover, a Horatio Alger award, the admiration of the masses. He took pride in his new clothes, new face, new dental arrangements, and in the stately bearing these brought to him. He was perhaps too overweeningly proud of his education, as recorded in the biography that Mary Barton had written, and he found incalculable fulfillment in the way Maerose—that is, Mary—looked at him when he commanded a table from the maitre d'hotel at the hotel restaurant across Mount Street in London. They ate Italian food only at home now, were never seen entering an Italian restaurant.

Charley appreciated the jigsaw puzzle of modern trendiness and of the many-layered culture that had made his instant acceptance possible. His wife had assembled a totality of new meaning within him, which had brought with it a bottomless faith in all instant labels. As each day went over the abyss to fall into the bottomless past, he became deeply set within his new carapace and more certain of his right to be cloaked in all things respectable.

But also, for the first time in his life, he was enjoying himself. No more dull routines of being expected to set the street prices for cocaine and pot every Monday morning. No more the depressing responsibility of zotzing his fellow men. He had the feeling that he could almost see over the horizon. His life, which, before the great changes, had been like being locked inside a junked refrigerator that had been dumped into an abandoned empty lot in the South Bronx, had suddenly become limitless, open, and admirable. Everything felt right. He could spend his money without being indicted by the IRS. He was a Rolls-Royce owner. He rarely had to hose fear on anyone in the new life. Women, who were sensitive to grotesque amounts of money and power, got the hots for him whenever he walked into a room. Nobody pressed him into the rut that had been his old life, and he thrilled to the freedom to expand endlessly outward like a musical note from an oboe to seek the edges of the (known) universe. Instead of the old routine—the conversations about how the Mets were playing nice ball and the mo-notonous daily demands of what he should shop for to make his own dinner—he had travel, the sort of food cultured people ate, even though what they were eating cost an arm and a leg, and he was somebody.

An expression of Mary Price Barton's long-deceased mother, "It is fiddly work making houseflies, said the Lord," had been constantly on Mary's mind as she had struggled through Charley's metamorphosis, but, at last, Charley was re-created: a walking dichotomy, a man who was capable of being nostalgic about two different pasts, like the way, in America, white people viewed the blacks. As Charley assimilated his new character and culture, she felt power as she had always dreamed of feeling the force of power. Even her grandfather would be in awe of what she was about to become.

Mary Barton was just a tad more than seven months pregnant, far along enough to have allowed the sonogram technician at the Princess Grace Hospital in London to tell her that she was going to have male twins. She carried the cargo well, as tall women can. She looked portly but not wheelbarrow pregnant. Charles Barton was made solemn and thoughtful by the news.

"Jehoshaphat, Mae," he drawled behind an outthrust chin, after grabbing her and kissing her with his new, wider mouth, "I am fifty-four years old, almost fifty-five, but I have made double of what most other people usually make."

"Twins come down through the female line," Mary explained. "My grandmother had twins."

"Blow my shirt!" He looked as if he did not really believe anyone else could have twins. "What shall we name them?" He spoke with those unflawed phonetic stresses whose doom was the burden of money, his jaw clenched shut in the Locust Valley manner because, when he lapsed, his wife kicked him in the ankle.

"I thought we should call them after the don and your father—Conrad Price Barton and Angier Macy Barton."

He stared at her in awe. "Conrad? Is that what the don's name is in English?"

She nodded. "But we're going to call him Rado. That will be his nickname."

"The *o* at the end. Isn't that a little Italian?"

"*Ital*ian? Good heavens no. It's very, very jet set."

"But what is Angier?"

"It's the French-American aristocratic equivalent of Angelo, which derives from the Sanskrit *angiras*, a divine spirit, and from the Persian *angaros*, a courier. In Greek it is *angelos*, meaning 'a messenger.' In Arabic the word is *malak*—Hebrew loan word. Angelos was first used as a personal name in Byzantium, whence it spread to Sicily, where there was a thirteenth-century saint of the name."

"Interesting," Charley said.

When the Bartons returned to New York, they brought with them eleven wardrobe trunks; the enormous Rolls; Danvers, a driver/valet, who had matriculated at the Rolls school at Crewe and who had studied pressing and sponge cleaning at the Tailors' & Cutters' in London; and a Sicilian lady's maid, Enrichetta Criscione, a woman with sewing skills who spoke no English and doubled as a waitress. She had never been off her native island before the Honored Society had graciously found her for Mary Barton. The Bartons had also acquired a housekeeper, Mrs. Ryan; a Swiss chef, Ueli Munger; a Chinese butler of enormous dignity named Yew Lee; and a Patek-Philippe watch that automatically registered the date change at each leap year and that had cost Mary Barton, as an Arbor Day gift to her husband, $27,812. All of these, and the Bartons, occupied a triple-front house on East Sixty-fourth Street, which had a seventeen-foot statue by Henry Moore in the garden and four enormously valuable paintings by James Richard Blake inside (two of these from the inexpressibly breathtaking Prism collection).

Before they had set the horizontal living quarters trend, requiring that the strivers within the nouvelle society abandon the concept of vertical housing to try to achieve horizontal housing within an extremely limited metropolitan demographic area, the record price of a triplex condominium had been $5.2 million, set by some Fort Worth people. The quadriplex of four private houses on East Sixty-fourth Street, redesigned and reconstructed into one magnificent dwelling with twenty-foot ceilings, had cost $9.6 million. It had a ballroom, an indoor jai alai court, a large quoits facility, and nursery air-filtering systems that circulated the scents of newly mown hay and deep green forests; nannies' quarters with wall-to-wall television and conveniently placed, hand-held electronic tickers for the stock and commodity markets; a nursery kitchen and a large walk-in vault for toys. Mary Barton, herself, after all, a former professional decorator, had conceived all the interior designs for the house from Switzerland and England, had approved or rejected, from photographs, all of the breathtaking Georgian furniture (and what *Architectural Digest* was to call "an important collection" of antiques); had fingered swatches of materials, wallpaper, and carpeting before they were installed, bringing off many startling effects such as the "living rug" in the main salon, which was an illuminated, channeled wall-to-wall transparent glass water tank that covered the entire floor, filled with tropical flora and brilliantly colored tropical fish that moved through the maze of invisible glass-walled channels and that would also continually divert guests from asking dopy questions about Charley's past.

When people were favored with invitations to attend the Macy Bartons' housewarming on May 30, 1992, four months after the birth of the twins, they came from the capitals of Europe, from Texas, from Hollywood, and from Washington, the proud elite of the old guard of New York's nouvelle society, to pay homage to an old friend, Mary Price, once New York's favored decorator (but hardly to be considered as only a *fournisseur*), the niece of Edward S. Price, front-runner for the Republican presidential nomination. Indeed, Mary Price Barton had made her place in New York's nouvelle society long before her brilliant marriage to the puissant Charles Macy Barton.

Charley was amazed to observe that, if anyone were asked a direct question about him, people got very nervous. It was the sort of nervousness that overwhelms any American group when a new person entering the group is said to control an insane amount of money. The most socially stable and sensitive people became unpoised and mechanical when they entered Charley's or Mary Barton's presence, harboring wild dreams of either of them suddenly behaving utterly irrationally, such as seeing the visitors' true value and bestowing a large-hearted sum of money on them.

As an ingrained Sicilian, Charley knew that the opposite side of the coin of hope is fear. Instinctively, he worked that edge. In a relatively short time, with the exception of very few people, including Mrs. Colin Baker, the arbiter of every crisis in the real society, no one would answer direct questions about Charles and Mary Barton until Mary Barton had cleared the questions.

On the third day in New York, although Eduardo was campaigning in caucus and early primary states, Mary Barton told her husband that the time had come for him to make his first appearance in the offices of Barker's Hill Enterprises as the company's CEO.

"How do you mean?"

"You go there and meet the people—your people."

"Alone?"

"I can't go looking like the Goodyear blimp, Charley. I typed out a few cards for little comments you can make at different occasions during the visit. There is nothing to it."

"What if they ask me questions about what they should do about running the business?"

"I have typed out safe, standard answers on the little file cards. Fahcrissake, Charley! Eduardo told you he never answered a direct question."

"How will Eduardo feel about me going in and just taking over?"

"Eduardo is out kissing babies in the heartland. And he personally named you as his successor."

Charley went to the Barker's Hill offices in the Barker's Hill building, which dominated a slight rise in the Avenue of the Americas, a rise that two full-time PR men and a professional briber were working to have officially designated as Barker's Hill on the city maps. Danvers

120

guided the Rolls into the especially private parking space under the building, a perquisite no one else enjoyed, which was five feet three inches from Charles Barton's private elevator to his offices at the top of the tower sixty-eight stories above the street.

Charles Barton rose to the command deck and accepted introductions to Miss Blue, his personal secretary, and to one Sestero and one Garrone, who had been Eduardo's personal vice-presidents. Not one of them recognized him, and they were people who had known him since he had come back from Nam in '67.

He was shown around the executive suite. He appreciated the private bathroom, dressing room, and shower, but he ordered the removal of the sauna and the whirlpool bath. "They breed germs and cause infections," he said sternly, consulting a palmed file card. "I could get hypersensitivity pneumonitis from breathing the contaminated air. *Pseudomonas aeruginosa* is rampant around hot tubs and whirlpool spas. Put a billiard table in here instead."

Edward Price's former office was furnished in the same austere PR "plain as an old shoe" style as the company's DC-10: harsh, uncushioned, country furniture; a rolltop desk, spittoons, all of it on uncomfortable, unpolished plank floors, with photo portraits of Enrico Caruso, Pope Pius XII, Arturo Toscanini, and Richard M. Nixon on the walls in stark gilt frames.

"What in tarnation!" Charley said, peeking at a palmed file card as he surveyed the room. "Where are we? On a movie set? Who thought this up, some press agent?" He ordered that the large, six-windowed, corner office be redecorated, telling Miss Blue to call his wife for instructions. "In the meantime, I'll use your office," he said to Carleton Garrone, who had been introduced as his general assistant.

He had lunch in the company's executive dining room, attended by its black-coated waiters, who themselves looked like bank presidents, with twelve of the thirty-one vice-presidents within the Office of the President, receiving them four at each course, in alphabetical order, greeting them warmly, and listening gravely to their immediate problems, promising early solutions. A vice-president named Kent Black, who was in charge of the Mass Communications Division, which was subordinate to Community Affairs, kept pressing Charley for solutions to his alleged problems to the point where Charley had to snarl at him to wait his turn, then hose him with the fear. The others at the table froze.

Everyone, except the dumbstruck Black, urged the Luxury Hamburger on him, a creation of Edward Price's. It was made with ground, inch-thick, New York sirloin strip steak with sterlet caviar used as a stretcher. Charley gagged on it. "What in tunket is this?" he said, choking on the food. Shocked by Charley's lèse-majesté, for the caviarburger was Edward Price's favorite dish, but greatly impressed by his palate, the four vice-presidents then at the table explained the hamburger's ingredients.

"It is not only garbage," Charley exploded, throwing the fear over them, "it is a sacrilege, mixing fish eggs with good meat. Take it off the menu." The incident took its place in the company's legends around the world.

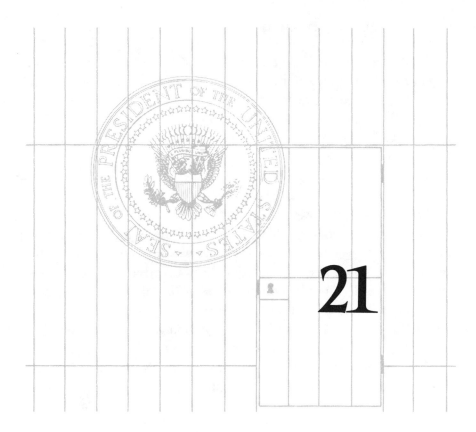

21

In the December of '91, before the *printemps* of their apotheosis, Charley and Mary were invited to lunch at Don Corrado's for a celebration of Mary Barton's gravidity and Charley's new face, which Angelo Partanna already had traveled in to New York to see, but which would be entirely new to the don. Angelo had thanked Mary Barton for having used his wife's name as the foundation for her new family name. "I just wanted to get everybody in," she said warmly.

Don Corrado was so overjoyed at the news of the twins and the choice of their names that, for the first time in man's memory, he had invited a woman to lunch with him. Maerose had heard much of these legendary lunches from her father and Charley. She accepted the invitation as the final stroke of her achievement of her place as the invisible *capa* of the Prizzi family.

It was truly a family party: Don Corrado, Maerose, Charley, and Angelo Partanna, with Aunt Amalia darting in and out of the kitchen. When they arrived at the front door, Charley started a big hello for Calorino Barbaccia, but Mae kicked him in the ankle and walked on his lines. "Calorino!" she cooed. "How nice. This is my husband, Charles Macy Barton."

Calorino touched his forelock.

"How is your son?" she asked.

"Back in solitary, Miss."

"Sorry to hear that." They moved into the house to greet Aunt Amalia, *who did not recognize Charley.* He was thrilled. He knew then that it wasn't all entirely out in front; he was carrying the whole new image deep inside himself; he felt different. Amalia had attended his christening and had slipped him pocket money when he was eight years old; she had written him once a week in Nam; she had supported his first marriage and had mourned when his young bride had passed away.

Charley leaned over and kissed her cheek. "It's me, Aunt Amalia," he said. "Charley." She stared at him, totally bewildered; then she remembered that she had known since Charley and Mae had gone to Europe and she began to weep and giggle at the same time.

She led them up the two flights of stairs to the door to the don's huge room, then hurriedly left them to get back to her stoves.

The don hadn't seen Charley since he had become the new Charley. It made him nervous and overexcited at the same time. Nervous because he couldn't believe it was Charley and he was confused as to how a stranger had appeared for lunch with him; overexcited because he knew it must be Charley because he was with Charley's wife and Charley's father and, tellingly, they had introduced him as Charley. The don insisted on a toast to the bride and the two sons packed inside her. He rushed to a bottle of Leonforte, which ran to 14.5 percent alcohol, which was waiting in a cooler. "This is from the mountains at the middle of the island near Enna," he said larkily. He filled each glass for each of them and for himself, lifted his own, drank it down, and filled it again. "You done a terrific job on him, Mae," he said. "I can't believe it's Charley. There is something familiar about him, not that he looks like Charley, but he looks like some other people I musta known once. And the verce! The way he talks! The clothes! He makes Eduardo look like a used-car salesman. Whatta day! Twins! Conrad and Angie! How did you think up the names?"

"It's Angier," Maerose said somewhat coolly.

"And Rado," Charley said.

"I never heard such a name. You coulda knocked me over. I can hardly get my breath." He gulped down another glass of wine.

"Hey, take it easy, Corrado," Angelo said.

"Watch this," the don said gaily, and with a flick of the wrist, he tossed the last few remaining drops of wine in his glass into a vase across the room. "Hey? I can still do it. That's *kottabos*, a game of skill invented fifteen hundred years ago by aristocratic Sicilian Greeks. Jesus! I gotta sit down." He tottered to a chair and fell into it.

Amalia and Mae rushed to him. He waved them away, weakly smiling his awful smile. "It's nothing," he said. "It's just the news. I never had such terrific news since my father and my uncles sent for me and told me I was gonna be made." He stared at Charley unbelievingly. "Go ahead, Charley. Say something. I can hardly follow the way you talk now."

"Pshaw, *padrino*," Charley said, toeing the carpet precisely in the mating ritual manner John Wayne had used when he was propositioning the schoolmarm. "I am so very glad to see you again."

"You look so—so wholesome."

"Don't that beat all?"

"*Magnifico!*" the don cried. "Come, I can smell the food. Let's eat."

They sat down to a lunch that was as baroque and overassembled as the rococo room that contained it. It was the moment that Charley had been dreading since the invitation had arrived. They started with a tremendous beet salad, seven diced beets to a plate in nests of rugola and endive. "I wish I could tell you what beets do for me," the don said, "but there is a lady present." He began to eat as if the Turks were at the gates. The others, knowing the horror of nutritional doom that was to follow, nibbled at the beets or pushed them around the plate.

Platters of *pasta 'a Sfinciuni*,' noodles baked with bread crumbs, anchovies, garlic, parsley, and a tomato sauce, which was itself a creation of many ingredients, were laid down in front of them. The don ate with the speed of a vacuum cleaner, his face down out of the wind, his fork and spoon making rapid shovelsful to his mouth, pausing only to bite into the *caciotti,* small hot rolls filled with cheese, and to gulp the wine that he continually poured into a glass from a large bottle at his elbow before anyone else might get the same idea. Then came the *pesce in gelatina,* a mixture of lampreys and the meat of sea rays in vinegar-flavored gelatin. "I am made ecstatic by *pesce in gelatina,"* he sang, uncharacteristically, because he never spoke while he was dining. There was a second pasta course after that, spaghetti with finely chopped lobster and a drawn butter sauce, then what Charley saw as sheer impudence on Amalia's part—a whole baked swordfish with an olive in its mouth, a dish honored in Agrigento, accompanied by stuffed artichokes and eggplant in a rich sauce of tomatoes, celery, onions, olive oil, pine nuts, and capers.

As he took the last forkful of the exquisitely baked fish, as he turned to ask Amalia what they would have for dessert, the don collapsed face flat upon his plate, as a samurai in days of yore and in ages and times long gone before might have fallen upon his sword. Maerose and Amalia screamed. Beautifully programmed, Charley yelled "What in *tun*ket!" and Angelo Partanna ran to the door of the room to call down the stairs for Calorino to get the doctor.

Amalia darted to the telephone and called the rectory at Santa Grazia di Traghetto. Father Passanante, who was having an all smoked codfish lunch, said he would be right over.

The Bartons lifted the tiny body gently and carried the don to his bed. They laid him flat on his back, the almost transparent eyelids half-closed, his skin the color of white Carrara marble when it is streaked with green. Calorino rushed into the room and began to rub his wrists, then took off his tiny shoes and rubbed his feet and ankles. He set up a screen, explaining, "I gotta change him," then took off the don's clothes and dressed him in a lavender flannel nightshirt with cerise stripes and combed the few strands of his white hair.

Father Passanante arrived within fifteen minutes with his death kit of sacred oils. He went behind the screen, spoke softly to the don, and administered the last rites of the Church.

Dr. Winikus got there before the priest left. He conducted an examination behind the screen, only to emerge shaking his head. "No sense in moving him," he said to the family. "It wouldn't make any difference." He shook everyone's hand, then left the room after saying that the screen could be taken away.

Eduardo was located by the Barker's Hill satellite. He was on the shuttle between Iowa, New Hampshire, and Florida within the clamor executed by the nineteen candidates for the presidential nomination fielded by the Party, their airplanes, motorcades; the chief advisers and lobbygows; the population of press agents and local committees; the vast camarilla of national press that attended them as the children had accompanied the Pied Piper; the portable public address systems and the high-speed Xerox machines; their women and their camp followers: their masseuses, astrologers, palm readers, and patch workers.

Eduardo flew to New York in the *Ronald Reagan,* reaching the don's bedside at 5:20 P.M.

As he came into the huge room, leaner and meaner from the months of hard campaigning that meant, centrally, the designation of the distribution of PAC money to the pols within the state, a knockout electioneering effect, Mary Barton was seated in a chair beside the don's bed, holding his hand, her tautened face made more beautiful by grief. The don's daughter, Amalia, sat weeping on the other side of the bed. The don, on his back, looked like a rag doll made out of used linen handkerchiefs. Angelo Partanna and Charles Barton stood at the foot of the bed.

Eduardo, unused to the new Charley, mistook him for Dr. Winikus, the don's doctor. "What is the prognosis, doctor?" he asked Charley anxiously.

"I swan!" Charley said. "Edward, how good to see you. I'm not the doctor. I am Charles Macy Barton, your successor."

Shocked, Eduardo backed away from him, bumping Angelo. He turned. "What did the doctor say?" he asked.

Angelo's eyes filled with tears. "He may have overeaten, he coulda had too much wine, Eduardo."

"That's not possible."

The don's little eyes opened. He turned to Maerose. "You are like me," he said. "You forgive nothing." His eyes closed.

He called for Amalia. She reached across the bed and took his hand. "My faithful daughter," he said. "How could I have lived without you?"

"My cooking killed him. Killed him," Amalia sobbed.

"Eduardo?" the don murmured after a while. Maerose called to her uncle, who came to the bedside. "I am here, Poppa."

"Eduardo—"

"Yes, Poppa."

"When they make the final deal for the nomination—" The don whispered the words.

"Yes?"

"Hold out for attorney general. I have talked to them, but you must remind them that we control 23,856 PACs spread across forty-three states."

"We *do?*"

"Talk to Angelo." The don closed his eyes again and called feebly for Charley. Frustrated, Eduardo took a step backward but remained beside the bed. Charley came forward.

"I am here, *padrino.*"

"You must do great things with the business," the don said. "I have made my will with fifteen witnesses including the governor, a justice of the Supreme Court, Henry Kissinger, and his Eminence, the Papal Nuncio. Fifty-one percent of the business will belong, in trust, to your sons." He paused to regroup his energies. "It is not a taxable will, you understand. It is just an old man's wishes. I own nothing."

Eduardo could not avoid overhearing his father repeat the dooming sentence. Now it was confirmed; in writing. Charley's whelps would get 51 percent of the $11 billion. Eduardo almost went blind with frustration and resentment. His father had taken everything from him: his Sicilianness, his own nose, his way of speaking, which was the way his mother had spoken. He had cast him out upon a sea of dishwater WASPS and, ripping Eduardo's birthright away from him, had forced him to become one of them, had driven him to administer the tens of millions of dollars that swept in upon them day after day like surf to build, alone and with his own hands and sweat—no, not sweat, gentlemen did not sweat—with his own mind to create the bottomless cornucopia, Barker's Hill Enterprises, which his father was going to give away on his deathbed to two po-faced, boobish babies. He looked to his father for some sign that it was all a joke, perhaps a wink.

Don Corrado seemed to be trying to rest for the next great effort. His eyes were shut when he spoke again. "Bring me Angelo," he said.

Angelo Partanna came forward to the bed. He had grown old the way a fine malacca cane ages. He was hard and supple and all about him was the sheen of elegance, a man in his eighties with dark skin, who weighed about as much as a cricket, with a beaked nose in the manner of a macaw, a widow's hump, and black eyes as expressionless as a teddy bear's. Corrado Prizzi, who had known some of the most labyrinthian minds of his generation, had called Angelo Partanna "the most devious mind ever to come out of Sicily, Israel, or Ireland." He had brought Angelo to New York from Agrigento fifty-five years before, and Angelo had, from that day onward, plotted at his side. If a poll could have been taken among the executives of the twenty-six Mafia families of the United States, Angelo Partanna would have been voted "the *consigliere*'s *condigliere*."

"Tell them to get out," the don said.

Angelo turned and looked at the assembly that was scattered across the enormous room either stoical or sobbing. They filed out of the room.

"Are they gone?"

"Yeah."

"Is the door shut?"

"Yeah."

"The will—my letter—" He closed his eyes.

"Where is it?"

"*La forza del destino*—Angelo! Lissena me. When it's over, you gotta promise me—the funeral—just the people who are here today. Don't tell nobody till I'm in the ground. Protect Eduardo and Mae's kids, your own grandchildren. Keep the money safe forever."

He sagged into a dark brown forest where dark brown dust filled the air gradually shutting out all light. He called out as he fell. "Swear it!" Then the blackness cradled him.

"I swear it, Corrado." Angelo felt the blow instantaneously. Don Corrado Prizzi, ninety-six, once an immigrant boy who had come to America, sweatless in December, with his little family and tiny nest egg, who had multiplied that pittance into an $11 billion fortune, had passed into the ages. He had been the most *mafiusu* of all of the *capo di capi* that the history of the *fratellanza* had ever known, and now he was gone to the angels. Angelo felt a great power of energy leave the room as when Santa went up the chimney on Christmas Eve. He crossed himself, wept for a few moments, wiped his eyes, and, as he had all of his life, kept his own counsel when he left the room.

In the hall Charles Barton was saying, "Jerusalem crickets! I never saw the don looking so badly. And that is saying a lot."

"He looks so badly and he felt so still that I have a terrible feeling," Mary Barton sobbed, holding up her Aunt Amalia.

Eduardo patted her shoulder. "No, no. Not at all. He needs rest, that's all. It's probably just a minor digestive problem."

"Oh, I hope so, Uncle Eduardo."

"I have to get back on the road, but you fellows can come cheer him up in the morning. Angelo, may I talk to you for a moment?"

Mary Barton knew she was only a few of the don's breaths away from her destiny. From the time she was twelve years old, she knew that one day she would take over all the powers of her grandfather and become the first woman don, the first *capa di famiglia* in the seven-hundred-year history of the Mafia. This was the day of the greatest triumph of her life no matter what else ever happened to her. This was why she had married her husband and was going to have his children. Suddenly a terrible thought entered her dreams of glory. Her grandfather had to die for her to take over his powers, but when he died, there would have to be a funeral and she and her husband would be expected to appear at the funeral of the most notorious of all organized criminals of all time. The world would see her for what she was. She would be exposed to all the rotten things the media was capable of showing. Her already extraordinary position in New York's nouvelle society would be at awful risk. She shuddered.

Angelo and Eduardo withdrew a few yards down the hall. Eduardo said, "My father told me to ask you about the PACs we control."

"I have a list."

"Is it—can it possibly be—23,856 PACs spread over forty-three states?"

"If he said it, it is."

"Public campaign financing is a complicated system. A candidate must meet certain conditions such as raising five thousand dollars in at least twenty states before the government will match the money any campaign puts up—and that could run to six million dollars and up for a well-financed candidate to the day the government money is freed in January nineteen ninety-two, next month. I have spent almost six million in fifty states, so I qualify."

"Your father was talking 23,856 PACs with twenty, twenty-five million dollars."

"My God! If we can make the transfer before December thirty-first, I can make it. With the matching money, I can have thirty, forty million dollars in the campaign chest. I can be president! Nobody in the whole field of candidates can raise more than five million for the homestretch campaigning—plus equal matching funds."

"Naturally, Eduardo, you know yourself all those PACs can't go to you."

"They can't?" His face went blank. "Why not?"

"Because we got to protect the two-party system. Half has to go to the Democrats. What would be the sense of having muscle with only one party?"

"Half?"

"Say you get twelve thousand PACs, they get eleven thousand. We can shade it a little."

"Can you meet with my people sometime tomorrow?"

"You are really going for it, Eduardo?"

He nodded. "It was my father's wish," he said stiffly. "I'm not a frivolous man, Angelo. You know that. I've been going for it since my first denial that I was going for it. And I can get it. Can we set up a meeting?"

It was impossible for Angelo to give something and get nothing. "Will there be something in this for Charley?"

"What do you mean?"

"I mean, if you make it, a good spot—recognition. Something nice."

"But Charley is the family Democrat."

"So if you win you'll be big about it. You'll call for bipartisan action."

"Like what for Charley?"

"Who knows? If you agree in principle, we can talk about it later. Quash a few indictments for him. Throw a coupla dozen defense contracts his way. Lose a coupla IRS files for him. Load him down with insider trading information. Move a little of that arms money for our Freedom Fighters into his personal account."

"All right." Accepting the idea really stuck in Eduardo's craw. God! Imagine being forced to appoint a man with Charley's background as ambassador to the Court of St. James's—but PACs were the name of the game. "Have the lists ready. And Angelo?" he drawled.

"Yeah?"

"I'd like to see that letter of my father's. Could you send me a copy?"

"If there are copies people could say it's a will. If it's a will, it's taxable."

"But I am entitled to read that letter."

"Sure you are. I'll show it to you. Then you'll hand it back to me."

Eduardo shook his head slowly as if he had seen a miracle: 23,856 PACs. He couldn't believe it. Then the realization hit him that his father had cheated him again. Half of those PACs had to go to the Democrats.

The don had been a student of what had to be seen as a possibly brutal side of American politics, that structure by which the Congress of the United States provided the means to have themselves openly and legally bribed. Corrado Prizzi had understood it instantly and had employed PACs from the first moment of their legal existence, even though it took away from bribery all the craft and skill that his people had been so many centuries learning. Not that he did anything differently from any other group that was now empowered to bribe its government. He had organized his people the way the American Medical Association PACs were set up, the way the American Bankers' and the Used Car Dealers' PACs had been organized. His national PAC mechanism source, under the warm-hearted law, was made up of the fifty-four principal crime groups of the country: the twenty-six Mafia families as well as the Blacks, the Hispanics, and the Orientals who constituted the national American merchandising force to bring forward the narcotics, gambling, vice, and the manifold other activities that the American people so zealously demanded. The PACs were all small organizations, truly the voice of the people: 23,856 PACs each offering up an average of $100,000 had yielded almost $25 million in political bribes, so it could be regarded as altogether certain that the bribed would show real gratitude to the bribers even as they had shown it to the American Medical Association and to the bankers, used car dealers, the toxic waste disposers, and so many others who celebrated the greenbacking of America.

22

At 1:47 A.M., December 12, before the dawn of the first day Corrado Prizzi would never see, two people forced the service door of the Prizzi mansion, found their way to the foot of the back staircase with ease in the darkness, and climbed the two flights with one of them carrying a folded stretcher. They entered the upstairs kitchen across from the top of the back stairs while Mariano Orecchione, Calorino's night relief, slept lightly in a chair in the hall outside the door to the don's room, a sawed-off shotgun in his lap. They faded across the kitchen, closing the door behind them, and entered the don's room. They lifted the lifeless body out of the bed and laid it on the pallet and carried it out of the room, across the kitchen and out into the back hall.

The morbid procession went down the steeply raked back stairs, silently passing the floor on which Amalia slept, taking the body out of the service entrance to a large truck that was parked at the delivery door. On its side was painted the legend, yellow on red:

TWO BOROS MEAT COMPANY
Refrigerated Truck.

One of the people activated the mechanism that lowered the freight lift platform. They rose to door level with the body, opened the door of the truck, and slid the body on the stretcher into the subfreezing temperatures, then walked to the driver's cabin, got in, and drove away.

The truck rolled out onto a deserted pier on the Brooklyn waterfront. A refrigerator freight ship, one of a Barker's Hill fleet, the RS *Jack Frost*, was tied up at the pier under sparse, harsh lighting that made shadows as heavy as those that fell across the river Lethe. The truck stopped at the freighter's open side port, level with the pier. There was a short work plank for boarding. The two body snatchers unloaded the stretcher from the back of the truck and carried it aboard the freighter.

They took the body along a long row of facing freezer-lockers, opening the fourth locker door and switching on the lights, to reveal hanging sides of beef, pork, and lamb, then slammed the door shut impatiently. They carried the stretcher to the next locker. As the door was opened, an empty storage cubicle was revealed. The stretcher was lifted to a shelf in the locker. As they left a large padlock was closed on the door; then they started down the companionway to encounter a ship's captain coming in the opposite direction.

"All set?" he asked.

The head ghoul said, "Don't fuck around with that padlock, Bocca, and you'll be all right. What's the first port of call?"

"It's a triangle run. New York to Brazzaville in the Congo to unload the meat and load fresh fruit, then to Liverpool to unload the fruit and take on cheese, then back to New York to unload the cheese and load more meat."

"When do you sail?"

The officer looked at his watch. "In fifty minutes," he said.

23

Calorino Barbaccia relieved Mariano Orecchione at 6:55 A.M. The men were old friends, an elite force, the palace guard of the Prizzi family.

"Did he have a quiet night?" Calo asked.

"Like a tomb."

Mariano propped the sawed-off shotgun up against the wall and, yawning, started down the main stairs.

"It's Lady Carrot in the fifth at Hialeah," Calorino called after him, then entered the don's room.

"Good morning!" he sang in a professional nurse's voice, a merry call. There was no answer. He went to the windows and pulled back the curtains, letting light into the room, and singing a chorus of "Pretty Baby" with a heavy Agrigento accent.

Whenna youse wake up inna mawnin'
Anna sun begins tuh shine,
Priddy Bay-bee

He turned toward the bed, stopping short.

"Don Corrado!" he said sharply. He moved past the empty bed to the bathroom and came right out again, calling the don's name. He went into the kitchen. He came back and opened closet doors. He looked under the bed, saying, "Come on, don't kid around, *padrino*. What the fuck is this?"

He went to the telephone and dialed Angelo Partanna's number. Angelo answered on the second ring.

"Yeah?"

"It's Calorino, *signore*. I come in at the don's and he ain't there. I looked all over. I don't see him."

"Where's the night man?"

"He went home."

"Call the laundry and send somebody for him. Get him back. But stay calm. We don't want nobody yelling about this. I'll be right over."

"Si, signore." He hung up relieved that it was somebody else's responsibility.

Angelo called Charley. Maerose answered, wide awake as soon as she heard his voice.

"Mae—Angelo. Lemme talk to Charley."

"Charley flew to Washington last night. He's got a seven-thirty breakfast with President Heller this morning."

"How come?"

"Heller found out Charley is our Democrat. About eight big businessmen are invited. Four of them run companies which Barker's Hill controls. They never met Charley, so they'll be knocking themselves out to make points with him, which will be hard on Heller."

"I gotta talk to Charley. Mae, lissena me—we got a problem."

"Whatsa matta?"

"Not on the phone. You think you can get Charley at the White House?"

"I guess so. Why not?"

137

"Tell him to get back to New York as quick as he can and go to your grandfather's house."

"Angelo, fahcrissake."

"Meet me there as soon as you can." He hung up.

He called Eduardo's private number, which had been installed primarily for Miss Claire Coolidge. The phone rang beside Eduardo's bed.
"Yes, sweedhard?" Eduardo cooed into the phone.

"It's Angelo. Get out to Brooklyn right away. He left us."

"He's gone?"

"Yeah. Meet me there. I'll bring all the PAC lists because there's no chance we can have another meet today." He hung up.

One of the Barker's Hill helicopters had picked Charley up at the East River heliport and landed him at the National Airport in Washington at 7:02 A.M. Charley thought that perhaps he ought to be more awestruck about being summoned to breakfast by the president of the United States in the private quarters at the White House, but the country was still groping its way out of a heavy steam of corruption that had settled over it during the administration of the spry, elderly president who had preceded Heller. He was a man who had been so reflexively amiable, so defiant of the laws of morality and consequence that, by being all things to all men, he had insured anarchy in his government with his unrelenting charm and disregard for the Constitution and the law.

Charley knew it must have been full-time work for the elderly astrologer-president, just as it had been for Corrado Prizzi, in a slightly different way. But through all the studied diffidence and the boyish matinee-today-as-usual shrugs, 162 cabinet members, White House aides, a cherished family press agent, deputy secretaries, political lobbygows, military officers, cronies, and nominees of the old gaffer had been publicly charged with, indicted for, convicted of, or had resigned because of conflict of interest, influence peddling, perjury, illegal profiteering, fraud, conspiracy, felony, obstruction of justice, and many uglier offenses. There had been so much corruption in the highest places that, simultaneously, six separate investigations by as many government-appointed separate investigators had been required.

The old geezer had been more like a *capo di famiglia* than a president, Charley recalled fondly, but when asked to describe the legacy he would leave the nation after eight years in office, the old wool-gatherer had said, "I hope that the imprint would be one of high morality." He urged schools and parents to impart "the right and wrong of things to young people."

The holy men for whom the dear old clotheshorse had secured such exalted and profitable television pulpits inside the checkbooks of the American pious had fallen effortlessly into the ways of Sodom and Moloch and were indecently exposing themselves as moneychangers inside their own electronic temples. A wee television kirk in Fort Hill, South Carolina, with its 13 million worshippers, was not only $66.7 million in debt, but $92 million of its plate money had gone missing, disappointing the old bungler because he had made the television clergy his henchmen.

The Gipper, idolized by his people, had, in the dire times of the historic budget deficit that he had crafted and that threatened the safety and sanity of the country for generations to come, tripled the amount of unaccountable secret funds for his departments of defense, state, the CIA, and the White House to the point where such secret funds were the fastest-growing major sector of the federal budget.

Many of the dear old coot's patriotic defense contractors had defrauded the country out of billions of dollars, just passing the time while they waited deep in the bushes under the shade of the money tree for the old outlaw's promise of riches untold to come true with the glorious Star Wars opportunity that everyone but the money-eaters said could not work but that was guaranteed to cost almost as much money as the bastion of democracy could print.

While the old gent napped away the afternoons upstairs in the White House, a light colonel of Marines had run a secret government in the basement with his own private treasury, army, air force, diplomatic corps, covert operations, and foreign bank accounts, all of it funded by the taxpayers of the United States, who lived in numbing fear that Nicaragua, like Cuba before it, would attack and ravage the United States.

The elderly waver's roster of corruption was so heinous as to make the malfeasances of U. S. Grant, Warren Harding, and Richard Nixon, separately or combined, seem to be little slips in comportment or innocent, forgivable slips of judgment, but all of it had the effect of making Charley feel as much at home in Washington as if he were back in Brooklyn in the old days. He had to admit that the Prizzis weren't in it at all when compared to the old dreamer. The dear old man, shuffling through history, had been more instantly lovable than Corrado Prizzi, but the overall effects produced had been the same. Both had offered diversions for the people, whether they had come packed in cocaine or wrapped in the folds of an enormous American flag. Neither of them had been able to do anything wrong in the public's heart of hearts, particularly the old actor, no matter what crimes had been committed behind the dense hedge of lieutenants. Honor in government had become a sardonic phrase. *The New York Times* was moved to write, "No President in modern times has put up a more moralistic front and has done less to enforce ethical standards in government."

Frantic to find safety from the shriveling blast of the president's charm, the people couldn't stop running and the poor were always underfoot. Foreign policy was made on what was best for the counting rooms, creating a perplexity in the country, which wondered why most of the world was its enemy. A nation starved for hope and heroes had either eaten its illusions—the cannibalism of the twentieth century— or had embraced its own image in a sky-high distorting mirror.

The president was waiting for Charley in the family quarters at the White House. Franklin M. Heller was the antithesis of his predecessor, the Old One. He had never been known to wave. As far as was known he did not know a single anecdote. His wife was only seen by the media on Christmas Day and even then cloaked in a black *chador*, the long head-to-foot garment of Islamic Iran, worn symbolically as a reminder to the incumbent of the awful mistakes that could be made. Heller had four children and they all lived at home. He smiled only at funerals and even then with a spamodic twitch like the opening and closing of a camera shutter, vanishing before he could be caught in the act. A black swag of skin hung under each eye in formal mourning for the national budget deficit.

On the morning of Charley's visit, he was massively avuncular. He shook hands like a Sumo wrestler, put an arm around Charley's shoulders, and said, "We can talk on the way down to breakfast." Charley was stiff with awe of his new surroundings, if not the resident. He was standing where the American history he had studied in high school had been made. Thinking of high school made him think of a Puerto Rican woman he had known there, a fantastic dresser, but he shook the thought off. Presidents had always been people on the tube, the headliners of the greatest showbiz—now this one had an arm around him. "I was glad to read that you are a faithful Democrat, Charley," Heller said as they waited for the elevator. "What I wanted to tell you, the first chance we had, is that it takes two hands to get them both washed. If you pitch in and organize the business community for me, when I'm re-elected, you are going to get recognition, you follow me? For example, do you want Treasury?"

"My stars and body, Mr. President. You have my one hundred percent support."

"We can use however many PACs you are able to get together, Charley. Let me send some of my people to see you in New York so we can make the allocations."

"Anytime, Mr. President."

They went in to the breakfast room. Eight earth-tremblingly puissant men stood up.

The White House operator told Mary Barton that she'd get the message to Mr. Barton as soon as he came out of the breakfast meeting. Mary Barton ordered the car to meet Charley at La Guardia, dressed rapidly, drank two glasses of pink grapefruit juice, then went out on the street to find a cab. It took her almost forty minutes to get to the don's house.

Charley was handed the message as he came out of the breakfast room at the White House. He was in a sour mood not only because it had been a fucking prayer breakfast, which he thought had gone out forever with Nixon and Carter, but because he was boxed in by the four executives who headed the colossal companies that were controlled by Barker's Hill, each one crowding for a position at his elbow, but whom he had never met. They were giants of American industry. "Gimme room, here!" he snarled, laying the fear on them. They recoiled with the shock of his glance and stepped away. Charley read the message.

"I gotta get outta here," he said and walked rapidly to the coat-rack, then to the South Portico. On the lawn beyond the driveway he

141

said a few convincing words of strong support for Franklin M. Heller on behalf of the American business community into the permanent installation of television cameras, which kept an eternal vigil there for the evening news. The man from *W* magazine demanded to know whom he would support for chief of protocol in the upcoming administration. Charley handled him with kid gloves because he didn't want Mae on his back. A White House car drove him to the airport.

Barker's Hill kept a few fast six-passenger Sikorsky helicopters for the short intercity trips, but that was too slow for Charley. He caught a shuttle. Mae had the Rolls and Danvers waiting for him at La Guardia. He got to the don's house at 11:35 A.M.

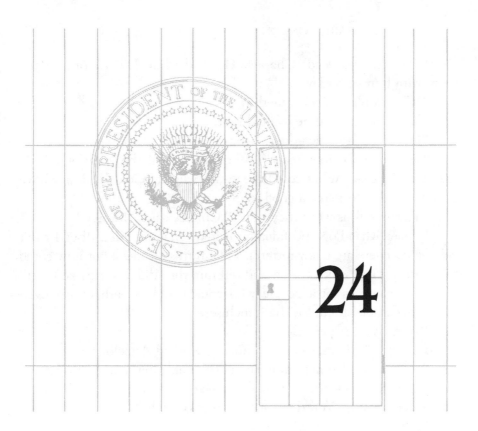

24

Mariano, on the door at the don's house while Calo sat in despair upstairs, didn't recognize Charley (who had been the hero of his boyhood), so he dummied up, pretending not to speak English, and pushed at Charley's chest with the length of the sawed-off shotgun. Charley hit him with the fear. "Take the weapon off the threads, creep. I am Charles Macy Barton," he said, and walked across the hall and up the stairs.

Pop and Mae sat facing each other. Maerose was wearing a scarlet sweater and a black skirt. Pop, in his black suit, had his head back, his eyes closed. He sat up as Charley came in.

"What happened?" Charley said.

"Somebody snatched the don."

"Whaaaaaaat?"

"Only he was dead, Charley. He died while I was alone in the room with him yesterday."

"Why didn't you say something?"

"He didn't tell me he wanted that."

"Jesus, Pop, I've heard of *omertà*, but—"

Maerose broke into tears. "Who would steal the body of a little old man like that? What could they want with it? God, he didn't have enough on him to make a good soup."

"They'll tell us what they want," Charley said. "Money."

"That's what Pop and Eduardo think," Maerose said. "But I can't believe it. There are a few rotten people in this business, but how could they face a priest at confession and tell him they did a thing like that?"

"There was a lotta people who coulda took a oath to get even when we dumped them for the franchises."

"Watch your speech, Charley!"

He gulped. "Is that not so, Pater?" he asked Angelo.

"Maybe, but I don't think so. How could they know he dropped out? Even we didn't know he was sick—he just went."

Maerose said, "You think it was an inside job?"

"I didn't say nothing."

"Six people knew—the three of us plus Eduardo, Amalia, and Calorino. The doctor is out because the don was alive when the doctor left. Amalia is the only one who didn't leave the house after the don collapsed. It wasn't Charley. It wasn't me. God knows it wasn't you, Angelo."

"It wasn't Eduardo—he's running for president," Angelo said. "It would look bad if it came out he had snatched his own father's body."

"Where is Eduardo? He ought to be here," Charley said.

"He was here. He hadda go to Iowa."

"Iowa?"

"The campaign."

"Amalia's out," Mary Barton continued. "That leaves Calo."

"Calo is too dumb to think like that, and he loved the don," Charley said.

"So that means nobody done it, but the don ain't here," Angelo said.

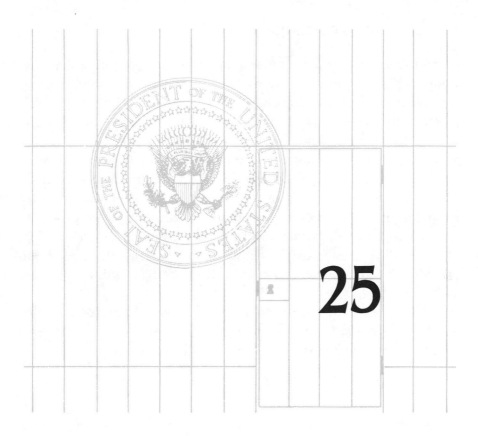

25

Edward S. Price was taking his run for the presidency seriously. He had lured away the former chairman of the Republican National Committee to become his principal campaign adviser. He had announced his choice for the vice-presidency on the ticket as Caspar P. "Junior" Lear, the billionaire agro-industrial farmer. He had formed and had announced a shadow cabinet, carefully weighted with gloriously prominent men and women, one black, one yuppie, one astronaut, a former secretary of state, and a champion of women's rights, among the power brokers, deal makers, and technicians, each one chosen for the number of PACs he could guarantee to bring into the campaign.

The looming presence of presidential primaries in a third of the fifty states had changed all campaign tactics. Times had changed since money could be spread around among local political bosses in 90 percent of the states for a guarantee that the right nominating delegates would appear at the convention. Nineteen ninety-two would be the first election where the process would be refined to the point of (almost) constituting an open nomination in both parties, and Franklin M. Heller, the incumbent, running unopposed, already had it sewn up for the Democrats. At least 66 percent of the total Republican delegates would be determined by the finish on Super Tuesday, March 8, 1992. So, for one thing, victory, state by state, depended upon the candidate having a lot more money to spread around than any other candidate and not only for advertising and legitimate campaign expenses. Blocs of nominating votes could be delivered in the states that didn't run primaries and the people who could deliver the blocs still cost an arm and a leg.

There were early primaries and late primaries. A candidate needed a war chest of from three to six million dollars to finance the former so that he could have the stamina to hang in for the latter.

12,856 NEW PACs SWING
BEHIND PRICE CANDIDACY

MARSHALTOWN, IOWA, December 29—In a simultaneous vote of confidence from Political Action Committees in 43 states, representing groups as various as the Alaskan Field Hockey Association, the Italian-American Baptist League and the United Fruit & Berry Pickers, what appeared to be the widest pre-election swath of voters in the nation's history committed their support en masse today for the Republican Presidential slate of Edward S. Price and Caspar P. Lear, Jr. This extraordinary avowal will add thirteen million dollars to the campaign chest of the already widely supported ticket of one of the country's most acclaimed businessmen and the billionaire farmer who seeks the nomination as his Vice-President. The nation-wide support of the 12,856 PACs will swell the Price-Lear ticket's estimated available Republican campaign funds by the addition of assured Federal matching funds to more than sixty million dollars.

The candidate who is a far-off second to Price's campaign expenditure is Connecticut Governor Gordon Manning who, until today, was rated as the front-runner. "There is something very fishy about this sudden rush of PAC money to Price," Governor Manning said, "but we can't put our finger on it."

"While the meaning of this great tide is overwhelming in terms of financial support," Edward S. Price said, "what it really means is that millions of American voters have put their money where their hearts are."

"Until this morning," said Carter B. Modred, former chairman of the Republican National Committee, now chief political adviser to the Price-Lear candidacy, "this looked like the first election in modern times with a really open nomination in the Party, but that is over now. Ed Price and Junior Lear sure look like they have it locked up."

(continued on page three)

WHITE HOUSE ANNOUNCES
11,488 PACs FOR HELLER

WASHINGTON, D.C., December 29—An election bombshell was thrown into the arena today when the White House announced that 11,488 PACs with swelling electoral funds, in a national coalition of support by such voting groups as the Farmer's Benefit Sodality, the Friends of Afghanistan, and the Steeple Jacks of America, threw their unanimous support behind the reelection of Franklin M. Heller with twelve million nine hundred thousand dollars of concentrated support.

"Never in the history of our great nation," the incumbent candidate said to the assembled press, "has such totally simultaneous partisanship been accorded to a candidate for the highest American office. The action brings further proof, if such were needed, that the Democratic ticket will sweep to victory in November."

(cont'd page 3)

Charley was summoned to the White House on the afternoon of the announcement. The president saw him alone in the Oval Office. The president, with those great salt tears that had made him so celebrated as a politician filling his eyes, said to Charley, "Never have so few been given so much by so many. You and your people have won my gratitude, Charley, and I think you know what that means—you can have anything you want that is within my power to give you."

"Godfrey and ginger, Mr. President! That's just the beginning."

"By God, you warm my heart, Charley!"

"The law also allows us to make unlimited contributions to the party's individual state organizations, and I've just been waiting to do that under your direction."

"Well, then! I'll send my people to you in New York!"

147

"There's something else, Mr. President—if I'm not being too presumptuous—"

"Presumptuous? You are manifesting the American way of life!"

"I've also been able to get together an unmarked fund of five million dollars for street money, Mr. President." Street money was the green cash that the vote brokers, who merchandise and deliver blocs of votes, spend (and hold out) to move large single-minded units of neighborhood voters into the polls. The money is delivered to clergymen, young lawyers, scoutmasters, and schoolteachers, who, in turn, distribute ten- or twenty-dollar bills to the voting blocs to which they have been assigned. Street money had swung key districts, even key states, in close elections.

"Call me Frank," Heller said hoarsely, choking up with the emotion of this man's generosity. "And you gotta know that I'm not going to forget this."

The week following the disappearance of Corrado Prizzi's body, while being the best Edward S. Price and F. M. Heller had ever known, was the worst Angelo Partanna, Amalia, and the Bartons had ever experienced and that included the Appalachia meeting. The matter of the body's disappearance had, as a matter of family policy, been kept away from the attention of the police. Angelo had made discreet inquiries throughout the American crime community about any news concerning the snatching of any dead bodies of prominent people, but he drew a blank.

Charles Barton checked with his father twice a day. Amalia waited beside the phone at the Prizzi mansion for three weeks, but no call came. Mary Barton, insofar as her pregnancy permitted it, sat vigil with Amalia, trying to persuade her to close the big house and to move into the Barton quadriplex in New York, trying to bribe her with the promise that she could do all the cooking, but Amalia would not hear of it. "Close the house? So how could they get in touch?" she said. "And Calo will stay on the door, so don't worry about me." After making that effort, Mary Barton seemed to disappear from view. She stayed in her bedroom at Sixty-fourth Street most of the time, ate very little, and grew gaunter and more haggard with worry about the indignity that had been dumped upon her grandfather's body, wherever it was.

148

Perhaps Charles Barton was the hardest hit by the body-snatching. For all the years of Charley's (former) life, Corrado Prizzi had been his hero, just as Angelo Partanna had been his model. He could not conceive of anyone having the barbarism to violate the don's body when he had been alive and the horror doubled at the thought of anyone desecrating the meaning of such a man by denying him burial in consecrated ground when he was dead.

Charley stood in front of his surrounding mirrors in his changing room at the top of Barker's Hill and the various bathrooms of the great house on Sixty-fourth Street and spoke binding oaths of vengeance upon whoever had committed the sacrilege against justice. He vowed to hunt the perpetrators down if the doing consumed all the days of his life, in his spare time. He pressed his father for news of the netherworld, for wisps of information from any and all rumors, but each day erected the blank wall of hopelessness between the possibility of a Christian burial for his don and the necessity for inflicting terrible punishment upon the desecrators.

As Charley brooded, his hero, quite blue, slept on at flashfreezing temperatures, belonging to the ages, as his host ship made the long diagonal run from New York to Brazzaville in the African Congo.

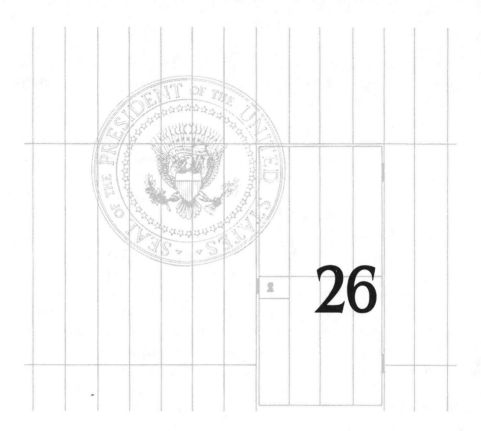

26

Eduardo succeeded in arranging the meeting with Angelo to read his father's last letter of simple wishes for his family by sending a limousine to bring Angelo from Brooklyn to Newark Airport and instructing his pilots to land the *Ronald Reagan* for a forty-minute stopover between Baton Rouge, Louisiana, and Bangor, Maine.

The two men sat in the office section of Eduardo's campaign plane behind a locked door. Angelo produced the letter and handed it over. Eduardo adjusted his reading glasses to study the letter.

> *TO MY BELOVED FAMILY,*
> *I have very little to leave you except my love. My clothes, my personal effects, my paintings, furniture, and phonograph records, together with this house, were all given to the Blessed Decima Manovale Foundation*

150

long years ago for, you see, I wish to leave this world as I had once entered it: without possessions. You have all done so well in this new country of ours that I am filled with pride of you. How wise you were, Amalia, to save that nest egg of $500,000 from which you will have the interest for the rest of your life, then to pass that interest on to your son, Rocco. How generous you were, my Eduardo, son of my hopes and dreams who realized every one of those hopes and every dream, to form the Price Foundation at the very outset of the establishment of the Barker's Hill Enterprises which will provide, in the majority sense of 51 percent, control of its funds and purposes by my great-grandsons, Conrad Price and Angier Macy Barton, to be administered by their loving parents until the brothers reach the age of thirty years. That you retained 20 percent of the funding of the Foundation for yourself is as I would have wished it, my son. May happiness and glory be yours for all of your days. My grandchildren, Maerose and Teresa, Arthur and Rocco, being of sound minds and bodies were successful in their own rights and to them I wish every continuing happiness, but to my grandsons I leave, to Arthur, my Ingersoll pocket watch, the timepiece of railroad engineers, and to Rocco, my John F. Kennedy PT boat tiepin.

(Signed) Corrado Prizzi

Witnessed by: Batsford Glick
Governor, State of New York

Carter B. Kilgore
Chief Justice, U.S. Supreme Court

Cencetto Balugi
Papal Nuncio

Patrick Joseph Mulligan
Secretary-General, United Nations Organization

Eduardo's eyes were filled with tears. He could not read on through the list of the other twelve witnesses to the intimate note his father had left behind. As he wiped his eyes he thought again that, more than ever, he had to find some way to offset his father's parsimony in some forthright tax-free way, not that the money itself mattered, but just to get a little back to show that he was not entirely that easily outsmarted, even by such a Sicilian as his father.

"I'm just a little surprised that he didn't remember you with a little something," he said to Angelo.

"He let me have eight percent of the franchise operation. I mean, what more do I want? I never travel and I don't even eat out much anymore."

"Eight percent must be a rather good piece."

Angelo shrugged. "Fifteen, sixteen million a year."

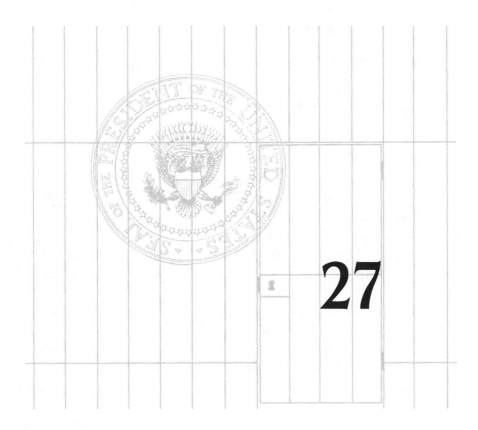

27

Mary Barton was so preoccupied with the disappearance of her grandfather's body that it was not until Christmas Eve that she realized she had not had a report from Charley on his power breakfast at the White House.

They had a quiet Sicilian sort of dinner, cooked by Charley in the Sixty-fourth Street house after refusing twenty-three social invitations because, quite suddenly, Mary Barton, in addition to the shame and grief over her grandfather's disappearance, had begun to show her double pregnancy in a spectacular way.

"What happened at the breakfast with Heller, Charley?"

"At the breakfast, nothing. Four of the other people he had there froze out the president trying to make me notice them."

"You never got a chance to talk to Heller?"

"Before. They sent me upstairs to where he lives. He was genial in a sour way."

"Of course he was genial and sour. He's a politician. What did he say?"

"He said he would appreciate my support."

"He wants you to set up some PACs?"

"Yeah. What's that?"

"Political Action Committees—a license to bribe."

"Where do I get them?"

"Pop has them."

"Anyway, he's going to send his people to see me in New York for the pickup. And he asked me if I wanted Treasury in the next administration."

"Treasury? What kind of a dead end is that?"

"Dead end?"

"Did you ever hear of anybody ever going from Treasury to the White House? And I am talking even Andrew Mellon."

"I never followed that stuff." He straightened up with alarm. "What do you mean?"

"I mean Herbert Hoover went from Commerce to the White House, but that was a freak thing. Through the cabinet is the wrong route."

"Wrong route for who?"

"You."

"Me?"

"Why not? Eduardo isn't going to make it—he has a lousy personality and he's a widower. Eduardo is the next attorney general, but, even if I'm wrong and he does make it, by law he's good for only eight years. You'll be only 64 in the year two thousand and one, which is exactly the right age for a president."

"What the fuck is this, Mae?"

"Watch the language, Charley. And my name is Mary, remember? You'll have eight years experience at running Barker's Hill. How is running Barker's Hill different from being president of the United States? But we've got to bring you up the right way—like if you started as vice-president—Coolidge, Truman, Johnson, Nixon, and Ford made it on that route—or through solid foreign policy experience, like ambassador-at-large, because the voters will know that you know the domestic thing."

"Mae, lissena me—"

"I'm not saying you should get State. After all, they gave Al Haig State and look what happened. Let me think about it for a while."

"Are you nuts, Mae?"

"Charley, fahcrissake! Anybody can be president! Look at Reagan! When are you going to understand that all it takes is an organization to keep up the heavy day-and-night PR, big PACs, and some good comedy writers. Hype and money. And we got both of those more than even Reagan ever had."

The twins were born on February 16, 1992. Suddenly, to his horror, Charley was on his own. Mary Barton lost all interest in Barker's Hill operations, in Charley's career, in the pressing decisions he had to make every day with which she had always helped him, even during the chaotic period of her grandfather's disappearance. For three months, ever since they had returned to New York, their routine had been to confer on the problems of Charley's day from 4:00 P.M. each afternoon until dinner, then for three hours after dinner. They had refused invitations. Mary Barton just dropped out as her husband's counsel, seeking forgetfulness of the shame that had happened to her grandfather by using her babies as an excuse.

"Charley, fahcrissake!" she said when he protested that he needed her to make the right decisions. "They're your kids, too! You think I'm gonna let them eat cow's milk when I got these two jugs on me?"

"But millions of dollars are involved here!"

"So the company will only make seventy million tomorrow instead of seventy-two. What is this? You are surrounded by the most expensive business talent in the country. So if one of them asks you a question, you ask one of the others for the answer. How do you think Eduardo ran the company?"

Mary Barton spent most of her waking hours with her children. She rolled them in the double pram to Central Park every morning and every afternoon, trailed by Al Melvini for security. Melvini was in his early sixties. He had a big paunch and heavy jowls. He was devoted to Maerose, whom he no longer dared to call Maerose, but Mrs. Barton. He carried two pieces, one in a back holster and one at his ankle. He kept ten to fifteen yards between himself and Mrs. Barton. She sat on a park bench, rain or shine, while the babies got their required time in the open air. She talked to them, beamed at them, and on mild days, changed their diapers in the carriage. At home, she supervised the nannies and took no calls until the babies were sleeping. She knitted their garments, sat up with them if they cried at night and, endlessly, plotted their future, having enrolled them at Groton and Harvard at birth.

And Charley came into his own. He felt the power. He was no longer the petticoat president of Barker's Hill Enterprises. After the twins had been weaned, Mary Barton turned her terrible concentration upon New York's nouvelle society to launch herself (and her husband) in fullest battle regalia.

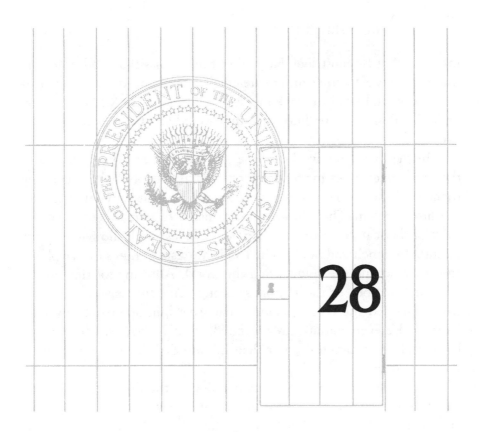

28

Except when it was raining, Charley didn't use his car and driver, which rolled along silently four feet behind him so that he could listen for the cellular telephone as he walked to the office, leaving Sixty-fourth Street at 6:45 in the morning and arriving at the Barker's Hill building at 7:04. Once he was delayed en route because he had to beat up a mugger who had obviously mistaken him for a mark, so most mornings he left the house with Al Melvini, the reliable strongarm. Seven hours sleep was enough, Mary Barton had explained to him, and he had to stay on top of the new job, hence the shocking hour of departure from the house. She had organized everything, at the office and at home, so that no sweat was involved. Each night before he left the office, he called for different files to take home. He didn't read them at home, but he had them at his desk early the next day because Mary Barton had drilled into him that he must look busy at all times. Miss Blue had been told that no one was to enter his private office unannounced, so that, whenever people did need to come in, she would sound the warning button under her desk with her knee, and they would find Charley poring over papers.

In the first three weeks on the job, he held meetings with all of the senior executives in the home office, fifty-four specialists, granting them a half-hour each and receiving the next one at sixty minutes after the first one left. This allowed him to listen to four executives a day (in alphabetical order of their fifty-four names) and allowed fifty-five minutes for lunch and one hundred and thirty-six minutes for telephone calls from around the country and the world. Allowing for time in the john and in front of the mirrors swearing vengeance against whoever had vandalized the don's memory, that gave him approximately nine hours and eleven minutes in the building each day, which was four hours and three minutes longer than Edward S. Price had spent, Mary Barton told him.

"Well—yes," Charley said, responding to the Price erg rate. "But Eduardo didn't have to see four executives a day at such fixed periods and he probably had his lunch in the office."

"Eduardo never ate lunch in his office, Charley."

Mary Barton had laid down a fixed routine for Charley to follow at each individual senior executive meeting. He would ask them to explain their jobs as they saw it in ten minutes. Halfway through the explanation, Charley would spray a little fear over them, engendering fright mixed with guilt in some cases, and, in the guilty cases, they would begin to backtrack on what they said, helping him to judge them. The method let Charley winnow out the reliable from the flaky, to mark at least two of them for transfer overseas, one of these to the company's spice manufactory on Devil's Island.

The second ten minutes were given over to suggestions from the men for streamlining or generally improving their operations. Charley stared at them implacably throughout these recitations, nodding at rare intervals. In the last decant of the meeting, the men were encouraged to bring their problems to Charley, which he would then ask them to repeat in memorandum form and to have the memo on his desk within twenty-four hours.

As the memoranda came in, Charley would turn them over to each of his two executive assistants, Chandler Sestero and Carleton Garrone, requiring that they return with a written answer to the problem by the end of the day. When the operational answer was on his desk, Charley called the senior executive who had raised the matter as a problem and gave him the solution, verbally, never in writing in case the recommendation turned out to be faulty. It was standard operating procedure in the corridors of power, whether in business or politics, a ponderous system that Mary Barton had soon made more effective by insisting that individual computer work stations be installed at each senior executive's desk so that the solutions could go out from a central computer in the Office of the Chief Executive to each work station, eliminating palaver and conserving Charley's time. As time went on she brought the Omaha-based Cray 3 supercomputer into it so that Charley—or someone delegated by Charley—could issue instantaneous solutions to policy problems directly to desks of the senior Barker's Hill executives in 74 cities in the continental United States, then, later, via satellite, to the individual stations in the 117 Barker's Hill offices in the world.

During the first year of Charley's leadership, Barker's Hill raided then took over eleven large companies worth $14.2 billion, instantly earning $4.7 billion by the raids. Working through its four brokerage house/investment banking firms on Wall Street, BH made $317 million from insider trading made possible by the foreknowledge of the takeover transactions. Its junk bond flotations and leveraged buyouts had further increased earnings by means so shady as to have made Charley flinch if no one else in the firm. Its enormous Department of Defense contractors, who remained fixed in place no matter what heinous revelations were made concerning the shoddiness of their products or the towering amounts of profits they made on the unit prices charged, showed an annual increase, under Charley's leadership, of $5.1 billion. Through it all, he made all the Barker's Hill companies toe the line and was gratified that they delivered an increase of 17.3 percent over the yields produced by Edward Price's stewardship.

Throughout all of Charley's first year on the bridge at Barker's Hill, the company's superb public relations department, the 117 people of the Community Affairs division, concentrated on establishing Charley in the minds of the American people as one of the greatest business leaders of history. The public relations department of Barker's Hill, like that of Ronald Reagan, could be compared to the Lords of Shouting of the Old Testament, consisting of 1,550 angels "all singing glory to the Lord." It is written that, because of the chanting of the Lords of Shouting, "judgment is lightened and the world is blessed." Charley, like Ronald Reagan, left golden footprints wherever he walked amid the hosannahs that confirmed his glory.

Charles Macy Barton showed up on the evening news rotating across the five networks, about three times every month. His byline over his recorded opinions on absolutely everything that was the currency of the day seemed to live on the op-ed pages of the great American newspapers. No Sunday morning was complete for the American family without seeing and hearing Charles Macy Barton and his breathtaking tailoring on the talk shows. Sam Donaldson beamed upon him. William F. Buckley, Jr., purred over him. If there was a national crisis of any kind, McNeil-Lehrer called him before their inquisitors. He made pronouncements regarding acid rain, the strength of the dollar, urged a close economic alliance with Japan providing it was brought to its knees, discussed cures for stuttering, took a stand on surrogate motherhood, abortion, and school prayer, condemned the Soviet while praising *glasnost* to the skies, and, through it all, his PR people never stopped selling him as the greatest organizer of American history. Over and over again this image of Charley reappeared in the print and electronic media of the world, until his name became a household word. Charley was instantly recognizable to the American people, and universally known, as the Great Organizer. The business schools of great universities used case histories in which Charley's towering judgment dominated: he was the sublime model of the American business executive as reflected in the claims made by his PR people. It was the American way because it revered the holy Bible. The Lords of Shouting had returned to bring salvation to the pious.

A growing amount of time, usually on Saturday morning or at the Sixty-fourth Street house at odd hours, whenever the president wanted advice or information, Charley (and Mary Barton) would need to turn their attentions to that set of problems. Not altogether slowly, Franklin M. Heller and Charley had built an intimate relationship in that election year of 1992. Heller had convinced himself that Charley had vital information at his fingertips and could get it faster than the White House staff could get it, on certain issues such as Republican Party strategies.

When the White House had to have instant information on projected Republican moves, Charley would call Pop at the laundry in Brooklyn. Pop would call Eduardo wherever he was; then Eduardo would turn the matter over to his principal campaign adviser, Carter B. Modred, former national chairman of the Republican party, to get the information in all partisan innocence. Eduardo would call Pop with it. Pop would pass the word immediately to Mary Barton, who would tell Charley. Charley would then call the delighted president.

If the Republicans planned a major offensive relating to international trade or planned evasive tactics to avoid vitally necessary increased taxation, before they could announce it, the White House was able to call in the media and lay down a superseding program of its own. The same happened in all the major campaign areas: foreign policy, defense positions, and election year promises on the support of the Freedom Fighters no matter where they were bleeding for democracy in the world.

"I don't know how you do it, Charley," Heller said every time. "The opposition is absolutely emasculated. Your information is always better than the stuff my staff gets and twice as fast."

Two months after the breaking-in period in New York, Charley and his personal staff of seventeen troubleshooters took to the road in the wide-bodied company jet to attend the get-acquainted meetings Mary Barton had insisted be organized in fifteen key cities, drawing an average of five Barker's Hill field office senior executives into the key cities of their region. The procedure was fixed: Charley took over the office of the head BH honcho in each key city and received delegations of up to twelve senior field executives to whom he gave a short talk that had been prepared by Mary Barton and that drove home the new quotas and raised objectives of the new headquarters management. It was a short talk allowing just enough time for Charley to spray a light steam of fear over those attending the meetings; then he would leave the meeting to the home-office executives concerned with the assembled divisions and go off to look at the branch's computer installation, its squash courts, and its Jacuzzis.

In California he had the chance to renew his old friendship with the lieutenant governor, Arthur Shuland. Not that he was able to reveal the basis of their lifetime friendship, when he had been Charley Partanna. He was the new head of Barker's Hill Enterprises. That was enough. Shuland was so pleased to take Charley's call in Sacramento that he flew to Los Angeles at once for a closed door luncheon meeting in Charley's hotel.

"I'm gonna make my pitch for the Senate," Arthur said. "State politics are all right, but the national arena is where the money is."

"You need money?" Charley asked with surprise.

"I'm not hurting. And someday my grandfather has to leave me a bundle. But that could be twenty years from now. In the meantime, I'll stick to politics for a living."

"Say the word, Governor," Charley said, "and we'll surround you with a couple of thousand PACs. But don't move too fast. Give me till after this election. I might have something very nice for you."

Charley had arrived late at the hotel in Detroit and had to wait more than twenty minutes in the lobby until he could get into his suite, greatly enraging his entourage, who fell just short of beating up on the hotel manager. By some thoroughly rotten mismanagement, Charley's suite had been rented to one of the greatest rock stars of the international culture. While Charley's people battled it out with the manager, Charley went to the newsstand and bought a selection of magazines to carry him through the off-hours and to sharpen his conversational gambits. Twenty minutes later he was eating his room service dinner in the Presidential Suite, with his security detail, when, one after another, two blips flickered across the far right of his peripheral vision.

"Somebody just went into the bedroom," he said to Al Melvini, the security man in charge of the detail.

"I didn't see nobody, boss," Melvini said.

162

"Get in there!" Charley snarled, trying to eat a medium-rare cheeseburger.

Melvini took out his piece and went into the bedroom. Within five minutes, he came out again, herding two middle-aged women ahead of him.

"How about this?" Melvini said. "They were hiding behind the drapes. They hoped they would get lucky with the singer."

"Ladies!" Charley said, shocked. "You are old enough to be his mother!"

Melvini kept them moving toward the front door. "The great man was moved outta here because he didn't belong here," he told the women. "This is our suite." Just before they passed out of view one of the women turned and faced Charley, pointing a quivering finger at him. "If they put Little Caligula out of this suite for him, who is he? Who is *he?*"

"I am Charles Macy Barton," Charley said simply.

The woman blanched, then lunged toward him. "My God!" she moaned. "The Great Organizer!"

163

29

Angelo Partanna had lines out all over the city, high up and low down, trying to find the don. As the weeks went on, he stayed on the telephone, asking discreet questions because he had to be careful not to let anybody know of the catastrophe and following hunches up blind alleys. There were rumors that a crooked undertaker had tried to sell a body in Cincinnati, but the body turned out to be his brother-in-law's. A tiny, wizened old man showed up on the beach in British Samoa spending American dollars like water, but he turned out to be a vacationing Iranian mullah.

Pop never gave up the search during the months after the don's body was lifted. While the RS *Jack Frost* was rolling north along the coast of Togoland, the don in his eternal crystallizing sleep, Angelo

164

had a visit at the laundry from Santo Calandra, who was in charge of enforcing the collections on the metropolitan franchises.

"Whatsamatta?" Angelo asked him.

"I got a beef, Boss."

The vats were turning on schedule, seven minutes before the hour, in the laundry outside Angelo's office door, and thirty-one vats filled with crashing water, turning in unison, made so much noise that the conversation had to be shouted to be heard.

"The Hispanics in East Harlem and the Busacca family are in a hassle over which one controls the Riker's Island market, but that ain't the beef."

"So what's the beef?"

"They want Don Corrado to handle it, but they can't get him onna phone."

"I'll handle it."

"I told them you'd handle it, but"—Santo shrugged—"the Busaccas said, of course, okay, but the Hispanics only know the don and they say he's gotta rule on it."

"Jesus, that's the trouble doing bidniz with foreigners. Whatta they know about the American way?"

"Listen, they can hardly speak English."

"They can't see him. Nobody can see him."

"I figured that."

"Tell them the don has to rest—doctor's orders—tell them that for thirty years I been the one who handles shit like this. Tell them there is no way they are gonna get to the don on this."

"I already told them."

"Who heads up the Hispanics?"

"A Puerto Rican. Jesus Salvador."

"Jesus *Salvador*. That must be his stage name."

"Whatever."

"Hit him."

"That could make it a bigger beef."

"Then tell both sides that the don says Riker's Island is an open territory."

"In three months, we do that, and they'll be shooting each other."

"Then nobody gets Riker's Island. We'll sell there ourselves."

"That could be the worst. All the franchisees would say we are back on the street after we told them that we were selling the street to them."

"Santo! Fahcrissake! Whatta we supposed to do here?"

"Well, I don't know what I'm saying, but like if I was the don, and I felt good enough to talk to them, I would tell them that the Busaccas can have the franchise to sell the hard shit and the Hispanics can sell the speed and the ganja."

"What's the difference between that and making the island open?"

"It gives them a ruling. They don't care which way it goes; they wanna know that they follow the rules or they lose the franchise."

"So tell them. In the don's name."

"He can't last forever," Santo said. "Nobody in this business ever lived so long as the don. It's even money that he's gotta go sometime, and when he goes and we throw him a big funeral, then they'll all know the don can't settle anything and they'll listen to whoever takes over."

"A funeral."

"A tremendous funeral."

Angelo called Charley on his private line and set up a meet for seven o'clock that night at Angelo's house in Bensonhurst. Charley called Mary Barton and told her he would be late and why. Mary Barton called Angelo.

"Pop? Mae. Charley called me."

"I gotta talk something over, Mae."

"What?"

"Not on the phone."

"Then have the meeting here. On Sixty-fourth Street."

"I'm not coming all the way in from Brooklyn, Mae. Not at this time of night. Them muggers like old people."

"I shouldn't have said it."

"You stay with your kids. I'll tell Charley, he'll tell you."

"All right. But tell him you told me you would tell him to tell me or he'll clam up."

"I'll tell him."

"Also, while you're telling him that, please remind yourself that he's not Charley Partanna anymore so don't forget yourself and give him some work to do."

"Not on the phone, Mae." They hung up.

Charley had grown up in his father's house in Bensonhurst. He had been a boy there; his mother had been alive there. It had all seemed very respectable to him, no matter what the don and Maerose might have thought. Mae was 47. Counting the time she had been away at school, she hadn't really lived in Brooklyn for almost thirty years, so that was why she had put the heat on her grandfather to be respectable. Mae was respectable to the people she hung out with in New York, but he knew there were people in Brooklyn, the old people who used to fill the Palermo Gardens in the old days, who didn't think she was respectable because she hung out with a lot of people who did nothing but go to hairdressers and dressmakers and spend their time either sleeping or going to parties. Charley knew one thing: he didn't feel any more respectable going back to Bensonhurst than he felt about going to East Sixty-fourth or to Barker's Hill, where he was stealing money and running rackets just like he had never left the laundry. He had found out that being respectable, *very* respectable, was a matter of who had the most money to show, not necessarily who had the most money. If the don had only known it, he could have been more respectable than the Pope. The way Mae saw it was that if she began to show her grandfather's money around, right away she'd be in trouble with the IRS, which was not respectable, but she decided to show it in a big way anyway and drop a little awe on the people she wanted to be respectable for; then she could take it for granted that she was respectable.

It had been a rough route. She had had to buy Charley a new face and teeth. There was a new house and servants and a different kind of work for him—well, not a different kind, just a different style of the same thing—and sometimes he thought she had bred the two kids so that her grandfather could have a newly made receptacle in which to leave his money so that Mae could show it. The more of it she showed, the more respectable she became. It wasn't natural, Charley figured, and someday the whole thing was going to turn around and bite her on the ass.

He hadn't been back to the Bensonhurst house since he and Mae had left for Europe and they had held the Charley Partanna funeral. The house in Bensonhurst was maybe where he belonged, but he couldn't go back. Not that he wanted to go back with any longing, like the women in the stories in the magazines he read. He liked Bensonhurst, but he liked the surroundings on Sixty-fourth Street just as much. The main thing was to stay curious about what might happen, because Mae said that he was meeting a better class of people and that he was finally out of the old rut.

When he had been Charley Partanna, he had done what he had been told to do, but now, the way it was working out, nothing was different. As far as he could see, it was the same rut. Instead of Don Corrado, Mae now gave the orders. For now, it was all right that she gave the orders because she knew what went on where they were and he didn't. But he was finding out. Maybe sometime not too far away he wouldn't take orders anymore. He wondered how he would like that. A habit was a habit.

He wasn't so sure that he and his wife lived in the same country anymore. She kept herself far apart from where everybody else lived. She was like somebody up on the movie screen in the days forty years ago when he and Vito and Vito's sister Tessie had watched in the back row at the Loew's while they took turns giving Tessie a feel. The screen was the dream world. Tessie was reality. Mae had lost touch with the reality. She was working on herself with the intensity that she had worked on him to make him shape up as Charles Macy Barton during the year they had lived in Europe. They had it good being married to each other except that Mae wasn't real anymore. He couldn't figure out what she wanted beyond that crap about respectability, but, whatever it was, whenever she got it she wanted more of it.

While they were still in Europe, he had thought the whole idea of the changeover was the don's idea, but he didn't think that way after a few weeks back in New York. Mae must have built every step of the stairs going up or going down, all the way, from the day she had decided she wanted to marry him, all the way. Ever since he had first met her, after she was grown-up, she had always acted as if she was living out some kind of master plan. She had talked about when this happened and when that happened they would have to be ready. Jesus, he thought as he rode across the bridge to Brooklyn and Bensonhurst, it must be a heavy load to be a Prizzi. Vincent had been a wreck before he was zotzed. Sal was a drunk. Amalia had zonked out on cooking smells. Only the don understood how to do it right, so it must be hard on Mae. The thing was, how would he know when she was going too far since, from the beginning, she had been rushing and struggling to get out to the end of the plank. But he figured he would know when she decided to go off the deep end because she would be wearing her Bill Blass diving suit and would find a trunk full of treasure at the bottom.

He wondered about his sons. Which one would be the Prizzi, or would they both be Prizzis, with the insatiable Prizzi greed for power and money, or would they be shaped by the new environment? He wasn't sure he liked his life anymore. But Maerose didn't use liking or disliking as the measurement. She saw her life as a single durable club to whack people with, and now, in a flash, he saw his life as something that had been mass-produced, the stereotype of a rich man that he would be forced to live out, because there was no place to get off the roller coaster his wife operated.

He began to feel that old urge for change, and whenever he thought about change, he thought about beginning the whole thing with a little incidental change in his women. Maybe he needed a little novelty.

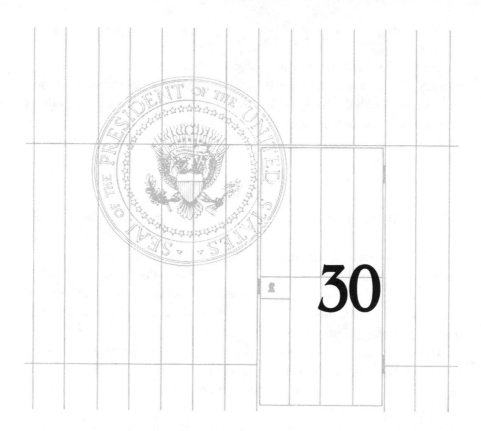

30

Charley and his father sat on either side of a large (commercial) pizza that had arrived from Vesuvio Deliveries five minutes before Charley. It had a very Neapolitan look, but what are you going to do? Charley thought. His father was uneasy talking to a face that claimed to be Charley underneath and that Angelo was fairly sure had to be Charley's, but it made him nervous talking business to a stranger like this, and he dreaded it when Charley started to speak, clutching all the sounds at the back of his throat as if he were being strangled, then releasing them like goo from a squeezed fist.

"It's about the franchises we sold them," Pop said.

"Yes?"

"The Busaccas and the Hispanics needa talk to the don about who handles the Riker's Island shit sales."

"Talk to the don?"

"I ain't satisfied the don is dead, Charley. I only thought he was dead when I said he was dead. We never had a doctor say he was dead. He could be alive, Charley."

"I don't think so, Pop. Even if he were alive when we left him that last day, it's not likely that he could survive the kind of winter this has been wherever he went in his nightshirt."

"Anyways, he ain't here to settle this beef and unless we wanna let all the franchises think we're some cockamamie outfit with no don we gotta come up with some ideas."

"We're not an outfit, Pop. We're a collection agency."

"We control the franchises."

"We control them as long as we can control them."

"I can't be the one to let it fall apart, Charley."

"Won't they talk to you?"

"No."

"Then tell them the don said the Busaccas can have the hard shit for the island and the Hispanics get the rest."

"I told 'em that already, Charley. That's not the point. It's a very small beef and it can be worked out. But sooner or later there is gonna be a big beef that it is gonna take a *capo di famiglia* of the family which controls the franchises to sit down with them and settle it. But we don't even know where the don is. Somebody else took control of our own *capo di famiglia.*"

"What do you want to do?"

"I wanna talk. Santo said it. He said that sooner or later the don had to go, then, when he went, there would have to be a new don to sit on top of this tremendous franchise business all over the world and when we had a don who could lay down the law to them, then everything would go back to normal."

"But we can't even prove the don is dead. How can we show them a new don?"

"Yeah."

"What else from Santo?"

"It follows. The way we prove the don is dead, we have a big funeral."

"Like mine?"

"If we had one, which is impossible, it would have to be bigger, Charley."

"But if the don's body shows up after his funeral, we're never going to get them straightened out."

"Maybe you better talk it over with Mae."

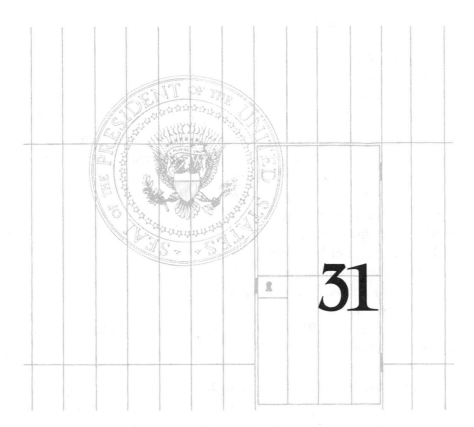

31

When Charley got back to the house on Sixty-fourth Street, a severe case of havoc had set in; the house was all shook up. Mary Barton's maid, Enrichetta Criscione, crashing into a nervous breakdown, had tried to sneak up behind her mistress and brain her with a large chair. She had had to be packed in wet sheets by Yew Lee and Maud Tinsley, Mary Barton's social secretary, until a doctor could be called in to sedate her with a huge hypodermic needle filled to the top of its tube.

When Charley came home, Mary Barton, faint with shock, was stretched out on a chaise longue in her boudoir with a wet cloth over her eyes. One arm was trembling like a crapshooter's warming up dice.

"Gracious evers, Mary!" Charley said. "What happened? The whole place is reeling."

"Enrichetta tried to kill me."

"Enrichetta?"

"She had a complete nervous breakdown, Charley."

"A Sicilian woman? A nervous breakdown? That's impossible."

"She had it, Charley," Mary Barton said. "And if I hadn't seen her in the mirror, coming at me with the chair raised over her head, she would have killed me. My God! You should see the room. She tore up the place, fighting three of us off. And I fought her for five or six minutes before Yew Lee heard the crashes and came in. He had to call in Maud to help us and finally Danvers had to whack her over the head with a lamp to quiet her down."

"But why? What set her off?"

"Nobody knows. She was incoherent."

"Where is she now?"

"At Lenox Hill. We had to get an ambulance. Oh, Charley, it was awful. What did Pop want?"

As Charley told her, Mary Barton only heard the part about there being mention of staging a fake funeral for the don. "Is Angelo out of his *mind*, Charley? If there is a funeral—any kind of a public funeral for grandfather—everybody in all the families would expect us to attend. How can we attend the funeral of a Mafia *capo di famiglia?* Your whole career would be ruined. We would be finished socially."

"Crickets, Mary, I don't know about that. Some of the biggest people in this country would attend Corrado Prizzi's funeral—senators, the mayor, the governor, the Papal Nuncio, the White House, South American and Asian dignitaries, the police commissioner, most of Hollywood—I mean we could even put a little pressure on the arbiter to get her to come."

Mary Barton was almost desperately emphatic. She said, "The public under*stands* that sort of thing. It's the way the political system works. But not private people. Not you or me."

"Eduardo went to your father's funeral, Mary. I don't know because I wasn't there, but he might even have gone to my funeral."

"Charley, lissena me. Forget it. I know about these things and you don't. We go to any funeral of the don's, fake or otherwise, and we will be ostracized."

"By whom?"

"By everybody! Think! Think of how hard everybody worked to keep Eduardo's connection with the family quiet because hundreds of millions of dollars are involved. This could even involve us with the IRS, God forbid!" Her voice was hysterical. "They'll have the FBI checking out everybody who shows up. Put it out of your mind, Charley. Not only is there not going to be any fake funeral because of a few crappy K's of shit for those losers in the Riker's Island can, but if and when my grandfather's body shows up there isn't going to be any public funeral then either."

"What's the matter with you? Are you sick or something? If it weren't for the don, we wouldn't have anything. I could still be in the old country, fahcrissake—the don brought my father over here. If there is a funeral, we're going to it."

Mary Barton began to weep, her head in her arms on a table. Charley knew something was wrong. He pulled up a chair beside her and put his arm around her. "What the hell, Mae," he said, "who is gonna knock anybody for paying his last respects to an old man at his funeral? And even if they did, we'd have to do it anyway. We owe everything we have to the don."

Mary Barton wept inconsolably.

At 4:00 p.m. the next afternoon, after he had settled the problem of Enrichetta, Charles Barton attended the semiannual meeting of the Ballet Council and met Claire Coolidge as she was getting into the elevator and he was coming out with Mrs. Colin Baker, the arbiter and a fellow council member.

"Claire, darling!" Mrs. Baker exclaimed. "How marvelous to see you again." The two women embraced briefly. "You must know Claire Coolidge, Charles?" Mrs. Baker said. "One of the most exciting ballerinas in our company?"

"I have admired Miss Coolidge for some time," Charles Barton said, "but we have not met." Looking at her, he began to get that old feeling. She was even more gorgeous than when he had given her to Eduardo almost six years ago. She had matured like *Parmigiana stravecchio*, ripened, full, redolent of pleasure, lovely. He felt the old-time stirring in his trousers.

175

"Mr. Barton is Edward Price's successor on the council," Mrs. Baker explained to Claire.

"Ah," Claire said. "How nice."

Charles Barton smiled at her. For a flicker, she thought she had known him once, long before. It was in his eyes.

32

Charley was bugged into electric insomnia by Mary Barton's disloyalty to her deepest obligation, respect for the family. He pitched and tossed around the bed, not even helped by the memory of the sly way Claire Coolidge had smiled at him, the way she had withdrawn her hand from his, so softly, so slowly, the flesh so warm and suggestive that she might just as well have laid down on her back on the marble floor in front of the elevator, made pyramids with her legs, and with a slack, panting mouth, pleaded with him to mount her.

He got out of bed, went into the gymnasium off the bathroom, and did four and a half miles on the exercise bike. Something wasn't kosher about the Enrichetta thing, he kept thinking. She was a stolid farm girl. She understood the Catholic sacraments and the benevolence of the Honored Society, how to sew and how to wait on table, and not much else, including how to speak English, so it wasn't possible that she had fallen in with some bad neighborhood crowd. How could she have a nervous breakdown? She was like a farm animal, a favorite ox or a faithful donkey. Things like that didn't have nervous breakdowns.

At eight o'clock in the morning, he got dressed. Danvers made him a light English breakfast of porridge, kippers, scrambled eggs and bacon, toast and tea, then drove him to Lenox Hill Hospital. Charley was on the board of the hospital. He told the desk who he was and asked to see the head nurse on duty.

The head nurse was a motherly, sweet-faced woman named Rose Hunt who knew instantly about Enrichetta's case.

"Miss Criscione needs a long rest and a complete change, Mr. Barton," she said.

"Have you talked to her?" Charley asked. "Did you find out what made her explode like that?"

"That is a difficulty, Mr. Barton. Miss Criscione doesn't speak English, and although we have people here who are fluent in Italian, Miss Criscione seems to be able to speak only some dialect so—so far—the psychiatrists haven't been really able to work with her."

"Do you think she's insane?"

"Definitely not. But she is very, very depressed."

"I have a man who may be able to translate for you."

"How did your wife cope with that?"

"She viewed Miss Criscione as a mute. She employed her because she wanted to help her—and of course Miss Criscione is highly skilled at her work. Ah—tell me, Nurse Hunt—is Miss Criscione pregnant? That might have driven her to despair. If she had been deserted, and so forth."

The nurse shook her head. "No. And she is—aside from this storm of violence she underwent—in very good health. Do you want to see her, Mr. Barton?"

"No. It might agitate her. And it wouldn't be of much use because I cannot speak to her. Let me send the man from my office. His name is Angelo Partanna. I'll see that he's here this afternoon."

Charley called Angelo from a candy store on Lexington Avenue as soon as he left the hospital.

"Pop, Charley. Listen, can you come into New York for lunch?"

"Why not?"

"Early, okay? Viandino on East Forty-sixth between Second and Third. Twelve-fifteen. You want me to send a car?"

"That car is too gaudy. People look and they remember."

"I'll send the Chevy van. I still got the van in my garage."

Pop was eating breadsticks when Charley got to the restaurant. "You know this place?" he said. "They got some nice old-fashioned things on the menu."

"The owner comes from Canicatti."

"Aaaaah."

They ordered lunch. Pop said, "What's on your mind?"

"Something fishy happened, Pop. You remember Enrichetta, Mae's maid?"

Pop nodded.

"She had a nervous breakdown yesterday."

"A nervous *break*down? Enri*chetta?*"

"She tried to brain Mae with a chair, then it took three of them to hold her down until they could get a doctor to hit her with a shot."

"Maybe she just went nuts."

"No. I went to the hospital this morning. I checked her out."

"What hospital?"

"Lenox Hill."

"It's very fishy, Charley." He stared off at a mote in the middle distance. "I went to see her when Maerose brought her over here. She's a good strong country girl. A nice, good-tempered woman. I knew some people from her town—where she grew up before her family moved to Agrigento. She grew up with the *fratellanza* all around her. Mae told me Enrichetta went to work for her because Mae is a Prizzi. Corrado Prizzi was Enrichetta's hero. She couldn't believe I knew him. When I told her I was Corrado's *consigliere,* she knelt down and kissed my hand. Jesus, it was like being back in the old country."

"She can't speak English. That makes a problem for the hospital."

"I know. But she speaks a very nice Enna dialect."

"So I told the hospital I'd have a man from my office who can talk to her go up there this afternoon. That's you."

179

"I'll go see her." He passed his hand heavily across his forehead.

"What's the matter, Pop?"

"Ah, nothing. Just that Corrado going like that hit me hard. I seen him like every day for over fifty years. We cut up a lotta touches."

Charley reached over and held his father's hand. "Ask not for whom the bell tolls, Pop," he said. "Shoot the bell ringer."

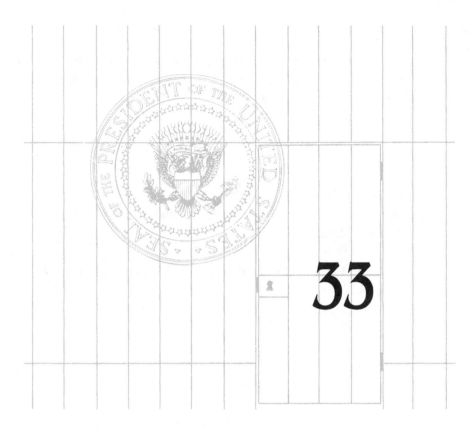

33

The insistent, prodding, overwhelming presence of Claire Coolidge in the same city almost violated Charley's mind. The memory of her primary and secondary sexual characteristics was so strong that once, while he and Mary Barton were looking at a channel 13 presidential retrospective that showed footage of Calvin Coolidge, Charley was so overcome with the marginal lust that swept over him merely at the mention of the name that, with a hoarse cry, he fell upon Maerose and ravished her upon the unborn Persian lamb upholstery of the enormous sofa in the brobdingnagian study at Sixty-fourth Street. Mae was extraordinarily pleased and, for once, utterly unsuspecting of Charley's motives. It was all Charley could do not to cry out Claire's name as he reached the dynamite apogee. It was so close a call that it forced Charley to do something about the danger. The lesson it taught him stayed with him until, the next morning, it pushed him into telephoning Miss Coolidge at the apartment in which Edward S. Price had set her up high in the Trump Tower off Fifth Avenue.

"Miss Coolidge, please."

"This is she."

"Ah, good morning, Miss Coolidge. This is Charles Macy Barton."

"Mr. Barton. How nice."

"Some people have been talking to me about perhaps proposing a new ballet and I thought of you."

"Mr. Barton!"

"Do call me Charles. Or, as the president says it, Charley."

"Whose ballet is it?"

"I thought we might chat about that at lunch—whenever you're free."

"As a matter of fact, I'm free today."

"How fortunate. So am I. The Russian Tea Room?"

"That would be really convenient."

"One o'clock then. The Russian Tea Room."

Charley hung up, wondering why he automatically thought of the Russian Tea Room whenever he wanted to have lunch with Claire Coolidge. He knew why. Mae would be lunching at Le Cirque or La Grenouille. The West Side was out-of-bounds for his wife, castewise.

They had the same booth as they had had their first luncheon.

"My lucky table!" Miss Coolidge exclaimed. Charley finessed it.

"There is no music yet and, of course, no set designs," Charley said easily, "but this young Argentinian librettist, Santo Calandra is his name, has this rather gripping conception for a storyline."

"Really."

"The ballet would be based on the Cherokee tragedy, the Trail of Tears, along which the Cherokee nation was forcibly moved by the United States Army in eighteen thirty-eight to be resettled on the Oklahoma strip after the disastrous Cherokee wars." Charley had heard the arbiter, Mrs. Colin Baker, mention the possibility of such a ballet and he had dug the rest out of the *Encyclopaedia Britannica*.

"How exciting."

"Very sad, actually. Out of eighteen thousand Cherokees, four thousand died along the way, and when they got to the reservation in Oklahoma, feuds and murders with the white settlers began."

"How perfectly tragic."

"But it does have the makings of a moving ballet."

"Oh, yes." Miss Coolidge wasn't taking any of this seriously. She was waiting for Charley to make his move.

"Do you think real tragedy can be expressed in the dance?"

"I think anything can be expressed in the dance, Charley." She covered his hand with hers for an electric moment. The voltage she generated hit Charley as if some hooded executioner had pulled a switch. He stiffened, arching his back.

They stared at the menu silently. Charley ordered. Miss Coolidge said, "I have the most uncanny feeling that we've met before."

"Before who?"

Miss Coolidge smiled. "I suppose you know about me and Edward."

"People do talk about beautiful ballerinas."

"Have you known Ed long?"

"Yes. I suppose so. In a business way," Charley said. "I advised him on mergers and acquisitions for a number of years."

"Do you think he'll get the nomination?"

"Oh, yes."

"The election?"

"I'm a Democrat, my dear."

"I think he can win it. And, of course, if he wins it, I lose him."

"Oh, I wouldn't say that. Any number of our presidents have maintained their dear friends. Thomas Jefferson, for example. And it is said that JFK had outside friends."

"Edward doesn't have that sort of flair."

"Well, he has a lot of things against his winning the election, too. He's a widower and Americans like to think that a man has a wife who is really running the country. He's an Eastern establishment banker. And he certainly doesn't have what one could call a charismatic personality, does he?"

"I suppose not. But he's sweet."

"On the other hand he does have money."

"God, yes."

The food came, the wine was poured.

"Would you like me to see if I can—uh—mount—that ballet for you? The Trail of Tears, that is?"

She stared into his eyes with the large green grapes that were imbedded on either side of her perfect nose. Charley swayed in his chair. He fought the madness. He had to stop these little adventures. He was fifty-five years old. "Do you think," he said slowly with a thick tongue, "that we might skip lunch and go back to your place?"

"That would be impossible," Miss Coolidge said. "Edward has made a friend of every one of those building employees, and the last thing I want to do is to break Edward's heart. Not right now. Not four days before Super Tuesday."

"I have to be in Boston next Monday. I can have a plane standing by for you."

"I will be dancing in New York at the Monday performance."

"Do you have any objection to perhaps some champagne in a suite at a hotel?"

"Hotels are such an impermanent arrangement, Charles. But . . ."

"But—what?"

"Let's wait out Super Tuesday. If Edward comes out of that with a clear chance at the nomination, then, well, he is really going to need me to help him through to Election Day."

Eduardo did very well on Super Tuesday. He split twelve states evenly with Gordon Manning: the nominating votes of seven states went to Manning and six went to ESP. In terms of delegates, he was still very much of a contender for the nomination. Manning sent a team to offer him the vice-presidency if he would withdraw in Manning's favor, so Eduardo sent his people to Manning to offer him a place in his administration as chief of protocol, an equally meaningless job, if Manning would withdraw.

34

Mary Price Barton, once the supreme New York interior decorator, celebrated as the niece of Edward S. Price, had been a familiar presence in the nouvelle society of New York for over twenty years, since she had been exiled from Brooklyn by her father in 1967, when, by her grandfather's order, she had become Mary Price. When she took up her exile in Manhattan, through her uncle, a leader of the old guard of the nouvelle, she sought out the leaders of the nouvelle for the growth and steady continuance of her decorating firm. She had been a cultivated young woman, beautiful, rich (in addition to her decorating business, her grandfather had given her 5 percent of the income from the city-wide restaurant and bordello linen supply business as an allowance), well-educated, with an incomparable knack for making clothes seem as important as great literature. She knew French and Italian. She was a renowned gourmet and opera authority, so that, at the end of the 1970s, when she ascended to the right hand of Edward S. Price as his executive assistant in the direction of the manifold financial complexities that he controlled (and in the administration of the institutional mercies that were his far-reaching philanthropies, and in his earnest cultivation of the arts, from within the shelter erected by the crazying amounts of his ever-burgeoning fortune), her position in the nouvelle was quadrupled in strength. She became one of the four instantly recognizable women in *W*, that indelible record of the nouvelle peerage and of the dressmakers of North America.

Therefore, when she compounded the increments of her glory with a brilliant marriage to Charles Macy Barton, successor to Edward S. Price, who had become a candidate for the highest office in the land, it was, by the measurement of the nouvelle, as if she had been beatified.

While the vast PR staff at Barker's Hill built the mountainous public record of the Macy-Barton ascension in all the media, from the day of the Price-Barton wedding to the moment when they moved into the quadriplex of houses on East Sixty-fourth Street, the nouvelle of New York waited with dread that any one of them might not receive invitations to Charles and Mary Barton's housewarming.

The moment came on the thirtieth of May 1992. One hundred invitations for two hundred of Mary Price Barton's closest friends had gone out by Federal Express. One hundred and ninety-three couples who did not receive invitations left the city for doctrinaire Memorial Day weekends. The hotels and motels at Gettysburg and Richmond were packed out. The one hundred to whom had been accorded the peace that exceeds all understanding poured out their gratitude in the form of commissions to the dressmakers for which the nouvelle existed and nailed down instantly the longest of the city's available stretched, rental limousines.

It was a transcendent night for every one except Charles Macy Barton. His wife had danced again and again with a man whose looks Charley didn't like, a youngish man who looked sex-crazed and was too handsome, maybe even a little gay. At twenty minutes after two on the morning of May 31, Charley confronted his wife as they prepared for bed.

"Who was the guy?"

"What guy?"

"Don't jerk me around!" Charley snarled.

"You mean Jake Hapworth?"

"I mean the guy you kept dancing with, pressing your hips into him, staring at his face as if it would go away and your life would be ruined."

"Oh, Charley, fahcrissake, he's a seeded walker."

"What's that—a walker?"

"What's the matter with you?"

"No more parties."

"What's that going to solve? If you have decided that if we went to parties that I would spend my time with Jake Hapworth, then what's to stop me from seeing him if I don't see him at parties?"

"You're a married woman. You have two children."

"You feel the knife, Charley? Good. I felt the knife for twenty years. Every time you looked at a woman, I thought I would lose you. Now, it's my turn."

His eyes got wild. "The don is dead, Mae. I don't need to keep doing what I'm doing for a living with all my working time. I don't even know Jake Hapworth, but if you start screwing around with him, he isn't going to last long."

"You think you can go back to being Charley Partanna? You can't. He's dead. You haven't got anywhere to live except inside your new skin. You can't take Hapworth out or anybody else because you are stuck with being legit, Charley."

"There were plenty of women with big eyes for me tonight."

"So—that's up to you. But remember one thing. Every time you take on a woman, and I'll know every time you do, I am going to take on two men. You're fifty-five years old and I'm stronger than you. It's time you put the fires out."

"I haven't done anything!"

"My intuition tells me that you've been thinking about doing something. Let my moves with Jake Hapworth warn you that you had better not make that one false step because I'm on my way to take over this town, Charley. The arbiter can't live forever and I'm going to be the arbiter. I'm going to run the nouvelle, the opera, the ballet, the theater, the museums, the libraries, the universities, the choice committees, and the big charities, and I can't do that if I have to think every minute of the day that you might be sniffing up the skirts of some woman. I won't need you any more if that's the way you want it to be, Charley. You can shape up or ship out. There are plenty of Jake Hapworths."

Charley looked at her and knew she meant it. Reluctantly, he pushed Claire Coolidge into a far closet of his mind and locked the door. He wondered if he could have some kind of operation to get the stone out of his private parts.

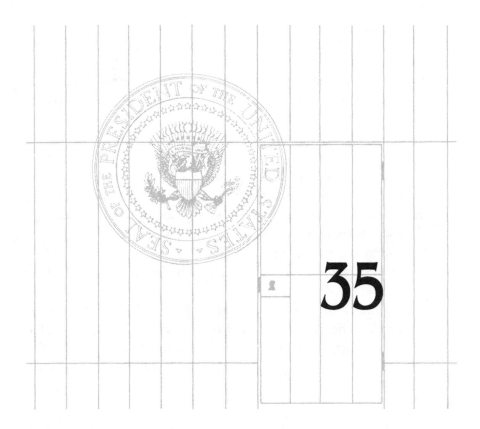

35

Charley waited nearly two days to hear from his father about Enrichetta. He couldn't reach him at the laundry or at home, and when he called Lenox Hill, they always said he had just left. In the late afternoon of the second day, Pop called Charley.

"Hey, Charley, you wanna have dinner?"

"Sure, Pop."

"Can you meet me at Idlewild?"

"*Idle*wild?"

"Kennedy, I mean. The restaurant in the main building at eight o'clock. They probably don't have real food, but we can get a steak or something."

"How come the airport?"

"I'm flying to London at ten o'clock."

"*London?* You?"

"I know, I ain't been much of a traveler, but something came up."

"What came up? What, fahcrissake, could come up to get you to fly in an airplane for the first time in your life?"

"Not on the phone, Charley." Pop hung up.

As usual, Pop was seated at the table when Charley got to the airport restaurant. The noise was horrendous, as if the success of all restaurants depended on how much noise they could generate. Charley was agitated. Pop was as calm as Buddha on a good day.

"Pop, what is going on here?"

"Siddown. Have a drink." He poured Charley a glass of mainland Italian red wine.

Charley gulped the wine, staring at his father. Pop called a waiter. "First we'll order," he said. He ordered two steaks. He took a ten-dollar bill out of his wallet and handed it to the waiter. "This is extra. Not the regular tip, you folla me? I want you to stand next to the cook when he makes the steaks. I want charred on the outside, pink on the inside. You got it?"

The waiter gulped, nodded, and went off like a red-assed bird. Pop sipped the wine.

"I think I found Corrado, Charley," he said.

"Holy shit!"

"I think I'm gonna pick him up in England."

"But—how—?"

"I talked to Enrichetta. You won't believe it, what I'm gonna tell you. Her and Mae snatched the don."

"*Mae?*" It was a scream of pain.

Pop nodded.

"But how did they move him to London? They've been right here all the time."

"They packed him in a Two Boros Meat Company truck; they drove him to pier eighty-nine, where the floating ice-box Barker's Hill owns, the RS *Jack Frost*, was tied up; and they packed him in a freezer-locker. He's been on a merry-go-round from New York to someplace in Africa, then to London, then back to New York, then around all over again. The ship gets into Liverpool—that's in England—the second time around for Corrado—day after tomorrow."

"Why would Mae do a terrible thing like that?"

"Later. What I need from you right now is that you radio the captain of the *Jack Frost* and tell him to do anything and everything I tell him so I can get Corrado outta that icebox and take him home without shaking up the British media or their cops."

Charley was dazed. "Yeah. I'll go to the office tonight. I'll set it up through the satellite."

The steaks came. Pop looked at them. He sliced his steak at the middle. "You done good," he said to the waiter. "Please, take the ketchup away. Do we look like people who would use ketchup?"

Charley ate automatically. He had been raised by his father not to talk at dinner. Once he opened his mouth to speak, but his father shook his head slowly from side to side, chewed the steak and sipped the wine. At last the plates were taken away. Pop ordered coffee, no dessert, and Charley blurted, "So okay, why did Mae do a thing like that?"

"She just flaked out, Charley, I guess. Enrichetta don't know why."

"I shoulda known," Charley moaned. "I shoulda known."

"Why?"

"The way she threw such a fit when I told her we were talking about a fake funeral for the don to handle the Riker's Island beef."

"What did she do?"

"She went wild on the idea of a big funeral. She was afraid it would ruin her socially. Mae's got big dreams."

"So the day the don died she musta hung around, then went in to him and found out he was gone. Then the fear of the big funeral hit her. She panicked."

"She panicked all right."

"She needed some help and she figured Enrichetta hadda do whatever she said, so she talked her into helping her do the lift on the don. She probably hadda give Enrichetta pills so she could get her to commit such a sin, but Enrichetta lifted and pushed and did the work; then, after it was all over—the next day—it hit her what she did. She had denied Don Corrado Prizzi, the *capo di tutti capi* of her whole world, his right to a consecrated burial in the Holy Mother Church. It ate her. She is a simple woman. To save herself, the whole thing snapped inside her and she tried to zotz Maerose with that chair."

"Jesus, poor Mae. It must have broke her heart, the whole thing."

"Talk to her, Charley. She's gotta hurt."

"Yeah. She needed me but what could I do? I gotta talk to her and tell her it's all right, she don't have to blame herself anymore."

"That's good, Charley. But I gotta do this for Corrado because he woulda done it for me. But when you're dead, you're dead. What's the difference if somebody sends you on one of those cruises even if it is too late to get the most out of it?"

The coffee arrived. The waiter left. Charley drank the coffee cautiously. "There's gotta be a funeral, no doubt about that."

"Of course. But there's a right way and a wrong way."

"So call me when you have the don. Mae is gonna have to take a trip to Australia, where it's too far away to get back in time, when we have the funeral. Ah, shit!" he said, slamming his napkin down on the table. "Women!"

"She don't hafta go to Australia. We'll have a little funeral—you and Mae, Amalia, me, and Eduardo. We'll have Corrado inna ground before anybody knows he's dead."

"You would do that for Mae, Pop?"

"Not for Mae, Charley. I gotta do it for Corrado. I swore to him I would do it."

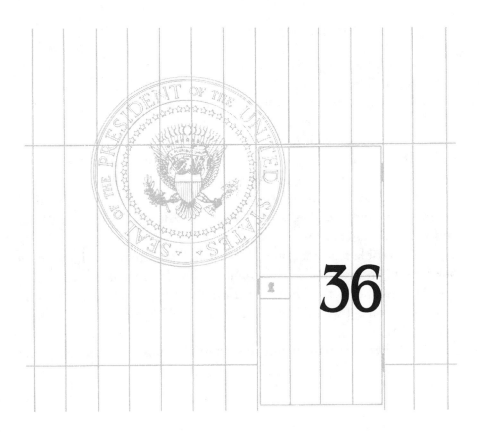

36

When Charley went into Mary Barton's bedroom that night, after he had talked to the skipper of the RS *Jack Frost* on the radio telephone bounced off the company's satellite, she was propped up on a pile of pillows watching a videocassette of "The Wodehouse Playhouse." She turned it off with the remote when Charley came in.

"What did Pop want?"

Charley sat on the side of the bed and stared into her face. "He found the don," he said.

Mary Barton closed her eyes. Her right hand went slowly to her face. She put the second knuckle of her index finger between her teeth and bit down.

"It's over now, Mae. You don't have to keep turning to stone every day. It's all right. I understand—Pop understands—what you did."

Her wild eyes implored him.

"Pop will be in England tomorrow. He'll take the don off, have him laid out in a casket, and fly him back here."

Tears ran down her cheeks, but she didn't make a sound. She gripped her knuckle with her teeth and made uncontrolled muted noises in her throat, the sounds of a small animal caught in a trap in a forest where any sound would be an anomaly.

"We'll bury him the day he gets here," Charley said. "A very small funeral. You and me, Pop, and Amalia and Eduardo." He reached out and touched her cheek with his full hand.

Her terrible fear burst free. "Oh, Charley," she sobbed, reaching out for him and pulling herself to him. "How I love you! I love you."

He kissed her, then held her until the sobbing subsided. "I think it would be nice if we also invited Enrichetta," he said. "It would mean a lot to her."

With her face pushed into his chest, Maerose nodded again and again.

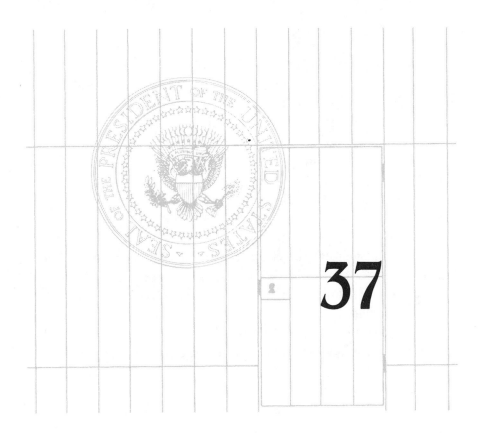

37

When Pop got back from England with the don's body, Charley met him at Kennedy. Pop seemed to be hearing an echo of his old friend's death, telling him to be ready because he was next. Charley felt his father's awe, which had come to him with three solid days of living with what remained of Don Corrado. He said, "What the hell, Pop. He had to go. Nobody beats that system."

"It's just funny how it all worked out. He come here from such a hot country. Jesus, I still can remember nearly dropping from the heat there. Then he lives in New York for seventy years, the most changeable climate in the world. But when he dies—what? Mae packs him in an icebox and sends him on a cruise."

Charley put his arm around his father's stooped shoulders. "Average it all out, temperaturewise," he said, "and where he went after he died has to have the perfect climate."

"I got a lot of papers to get the body in." He pulled a sheaf of documents from his inside breast pocket. "They done a really classy embalming job in England. The guy actually made a house call."

"I got people here to handle the papers," Charley said. "Mr. Dalloway?"

A brisk man with an entourage of two rushed to Charley's side like a cheetah. "Yes, sir?"

"See that this cargo is cleared, please. You had them bring a hearse along?"

"Yes, sir."

"Take the cargo to the Santa Grazia Funeral Home in Brooklyn. At this address, please." Charley gave him the papers from Pop's hand.

"Yes, *sir!*" Dalloway and his unit wheeled as one man and took off like arrows in flight.

"You want a cup of coffee, Pop?"

"I gotta go in and see Amalia. Did you tell her?"

"Not yet."

"Good. She's gonna take it hard, Charley. All this time, she thinks her father just snuck out of the house and went someplace on business."

"I got a limo outside."

"Not that flashy Rolls?"

"No. It's a rental from one of our companies."

They moved out of the terminal. The car was waiting. They got in and Charley rolled up the partition between the tonneau and the driver.

"Flying ain't so bad," Pop said, "if you discount the food, the movie, and the seats. Maybe I'll go visit the old country."

"We need you here, Pop."

"Your people were a lotta help getting Corrado in the box and outta the country, Charley. For a minute there, I thought I had blown it. I began to think I shoulda let him ride back to New York in the icebox, but your people took over. They set him up for the custom embalming job, and they put in the fix to clear him for the flight home." He sighed. "Jesus, when I found him he was still in his nightshirt, the way we left him four months ago."

Charley patted his father's hand. "It's okay, Pop."

"No, it ain't, Charley. Mae done a terrible thing here. Nothing is gonna be okay until we find out how Amalia is gonna take the news."

"You gonna tell her about Mae?"

"What for, fahcrissake?"

When they got to the don's house in Brooklyn Heights, Pop told Charley it would be better if he saw Amalia alone.

"I'll be at the office," Charley said. "When are you going to make the funeral?"

"Tomorrow. We gotta get him in the ground and get it over with before the papers start everybody walking down memory lane."

Amalia settled Angelo Partanna in a big chair in the main floor living room, which no one had entered, except Amalia, who watched television in there every night after the don had gone to sleep at seven o'clock. Because the don had never come downstairs, Amalia had let Maerose's company do the decorating. The living room was like a room in an English country house, comfortable and colorful. Amalia had added her own little touch. There were dozens of soft cushions scattered upon the many pieces of furniture.

"Where you been, Angelo?" she said with affection. "I ain't heard from you in three, four days."

She was a small, refined-looking woman in her late sixties with a trim figure and elegant legs. She dressed well, in the Bloomingdale's style. No one would have made her for what she had never ceased to be, a Sicilian country woman. "Take away the little moustache," Don Corrado had said to Pop time and time again, "and you got a show girl." Her eyes had the Prizzi intensity. For all her life, Amalia had been careful to view life from a distance, but she had seen it, recorded it, and measured it against what she knew to be the greatness of her father.

"Well—"

"You have news of Poppa! You found Poppa! Did you find Poppa, Angelo?"

He nodded.

"My God!" she said. "Where is he? Why ain't he here if you found him?"

Tears filled his eyes as he stared at her.

"He's gone? Poppa's *gone?*" Her hand covered her mouth tightly as if to keep her sanity from escaping. Angelo measured her shock and answered carefully.

"He's at Santa Grazia's Funeral Home. The funeral is tomorrow."

"*Tomorrow?*" She was deeply shocked. "How can it be tomorrow? People gotta come from all over the country. Fly in even from Sicily. Does the Cardinal know? He's gotta say the requiem mass. Jesus God, Angelo, thousands and thousands of people are involved here. How can the funeral be tomorrow?"

"It's better that way, Amalia."

"No! It can't be! You think we can just lose a great man like we're burying somebody's dog in the backyard?"

"Lissena me," Angelo said harshly. "He was my friend. I loved him. I wouldn't do nothing for him the wrong way."

"But—what the hell?—who is gonna be there if nobody knows? How can the people and the whole world pay their respect to him?"

"I was the last one to talk to him."

"It's not only the family, Angelo. History is involved here. A great man is gone."

"He made me swear that, if he died—and he knew then he was gonna die, Amalia—he made me take an oath on the immortal souls of my two grandsons that when he died only you and Mae and me and Charley and Eduardo and Father Passanante would go to the funeral. He said to me he had to be in the ground before the newspapers and the television found out about it."

"I don't unnastan. What about my son, Poppa's grandson, Rocco? What about Pasquale, in California?"

"Right after the funeral you can tell them."

"Rocco will go crazy."

"Lissena me! You think there ain't a lotta people who are gonna bleed over this? But, if it's only the five of us, then after a while they're gonna unnastan the whole thing."

"How does anybody know Poppa said that to you?"

"He wrote a letter. It's in the letter."

"Where's the letter?"

"What?"

"The letter, where is it?"

Angelo replayed the don's death scene in his mind. When he had told about the letter, he had used a kind of shorthand because he didn't have time for a lot of words. He had said, "The force of destiny."

"It's upstairs. In the sleeve of the record album, *La Forza del Destino*. I put it back there myself after I hadda show it to Eduardo."

"I wanna see it," Amalia said.

"Come on. We'll go up."

They climbed the stairs in silence. They entered the enormous room. They walked to the wall that held shelf upon shelf of record albums, several thousand of them. Angelo halted at the F's, then ran his finger along the numbered positions to slide out the album they sought. He held the front flap of the liner open and reached inside. His hand came out with a long white envelope. Before the Blessed Decima Manovale took over the house, he thought, he had to go through every record sleeve on these shelves. This was Corrado's special filing system. There could be some terrible secrets and a lotta spare cash in there.

Amalia stared at the open letter for a long time. "Well, if this is the way he wanted it, then that's how it's gotta be. But how come Mae and Charley if not Rocco?" she said implacably. "Mae is a granddaughter, but Charley ain't even a relative."

"Charley is the husband. The husband goes with the wife to funerals."

"So how come Mae if not Rocco?" Amalia said bitterly. "She is the granddaughter so she is going, but Rocco is the grandson and he is nothing."

"Charley's people found the don," Angelo lied easily. "So Charley knew first. He didn't know about what the don told me before he went, so, naturally, he told his wife. So she has to go."

"So does Rocco."

"Lissena me, Amalia. Five people are going. And five is a big risk. Rocco is gonna be so knocked out that the don is dead and he's the first one of the soldiers to know that so he's gonna tell evveybody. Tomorrow morning the television, all the papers. Ten thousand people will show up at the church plus eleven TV cameras. The FBI and the IRS. Then Eduardo will be through—washed up. You don't want your own brother to be president of the United States? The don knew what was gonna be if we didn't keep it quiet until it was over. You gotta do it his way."

"If Rocco don't go, then Maerose can't go. And if she don't go, then Charley ain't going. I am telling you, Angelo."

"All right. Charley don't go. Maybe that's good thinking. He is running a ten-, twenty-billion-dollar operation. What is a guy name of Charles Macy Barton doing at a *fratellanza* funeral, they're all gonna say."

"And Mae don't go."

"So that's it. You, Eduardo, and me. That's it."

"No," she said sobbing brokenly. "It ain't right. He was a great man and the mighty of the earth should come to his grave and praise him."

"You gonna spit on your father's dying wishes?"

"No. Whatever he ever wanted, that's what I want for him." But her face had changed and Angelo had spent his life reading faces and clocking body language. Deep in the eyes of the sweet, obedient, compliant Amalia, altars to malevolence were shining within the cathedral of her Sicilian resentment.

Her face settled into a mask of defiance. "You think I don't know nothing. You think I was some kind of machine who walks in and outta the room with cookies and grappa and the food? I listened to everything that went on in there—setting up little Sal Prizzi, telling Charley to zotz this one and that one, hearing Mae talk Poppa into—what?—being respectable, looking nice, walking a line like he was some American shithead instead of a *mafiusu* Sicilian! You think it didn't break my heart, hearing her talk to him and seeing him buy it, the whole thing? And now—on the day he is dying on his deathbed, he tells you, his *consigliere*, not me, his daughter, that he wants you to put him in the ground in silence, a secret from the people he made and the people who made him."

"With this kind of money riding, that's the way it's gotta be," Angelo said, reaching out to touch her arm.

She flinched and stared at him with contempt. "Where was he when you found him, Angelo?"

"In England."

Amalia crossed herself.

"Lemme tell you what happened to him," the old man said, all ready with a pack of lies.

38

Amalia stayed in her room upstairs. Angelo went down to the main floor and told Calo Barbaccia to get him a taxi. He went to his house in Bensonhurst and called Charley. "Tell Mae I'm comin' to dinner wit' choose," he said.

"How did Amalia take it?" Charley asked.

"Not on the phone." He hung up.

Charley met him at the door. They went into the drawing room, crossed into the cozy book-lined study that made Angelo think of the old One Hundred and Fourth Field Artillery Armory. It had a gigantic snooker table that no one had ever played on and a movie screen behind a Fra Angelico that could be cantilevered from the ceiling by an electric switch. "The Wodehouse Playhouse" was on the television screen to keep Charley

201

kosher about upper-class attitudes. Mary Barton was waiting—a different Mary Barton—more subdued, womanly again. A police report might have said there were no marks on her, but Angelo could see the marks, welts upon her soul endlessly bleeding in her punishment for what she had done to her grandfather. Angelo went to her and took her in his arms. "Like you always did, Mae," he said gently, "you was only thinking exactly like the don."

She clung to him until Charley said, "How did Amalia take it, Pop?" and Angelo broke away gently.

"Lemme put it this way," Angelo said. "She wanted a big public funeral with evvey family in the country coming in and all the Prizzi soldiers and their women doing their thing for the TV cameras and the FBI."

"Oh, Jesus," Maerose said.

"There was only one way to go. I told her what the don told me just before he went to the angels."

"What, fahcrissake?" Mary Barton said.

"That nobody should know he was dead until he was inna ground. That's what he made me swear. You and him think the same, Mae."

"Oh, *Jesus!*" She covered her face with her hands.

"But she held out that Rocco had to go to the funeral and I told her no. Anyways, we made a deal. Rocco don't go, you don't go, Mae. And if you don't go, Charley don't go."

"My stars and body," Charley said. "Who does go then?"

"Amalia, Eduardo, and me. That's it."

39

The small church was nearly empty. Three people stood in the front row. Father Passanante led the procession just ahead of the closed casket as it was rolled on its gurney away from the altar by the mortician's staff. The three mourners peeled out of the front pew and followed the casket down the aisle, Amalia between her brother and Angelo Partanna, the two men needing to support her.

The three mourners got into the only limousine that waited behind the black hearse in front of the church. The short cortege rode across Brooklyn to the Verrazano Bridge to the family's cemetery, Santa Grazia di Traghetto in Staten Island, swiftly following the route that Charley Partanna's funeral had taken so slowly almost two years before.

Father Passanante intoned the litany at the graveside and the three mourners repeated the words after him. The priest closed his breviary.

"I have known Corrado Prizzi for thirty years," he said. "There was no man who matched his qualities. He was a positive man. He was generous to those whom circumstances forced him to encourage or to chastise. He was a singleminded man who kept an openness to God and who husbanded the temporal power accorded to him with a kind of justice. He died shriven. He has gone to the angels."

The simple wooden casket was lowered into the grave. Father Passanante sprinkled earth upon it and intoned the ritual. The three mourners wept, the men bowed and uncovered on the perfect early spring morning.

When the service was over, the mourners returned to the limousine, which rolled slowly out of the marbled park. Father Passanante got into his Korean two-door and left after he had offered up his own prayers at the grave.

Amalia sat between the two men, staring straight ahead. "We are free of the oath which Poppa made you take, Angelo," she said with a dulled voice. "Now I can avenge what has been done to my father."

"What are you talking about, Amalia?" Eduardo said, thinking several hundred thoughts at once about the Republican nominating convention.

"You have respectability, you think, Eduardo. But it was laid over you like a blanket and it can be snatched away."

Eduardo leaned across her and looked at Angelo. "Do you know what this is all about?" he asked testily.

"Let her talk it out, Eduardo."

"I am going to take us back to where we all belong, to what our meaning is, to what we are."

"Please, Amalia, shut up. I have a lot on my mind."

"Listen to her, Eduardo," Angelo said.

"When I get to a telephone, I am going to call the television and the *Daily News* and tell them whose son you are. I am going to tell them who Charles Macy Barton is—that we are all Sicilians, *mafiosi*, and that we have become what we are at the pleasure of our father, the don of dons, Corrado Prizzi."

Eduardo stared at her with transfixed horror. "What's happening here?" He looked confusedly at Angelo across his distant, dreaming sister.

No one spoke until the car returned them to the don's house on the slope above the river. Angelo got out of the car and helped Amalia down. "Stay here," he said to Eduardo.

They went into the house. As Amalia walked unsteadily toward the stairs, Angelo spoke to Calorino Barbaccia. "Keep her away from the phone," he said. "And don't let her leave the house. I'll call you. Stay here."

Angelo went back to the limousine and got in. "You can drop me in Bensonhurst on your way to the airport," he said to Eduardo.

The car moved away. "Was she serious?" Eduardo said. "Because if she's serious I might as well shoot myself."

"She's depressed," Angelo said. "But Calo is with her and he's a solid man."

"I can't believe any of this," Eduardo said.

"Let me handle it. You got the convention coming up."

When Angelo got to his house in Bensonhurst he called Calo at the don's house. "How is she?"

"She's tryna get the phone. I hadda lock her in her room."

"Remember the time you had the meet with Melchiorre Vitale down at Long Beach?"

"Yeah."

"Show Amalia how it worked."

"Yeah?"

"Then go back to the door and wait till your regular relief comes in." Angelo hung up.

Calo went slowly up the stairs. He unlocked the door to Amalia's room and went in. She was on the bed, but she got up as he came in.

"Okay, Calo?" she said. "You unnastan what I gotta do? You're gonna lemme use the phone?"

He pushed her down on the bed. He put two of the bed pillows over her face, then lay across them. Amalia's lower body flopped around crazily. After the legs stopped moving, he looked at his watch with a technician's interest, then let ten full minutes go by before getting to his feet again. He lifted Amalia's body and took it to the center of the room. He let it fall to the floor. He smoothed the covers on the bed, fluffed up the pillows and put them back in their proper places; then he left the room to take up his vigil at the front door.

Mariano Orecchione, the night man, discovered Amalia's body at 7:20 A.M. the next morning. He went into the room to see if anything was wrong because, as regularly as sunrise every morning for the six years he had been on the job, Amalia had arrived at his post at 6:15 A.M. with a breakfast tray and a big pot of coffee. He called Angelo. Angelo called Dr. Winikus. On the death certificate Dr. Winikus gave as reason for death from natural causes instantaneous heart failure, and Eduardo had to fly back to New York for his sister's funeral.

The day after the don's quiet funeral, a short, paid announcement appeared in the death notices in *The New York Times*. The day after that, all the New York newspapers and all the networks carried flamboyant recollections of Corrado Prizzi, inserting his memory into the national mythology with gory accounts of the twenties and thirties, wistfully recalled, but the people, who had been conditioned to feed on a rhythm of instantaneous change that had come to be measured by the forgettable images on their television screens, were no longer able to harken back that far. He was only another old, old man from the bad, old days who had died forgotten in faroff farcical Brooklyn. The federal prosecutors and the media marked well that the don's death had signified the end of the Mafia in America, a nice gesture on their part.

The day after the funeral, Angelo Partanna drove out to the don's house in his old Dodge. He told Calo about the nice job he had set up for him in sunshine-filled, fun-packed Vegas. Then he climbed the stairs slowly to the don's room, emptied forty-one album liners of nearly-forgotten operas and burned in the fireplace everything he found except the forty-one thousand dollars in cash.

The day after the obituary accounts appeared, the Blessed Decima Manovale Foundation of the Little Sisters of Pain and Pity made their claim to take over the geegaw-packed Prizzi mansion. Within a week it was stripped bare of every bibelot and gilded frame. Walls were torn down and the bingo equipment and chairs were moved in. The don's great floor space at the top was given over to the storage of three hundred gross of short pencils and forty-two thousand printed bingo forms. A large sign was erected at the entrance, which read:

BLESSED DECIMA MANOVALE
WEST BROOKLYN BINGO CENTER

The bishop of the diocese of Brooklyn, The Most Reverend Patrick J. Girty, blessed the first drawing. When Charley read about the transformation of the don's miniature Sicilian museum into a gambling hall, he wondered: although the Church certainly thought a bingo parlor on the site of Don Corrado's greatest days was respectable, would Mrs. Colin Baker, the arbiter, rule that it was?

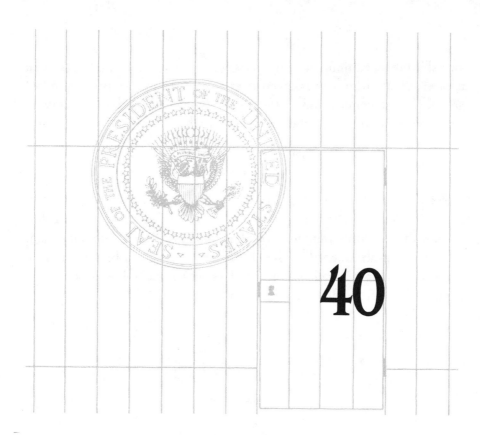

40

Edward S. Price (or Ned Price, as he was known in politics) had won forty-eight separate delegate-selection contests, beginning with precinct caucuses in Iowa and ending with the Delaware State Democratic Convention and primary elections in California, New Jersey, and Ohio. He entered the presidential nominating convention of the Republican party at Dallas as the leading candidate, having a delegate total of over 1,200 of the 1,505 needed for the nomination.

Wearing a bulletproof T-shirt and jockey shorts under his sublime tailoring, Ned Price left the Crescent Hotel in Dallas and made his way slowly inside a bulletproof limousine in a minimotorcade through a crowd of 1,800 people (police estimate) who were waiting at the hotel gates, to drive to the fair grounds, where he would spend three hours at a reception for Price delegates, under wall-to-wall banners and hoisted placards that read PRICE IS RIGHT! The candidate wanted to shake the hand of each of the men and women pledged to him, to let them know that he personally cared about individual human beings as long as they toed the line and knew their place.

That evening, at 9:00 P.M. Eastern Standard Time, starting late to accommodate the West Coast, the 3,353 delegates and half-delegates were assembled, a number that was swelled by the media representatives, security people, gate crashers, hookers, political aides, mutual fund salesmen, and floor managers to between 5,000 and 7,000 people milling about on the convention floor. The delegates were 66 percent male and 44 percent female; their age averaged forty-three years. Eleven percent were black, 48 percent were Protestant, 14 percent had Hispanic names, 2 percent were Amerinds, 54 percent were college graduates; all were faint with the heat, thinking with dread of leaving the air-conditioning in the building for the sledgehammer of heat that would fall on them outside.

Collectively, they did not have much power to nominate, but, individually, an amazingly small percentage within the bewitching definition of democracy did have that power.

A group of about fifty Republican leaders representing the visible constituencies—organized labor, women, blacks, conservation, the professional and industrial lobbies, gay rights, the electronic church, abortion-position surrounders, etc.—had met to recommend the optional nomination slates. However, that caucus of fifty could act only on options prepared by a smaller group of twelve, whose clients were a more powerful bloc than the visible constituencies. The posse of twelve included three full-time politicians who were paid by the party; two Washington attorneys, including S. L. Penrose; a power banker; three state governors; two senators; and the Republican minority leader of the House of Representatives.

The Twelve group maintained its staff of delegate counters and a spread of assembled tools: charts and blackboards to show the current delegate strength of each candidate; telephones directly to floor captains and delegation leaders; and hot-line phones to the principal candidates, who were waiting in their hotel suites for the word to race out to the convention to accept nomination.

Including the tight group of twelve controlling the convention decisions, it was the television networks who owned the convention. Their future problems had to be considered: the charisma-on-camera of the candidate; his wife's smile, style, and abject devotion; his height when standing beside other heads of state; his horseshit quotient; the state of his teeth when bared in smiles; and his stand on tax shelters. The networks would spend more than $27 million for the week in Dallas, while the Republican National Committee was spending only $2.18 million.

Therefore, due to circumstances which had been beyond his control from the day he had begun his run for the nomination, Ned Price, a five-feet eight-inch widower who was stuck with talking like Franklin D. Roosevelt, which had become discordant against the diction of around-the-clock television speech and was an absolute disaster when contrasted with the shouted, omelet-diction of the commercials, was denied the Republican nomination for president of the United States despite the overwhelming number of delegate votes that he had so painfully bought and paid for. His father, who had understood clearly who owned what and whom, had anticipated this and had made arrangements for the ultimate disposition of Eduardo's (and the *fratellanza*'s) ambitions. At the end of the first ballot, when the convention opened on the second night in Dallas, Ned Price was only 297 votes short of winning, but because he had become such a candidate of the wild-eyed religious far right, which had led to disasters for the party in 1988, and mainly because he had no wife to take the blame for any heinous mistakes that could be made during his administration, and also because there had not been a more Eastern establishment figure in politics since Averell Harriman, the professionals decided to fill a room with smoke and settle in to alter the destinations of American history in the usual manner.

The Twelve group met in a large suite in The Mansion on Turtle Creek, demolishing table after table from room service, and decided without contest that Ed Price was not electable. Two of them could not stop grinning because all of that PAC money had disappeared not quite in vain; a lot of the party faithful would be able to keep up the payments on their summer houses because of it.

After they had deliberated, the work was split up so that things could get moving. The floor captains and delegation leaders were given their orders over the direct-line telephones to the convention floor.

The convention's vote was swung behind Gordon Manning of Connecticut.

Price's supporters were allowed a forty-six-minute demonstration on the floor of the convention, after his conceding speech in Manning's favor, mainly because the networks had to fill the time if they were to realize the emperor's ransom of income from the commercials that made the convention possible. Ned Price was dumped.

Manning, governor of Connecticut and a crusading champion of the expedient, who understood clearly that '92 was not going to be a Republican year at the White House because the nation would need at least twelve years to recover from the old codger whose administration had vanished like steam, carried the convention by a majority of ninety-six votes on the next ballot, then was nominated unanimously on the third ballot.

The first move Governor Manning made after he had carried the nomination was to telephone Ned Price to offer him the key post in the proposed Manning cabinet as attorney general of the United States, which Ned Price accepted.

"The people have spoken," Price told the convention over the greatly flawed public address system. "The party now has given America the strongest and most electable candidate in its history, a great American, Gordon Godber Manning."

Humbled not at all, Ned Price left the convention hall, returned to his hotel, where he locked himself in, changed out of his visionary Woodrow Wilson dentures into a more homey set, the Adolf Hitler set, and telephoned Miss Claire Coolidge in New York. "It's over, baby," Eduardo said into the telephone, "and not only can nothing ever keep us apart again, but I am going to get you the lead in *Giselle*."

"Oh, *Edward!*" Miss Coolidge answered breathily and, while not entirely erasing Charles Macy Barton from her memory, she did put him on hold.

"Manning has offered me Justice."

"Have you been arrested, dearest?" Claire cried out.

"No, no. The Department of Justice. He wants me to be his attorney general."

"Oh, Woofy! You'll be *wonderful!*"

Reluctantly, Ned Price ended the conversation, feeling the sharpest of basic longings but unwilling to articulate them at his age. He stared at the telephone for a moment or two as if he knew he could reach into it and pull Miss Coolidge out of it, then began to think about his other major preoccupation again, the screwing his father had given him over his birthright, and, all at once, the devious plans he had been constructing inside his soul with a Sicilian lapidarian's precision came to a head like an angry carbuncle, and, with one telephone call, he lanced it.

He called his nephew, Rocco Sestero, in Atlantic City, grateful that his former secretary, Miss Blue, kept his address book up-to-the-minute. He would have placed Rocco in Brooklyn.

"Rocco?" Ned Price drawled into the telephone. "This is your Uncle Eduardo."

"Uncle Eduardo!" Rocco was awestruck. He had seen his uncle in the distance at family weddings, christenings, and funerals, but his uncle had never actually spoken to him. Throughout the evening, he had been sitting with his son in front of the television set at the fashionable New Jersey spa, watching history being made in Dallas, helpless with pride that a member of his family might be nominated for president of the United States; then, like it wasn't even happening, his uncle had called him on the telephone.

"What a magnificent speech!" Rocco sang. "But the American people were gypped out of a great leader."

"Thank you, Rocco."

"Beppino and me watched every minute of the convention here!"

"Beppino?" Eduardo hated immigrant names like that.

"My son! Beppino—your grandnephew. Anyway, what I wanna tell you is—maybe I don't understand politics, but I know enough to know you was robbed." Since he had been a boy, Rocco had hero-worshipped Eduardo; then, as a man, the feeling had been even more so since *People* magazine had identified Eduardo as one of the three richest men in the United States.

"No, no," Eduardo said. "The best man won. Rocco, as you know, I am in Dallas."

Who ever heard such a crazy accent? Rocco thought. This guy makes William F. Buckley, Jr., sound like Nathan Detroit. "That figures, Uncle Eduardo," he said.

"I'd like you to have breakfast with me tomorrow at my apartment in New York. Are you free?"

Am I free? Rocco thought wildly. What does he think, I'd charge my own uncle? "I'll be there, Uncle Eduardo." What an honor!

"Do you know where it is?"

"Not exactly."

"The Trump Tower. Eight-thirty tomorrow morning."

Rocco Sestero was Amalia's son, Corrado Prizzi's grandson. He was a demandingly acquisitive man in his early fifties who had been one of the three *caporegimes* of the Prizzi family. When the franchises had been sold, because he believed he was going to inherit millions through his mother when the don died, he had stayed out of the action with the result that he had had to accept an enforced retirement check for $418,652.39 from the Prizzi settlement and take work as a pit boss at one of the Prizzi casinos in Atlantic City. Rocco thought about money the way other Italians thought about pasta when they were hungry. Rocco was always hungry and money was the only food that could satisfy him. He was a Prizzi.

Eduardo checked the current-status address book. S. L. Penrose, a member of The Twelve, one of the foremost political consultants in Washington, and a head of one of the capital's largest law firms, was also the guiding force behind the National Landscapers Congress, formerly the *Unione Siciliane*, the *fratellanza's* lobby, in which the relatively newly established Black, Hispanic, and Oriental organizations held associate memberships. Eduardo allowed time for S. L. to finish his business at the convention and return to his hotel, the Plaza of the Americas. Sal Penrose had been a protégé of Corrado Prizzi. When Sal was a young law student at Tulane University, the don's sister, Birdie, married to Gennaro Fustino, Boss of the southern-southwestern rim of the United States, had recommended him to her brother as deserving of all the help the don could give him. The don put him through law school, where he was editor of the law review. After graduation, after four years of service in one of the great Barker's Hill Wall Street law firms, the don provided the capital for Sal to open a law office in Washington, which, in thirty years, had become one of the two greatest law firms in the city. S. L. Penrose was a considerable figure in American affairs, an adviser to presidents, an esteemed, and toweringly expensive, "political consultant," and the source of the *fratellanza*'s power in national politics, which ranked third in national consequence after the gun lobby and toxic waste disposal.

Although administratively, being a Barker's Hill lawyer, Penrose worked directly under Charles Macy Barton, he had, until Eduardo had retired to run for president, worked for Eduardo.

"Sal?" Eduardo said into the phone. "Ned Price. When the convention closes down tonight, come over to my hotel. I'd like to have a chat."

"Certainly, Ned."

"I'll look for you."

When Penrose arrived Eduardo only kept him for about twelve minutes. "Manning offered me Justice," he said.

"That's where the diamonds shine."

"I want you to get the committees in both houses ready for my confirmation. A two-thirds majority, no more."

"And if Manning doesn't win?"

"We'll cross that bridge when, as, and if."

"Justice. Jesus. We can really win with Justice."

Edward knew how much they could win. He would be sitting right on the sweet spot where he could force every crime family in the United States to amalgamate his way and really grow so that their profits could be reinvested and their regional companies could be brought under the Barker's Hill formula. Ask not what you can do for your country, he thought. Let the other guy be president. Glue me into that chair in the attorney general's office and let me write the nation's songs.

But his loathing of all those unwashed, crudely accented people in the *fratellanza* who would directly benefit from such policies choked in his gullet again. Whenever he thought of those people, he thought of his swinish brother, Vincent. He loathed being the force that would make all of those swinish people richer and more powerful. As if they could be. If he did do it, he was going to make some hard, hard deals through Sal Penrose so that at least he could know that he was making something substantial out of every enhanced dollar he would be helping

214

to let them make. God, he thought, imagining the CIA flying in drugs from all the contributing countries of the world for absolutely trouble-free entry into the market cities of North America. There were hundreds of billions to be made and the lion's share of it could be his. They could put cocaine in every household, as available as packaged bread. He decided to forget his objections to most of the individual members of the *fratellanza*. He would carry out his father's policy willingly and serve his government.

The *fratellanza*, when advised by S. L. Penrose, was, in all its innocence, unconscious of the hyperactive destiny that Eduardo Prizzi had in store for them and was pleased by the outcome of the nomination. Eduardo, they were told by their *consiglieri*, would be more useful to its directly patriotic interests than if he had won the nomination for the presidency in that he would be the chief law enforcement officer of the United States: after all, their principal business was breaking the law on behalf of a pleading public.

Those portions of the families that had been contributing to get Eduardo elected president were now told to switch their allegiance to the Manning ticket, while the other half of the families worked and spent for the candidacy of Franklin M. Heller so that the two-party system would be preserved.

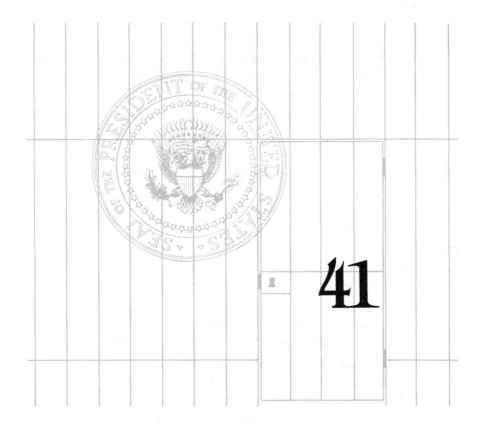

41

Rocco entered his Uncle Eduardo's security system on a high aerie floor of the four-floor Price apartment in New York's Trump Tower at 8:26 A.M. the following morning, requiring that he get out of bed at 3:45 A.M. to drive from the Jersey shore into the city. He was processed by Eduardo's security people and ready to enter his uncle's breakfast room at 8:37. He resented the whole thing. Rocco had been a resenter all his life, one of the people with cancer of the soul. He had made *capo* because his mother controlled what his grandfather got to eat, and his mother had been determined to make something out of Rocco. All his life he had figured that, when the don died, he—or his mother, which was the same thing because he'd get it in the end—would come into a fortune. He was Corrado Prizzi's grandson so—what else? But nothing happened when the don died. The don left his mother the income on five hundred thousand dollars and not a dime to him. Then his mother

216

died twenty minutes later, so he got it. What was it, the income? Twenty-two thousand nine hundred a year. Fahcrissake, he had spent more than that on a weekend at Vegas. What kind of a life had they handed him, the grandson of Corrado Prizzi, who got only the income on five hundred grand and a big line of horseshit?

Eduardo was waiting for him in the breakfast room. It would have been an imposing room for the state dinners of the Shah of Iran in his salad days. The furniture was made of solid silver, which shone capriciously in the morning sunlight, requiring a full-time staff of two to keep it polished. The powerful, not to say overwhelming, Rembrandt, *The Master Clock Maker,* valued by *Lifestyles of the Rich and Famous* at $8.7 million, which was quite large and *very* striking, would have dominated the room were it not for the glassed-in junglelike arboretum that filled the longest wall, in which families of rhesus monkeys swung from branch to branch or searched for lice in each other's fur. The arboretum was Eduardo's statement in support of worldwide environmental protection, a deeply personal, not merely political, conviction.

Eduardo rose and embraced his nephew. "I am brokenhearted about your mother."

They settled down to a reassuring Sicilian breakfast of *focaccia,* which were rolls with a filling of ricotta cheese and minced kidney; strong coffee; and *cubaita,* an expressive sweet made from sesame seed, sugar, and honey. Eduardo, of course, *never* ate Sicilian food unless he was with members of his family from whom he needed something, which was as seldom as it needed to be, so his people had been scouring the Sicilian food markets of the city since dawn to come up with something approximately suitable.

"This is tremendous, Uncle Eduardo. You must have a fucking genius of a Sicilian cook."

Eduardo shuddered lightly. He offered Rocco a selection of Zeno Davidoff's breakfast cigars. He passed a ruby- and emerald-studded Zippo lighter to Rocco, saying, "Keep it as a little souvenir."

"Holy shit, Uncle Eduardo!"

"As the surviving head of the Prizzi family, I've been thinking, Rocco, about how your grandfather had somehow passed you over in his few bequests."

"Shit, yes."

"I think you are entitled to more than the interest on the five hundred thousand dollars which was passed on to you from your mother."

"Shit, yes."

"I don't suppose the interest is very much?"

"A lousy twenty-two thousand nine hundred a year."

"Whaaaaaat? Good heavens I could do better than that for you."

"How much?"

"Say thirty thousand."

Rocco snorted. "Thirty thousand," he said. "I gotta work my ass off just to stay even."

"What do you do?"

"I'm a pit boss at the number three in Atlantic City."

"You must be on your feet most of the time."

"You can say that again."

"Well, by God, by my lights, it just isn't fair. You, the grandson, get twenty-two thousand nine hundred a year, but Maerose, the granddaughter, is the custodian of billions."

"Ah, *shit*, Uncle Eduardo," Rocco moaned.

"The injustice of the whole thing has been bothering me so that I can't sleep nights. Really. I've had to put on my thinking cap about it, and I think I have evolved a way in which you can pick up a million or two in a perfectly straightforward way."

"How?"

"Tax-free, of course."

"No kidding? How, Uncle Eduardo?"

"Do you know an absolutely stupid but reliable man whom you could enlist to sort of—front—this thing for you?"

Rocco thought. His mind wasn't as fast as an Olivetti 260 work station, but he got there. "Yeah. Santo Calandra."

"The collector for the franchises? The former *vindicatore?*"

"Yeah. He's like the stupidest anywheres."

"I see. Well! That's splendid. Now—this is what I want you to do. Down to the last detail. We'll go over it two or three times, but if there is anything about the plan which you do not understand, I rely on you to ask me about it now, because—except for one more time—we won't be meeting again." He smiled benignly. "In this connection, that is."

218

42

Rocco set the meet with Santo Calandra by inviting him for a weekend at the fanciest of the three Prizzi hotels in Atlantic City. When Santo got there on a Friday afternoon, Rocco laid on a gorgeous broad, stacks of chips, all the New Jersey champagne Santo could drink, a suite with a private steam room, and four hard-core porn videos. The whole hospitality knocked Santo out until three o'clock the next afternoon, which was when Rocco went up to see him.

Santo had worked in Rocco's regime during the years of Vincent Prizzi and Charley Partanna. He had a wary respect for Rocco, who not only had been the source from which all good things had flowed for most of his professional life, but also was a Prizzi on his mother's side, where it counted.

They sat at either end of an enormous sofa, smiling at each other.

Santo was wearing a light pink undershirt and orange shorts. He looked like the flag of an emerging African nation. Santo was a bulky man with a nose like a boxing glove who had so much respect for his skin that he only shaved every other day. Beardwise, Rocco thought, he could have took a shave every four hours. As long as Rocco had known him, Santo had stayed just busy enough not to have the time to clean his fingernails, or even to wash his hands for that matter. He could have grown Perricone grapes in the accumulation of soil at the end of each grimy finger. Most of all, just sitting around like this, he missed Santo's neckties. Santo's adventurousness showed in his neckties, which made him look as if he had encouraged people to break eggs all over his chest. His suits were too tight but looked a lot better than his underwear. Just the same, Rocco remembered wistfully, when Santo didn't have his feet up on the furniture like this he wore the most beautiful shoes in Brooklyn.

Rocco was a vertical of the right creases, old-school tie, button-down collar, and a charcoal-gray blazer with brass buttons. He wore a black mourning band on his left sleeve.

"They take good care of you?" Rocco asked.

"Sensational."

"How was the broad?"

"Sensational."

"Wait'll you see what I got for you tonight."

"No kidding?"

"Two. Real movie stahz."

Santo grinned, which, considering the state of his teeth, his stubble, and the size of his head, was not the most considerate thing he could have done.

"How did you make out downstairs?"

"Like I broke even, maybe won a little."

"I ain't seen you for a long time. Not since the franchises."

"Yeah."

"I got a tremendous proposition for you."

"Yeah?"

"For maybe three-four months I been asking around about who is the most natural leader to take over the family if the family was gonna go back into bidniz again."

"Whatta you mean?"

220

"I mean the franchise thing ain't right. We gotta take them back and operate them the way my grandfather set them up."

"But those other outfits paid like thirty million for the franchises."

"So we'll give them the money back."

"Where are we gonna get that kind of money?"

"Later. Don't worry about it."

"Where do I come in here?"

"You are the natural *capo di famiglia*. Everybody I talked to from the old setup agrees with that."

"No shit?"

"We're gonna call it the Calandra family."

"No shit?"

"What else?"

"Whose idea was this, anyway?"

"Angelo Partanna."

"Angelo?"

"But he wants you to stay far away from him until we get the whole thing set up."

"This ain't easy to follow, Rocco. It's coming at me very fast. So if we gotta pay thirty million to get the franchises back, then where we gonna get it?"

"That's the beauty part Angelo thought of. You know who got the money when my grandfather went?"

"Who?"

"My cousin's kids."

"Who?"

"Maerose's kids."

"So?"

"So you line up a couple of solid helpers and you lift my cousin's kids."

"What for?"

"For thirty million bucks."

"The don left that kind of money?"

"Then you get the franchises back and you head up the Calandra family."

After Rocco left, Santo went back to bed to think the whole thing over. It was a terrific proposition. The more he thought about it, the more he knew he needed to talk to Angelo before he made any moves on Maerose's kids. What he needed more than he needed the thirty million was a *consigliere,* and everybody knew Angelo was the best in the business, coast to coast. He lay on the emperor-size bed on top of an antique American patchwork quilt made by little old ladies high up in Vermont or maybe Taiwan, and he could feel the power inside his head like it was water on the brain, but even so he was big enough to admit that he owed it to Angelo to offer him the job because he never forgot how he owed it to Angelo, who had given him his start as a contract hitter when he had been a young guy just starting out. Also he wanted to lay it on Angelo a little because the time had finally come when he was about to move up from wiseguy to the top of the heap. The Calandra family! Jesus, he wished his mother was still alive.

Santo and Angelo met at the laundry on Tuesday morning.

"Look at it this way, Angelo," Santo said. "Nobody can say nothing against the Prizzis because there ain't no Prizzis. Also Charley is gone. No family honor is involved here. You are like the janitor for the operation, so nobody is gonna blame you."

"Janitor?" Pop said. "If I'm the janitor, what does that make you— the men's room attendant, you marble-headed wop stupe?"

"No offense, Angelo. It just gets you off the hook."

"I'm over eighty years old. That's the only hook I needa get off."

"What I'm saying is, it has nothing to do with you. Nobody is gonna blame you."

"But they're gonna blame *you,* Santo. The Blacks, Hispanics, and Orientals and the families who bought them franchises are gonna blame you. They paid out all that money to buy them businesses—how do you think you're gonna stay alive after that?"

"Because I am gonna give them back the money they paid for the franchises."

"Why should they sell it back for what they paid? Why should they sell it back at all? What the fuck you think they bought it for inna first place? You think they keep paying us the royalties if it wasn't making a shitpot fulla money?"

"I didn't say they'd sell it back. I said I'd make the offer to pay it back so I could have a position if it comes up in the Commission. Pretty good, hah?"

"If it comes up? *If?* And suppose they say sure, old pal, we'll give it back. Where you gonna get that kinda money?"

Santo hadn't expected such a question; then he remembered how Rocco had told him that Angelo had to be kept far out of this until the new Calandra family had been set up, so he improvised. What was the difference? Whatever he said, they both knew exactly what they were talking about. "Where? You are gonna give it to me."

"Me? Where am I gonna get it?"

"You're the only one left out of the whole Prizzi family. You got the money. So you give it to me, and I give it back to them."

"Santo, don't work overtime being a schmuck. You think the Prizzis put the thirty million from the franchises inna tin box and handed it to me? Use your head, fahcrissake."

"Whatta you mean?"

"I mean the Prizzis wouldn't let fifty bucks lay around without reinvesting it. The money was all washed. It's out working. It's been moved under a half dozen different names since it was paid in. Whatta you, some kinda *cretino?*"

Santo thought maybe he could be wrong thinking about Angelo as a *consigliere.* Where was the respect here? What kind of attitude was this? "So who got the don's money?" he said. "Maerose Prizzi?"

"The Salvation Army," Angelo said.

"Yeah? Rocco's mother told him Mae's kids got it," Santo said.

"Jesus!" Angelo said. "Now you give me street gossip. Santo, lissena me. You got a good thing going with the override on the franchise collections. What you were thinking you could do only looks good on paper. Forget it. And I'll forget we ever had this meeting."

"Fuck that, Angelo. I'm not running no collection agency for a lousy three percent when I can have the whole thing."

"So maybe we can work it out to five percent," Angelo lied. "That's a lotta money, Santo. That was the boss's cut in the old days."

"A lotta money? You know what's left after a hundred and thirty-four collectors get their end and the payoff money is taken out and I pay the overhead? Practically nothing, that's what's left."

"It's more money than you ever saw in your life," Angelo said. "And the way you wanna routine it, it's gonna be a very short life."

"So a buncha hoodlums are gonna get in an uproar. So there'll be a little war. Then everybody will go back to business."

"You are gonna sting Sicilians for thirty million plus and they're gonna forget it?"

"Maybe I didn't think it through, Angelo. But I will. And when I do, I'm gonna take over all that business. And you're gonna hafta decide whose side you're on."

"Think what through, you asshole?"

"I'm gonna get the money, that's what I'm gonna think it through." Santo saw that he would need to get back to Rocco to get this thing opened up for him a little more.

"How're you gonna get the money, you shithead?"

"That's what I gotta think through," he said stiffly, deeply offended. He stood up and left the laundry.

Pop swiveled his chair around and stared out of the window at the bricks and the cats in the garbage. After a while he turned back to the desk. He called Charley at the Barker's Hill office. "Something came up, Charley," he said into the phone.

"When do you want to make it?"

"Like now."

"The laundry?"

"Yeah."

Charley drove himself to Brooklyn in the Chevy van. He was wearing a gray flannel suit with the tailoring that Mary Barton said made him look like Gary Cooper around the torso, and a maroon Bohemian Grove tie. The Ralph Lauren alligator scuffies he had on had cost him more than the quarterly rent on the apartment at the beach in the old days and that was after inflation had set in. Pop was sitting too quietly when Charley came into the office, staring at a statue of St. Gennaro, a leftover from Vincent Prizzi's time. It was a nice summer day. There was a redolent breeze off the Gowanus Canal, three miles to the northwest.

Charley sat in one of the two chairs facing his father, who was behind the desk that held Vincent's fake bronze plastic sign that said: THANK YOU FOR NOT SMOKING.

"A nice suit, Charley."

Charley shrugged. "It happened in Europe."

"I used to be a snappy dresser. But—you get outta the habit, I guess."

"What came up, Pop?"

Angelo spoke mildly, watching St. Gennaro do nothing. "You remember I told Corrado that selling the New York franchises wouldn't work?"

"I remember."

"It ain't working. It's starting to fall apart, Charley."

"No kidding?" It was all very distant to Charley.

"Santo come to see me here. Prince Nowhere. He told me he's gonna organize the old *soldati* and go back into business the way it used to be."

"It's too complicated for Santo."

"You ain't kidding."

"How does the dummy figure they can get away with that? The other outfits paid us to get out."

"Santo said he was gonna give them back the money."

"What money?"

"The thirty million plus."

"Where is Santo gonna get thirty million plus?"

"That's what I asked him. He said he was gonna get it from the Prizzis. He had it in his mind that it was all in a little sack and that I could hand it to him."

"I know he's very stupid, but what happens when he understands he can't have it?"

"That's why I called you. He thinks the don left the thirty million to the twins."

"The *twins?*" Charley froze. Pop finally had his full attention.

"What he was telling me, although he didn't know he was saying it, is that he is gonna snatch the twins to get the money."

Charley turned to stone. He shook his head slowly, back and forth, denying the meaning of what he had heard, staring at his father. "That's how you figure it?"

"That's what he thinks."

"I'll hit him myself," Charley said thickly.

"No, no. I'll get people to hit him."

"First, it's my wife and my kids. Second, Santo's too tricky.

But I know him. I'll handle it. Like quick. Now—before he can get set."

"It's prolly the best way. You'll need a piece."

"Yeah, right."

Angelo got up and shuffled out of the room. He was gone about five minutes. He came back with a bundle wrapped in oilpaper. "This is a nice, clean piece with a noise suppressor," he said. "Also a harness."

He closed the door and began to unwrap the package on his desk, taking care not to touch the weapon. There was a pair of transparent surgical gloves under the piece. "Today is Friday," Pop said. "The Busaccas usually leave their royalty envelope on Saturdays, but it's summertime so they could change it. The daughter will answer the door. You tell her you brought the envelope from the Busaccas. She'll tell you to wait; then she'll go in and tell her father. You follow her in and do the job on Santo."

Santo lived in a big apartment house with his divorced daughter, Melba, in Sunset Park, between Bay Ridge and the Greenwood Cemetery. As Charley drove across from Bensonhurst, he felt like he was moving through a fog of time over which he had never had any control. His own wife, the don's own granddaughter, had set up the don to change them all from flesh-and-blood Sicilians into cut-out, coloring book Americans who lived in a world where respectable was everything. The land of Dick and Jane and their respectable little dog.

Charley was like some reluctant fallen angel, the only one out of the 133,306,668 fallen angels, according to the Cardinal Bishop of Tusculum in 1273, who had not wanted to leave the paradise on high where he had always existed, but who had gone along with the trend because the two men, his father and Don Corrado, who had made all the large decisions of his life, had ordered him to fall into the pit of respectability with Mae, Eduardo, and the twins. Now there was no going back. By doing the job on Santo he wouldn't be going back or changing anything. He would be giving it to Santo to preserve the respectability that his wife had lusted for, a lust, in fact, that must have been the central curse laid upon the Prizzis because the grandfather had lusted just as hard after respectability as the granddaughter.

It had reached the point where Santo, that dummy of dummies, had laid a threat on Charley's two children so that there was nothing he could do except what he was going to do. He was protecting the holy of holies of Prizzi respectability, his own two sons, who were preordained by the will of their mother and the bottomless purse of their great-grandfather to grow up to talk like Eduardo and learn how to play polo. Time was pouring all of their essences from chalice to chalice. Charley was suspended hundreds of thousands of miles away in lightless, freezing outer space, between a life now gone, which he understood, and a life that was measured by the tread of pomp in an unspeakable procession toward the altar of respectability.

He put on the transparent rubber gloves in the hall facing the Calandras' front door, thinking of another hallway twenty-five years ago when they had made him put Vito Daspisa away. But this was an entirely different proposition. He looked at his watch and rang the doorbell at a quarter to six. He could smell the *ragu* on the stove inside, a terrific smell.

Melba Calandra answered the door. "Whatta you want?" she said. She was a short, plump, bottle-blonde in a skirt like a pelmet.

"I brought the envelope from the Busaccas."

"Today ain't Saturday."

"We got a big weekend coming up. We're going to the beach tonight."

"Wait here." She slammed the door so quickly, Charley couldn't follow her in. He waited. Santo opened the door. "You from the Busaccas?" he said.

"Yeah. With the envelope."

"That's a nice suit."

"Barney's. Seventh Avenue and Seventeenth Street."

Santo held out his hand for the envelope. Charley's hand went to his inside breast pocket and came out with the bad news. He shot Santo through his left eye; then he stepped over the body, shut the door behind him, and went into the kitchen, where he shot Melba in the chest and, when she went down, in the throat. She was a heavy bleeder. He dropped the piece on her stomach, watched it bounce and somersault like an acrobat hitting a trampoline, then leaned across her body and dipped a rubber-sheathed finger in the *ragu* for a little taste. It was absolutely delicious. He turned off the low flame under the pot.

43

Charley got back to Sixty-fourth Street in time to change into dinner clothes, have a light snack, then, at ten o'clock, leave with Mary Barton for the October in Albania Ball in Southampton, which would be heavily covered by *W*, which meant that Mae had been dressing for it since four in the afternoon, surrounded by fitters, combers, and handlers, to wow the dozens of rich dressmakers who would be at the fete.

Danvers drove them to the East River heliport. They boarded one of the Barker's Hill eight-passenger Sikorsky choppers and were set down at Southampton twenty-two minutes later. It was really gala. The women were lined up in phalanxes behind their dressmakers to make it easier for the *W* photographers and caption people. They danced to an Albanian bagpipe orchestra and drank Diet Pepsi. It was a fun night, but they got away early because Mary Barton was chairing the annual meeting of the Public Libraries Association at 3:00 P.M. the next day after a policy lunch at Mortimer's with the arbiter, and, after the libraries meeting, she looked forward to her time with the twins in Central Park. Also, they couldn't stay on at the ball because Charley had an oil company takeover beginning at 8:00 A.M., which involved full control through an offer of $6.2 billion for the 45 percent Barker's Hill did not already own. Whether the $72 a share offer would be enough was still uncertain because the oil company's stock price had since risen above the bid, but it was only money and Charley was confident of reeling the deal in. But he had to be sharp. So they left the party early, Danvers met them at the heliport, and they were driven to bed at Sixty-fourth Street.

The hit on Santo Calandra reverberated throughout Brooklyn, with the outer waves immediately reaching Atlantic City. He had been one of the elder statesmen of the community, so secure in his place that the surviving professional population was aghast at what had happened. Except Rocco, who, in faroff Atlantic City, with his prior, intimate knowledge of Prizzi thinking, understood what had happened to Santo from the moment Santo called him to tell him that the Prizzis weren't going to give them the money.

"Who?" Rocco asked.

"Angelo."

"Angelo? You asked Angelo for the thirty million dollars?"

"He knows me a long time."

"How in Christ's name did you ever think Angelo would let you have thirty million dollars? I told you Angelo was the one who had figured out how we were gonna get it. He musta thought you were nuts." Rocco was talking on the telephone in the kitchen while his wife worked at the stove and his son, Beppino, ate his breakfast.

"I wanted to show him my appreciation that the family was gonna start up again and that he wanted me to head it up. He woulda got his money back plus he'd have his old job again. I woulda made him my consigliere."

"Holy shit."

Rocco vacillated between telling Santo to get out of town and telling him to forget the whole thing, that they weren't going to do what they had talked about, but in the end he decided that the best thing would be to let them move Santo out of the way so that a new plan could be made.

After the call he went back into the small living room and dropped himself on a sofa. His son, Beppino, came in and said, "Whatsa matta, Pop?"

"Nothing a Tums for the tummy won't cure," Rocco said.

The next day Beppino came back to the apartment star-crossed by the fate of men. "Somebody done the job on Santo and Melba," he said.

"*Melba?*" Mary Sestero said. "What did Melba ever do? What the hell is this, Rocco?"

"It was Angelo's contract," Rocco said.

"But—why Melba?"

"She musta saw the contractor."

"You think Angelo set it up?"

"I know it."

Rocco ate the lunch his wife had prepared; then he left the apartment and went to one of the three big Prizzi hotels on the boardwalk and let himself into the room he had been alloted on the fourth floor to get the load off his feet when his relief came on. He called his Uncle Eduardo in New York. Eduardo took the call on a scrambler phone.

"Yes, Rocco?"

"Somebody took out Santo."

"Somebody?"

"Angelo."

"How is that?"

"Santo went to the laundry and asked him for thirty million to start up a new family."

"I see. So?"

"So should I forget the whole thing?"

"Absolutely *not*, Rocco. You'll have to handle it yourself now— that's all."

"Yeah?"

"Then we'll proceed as planned, shall we?" Eduardo hung up.

The oil company merger pressure had slackened off by about one o'clock. Charley got most of what he wanted by giving in graciously to a few golden handshakes and platinum parachutes. At 1:20 P.M. Claire Coolidge called him.

"Mr. Barton, I feel awful about bothering you, but I wondered if you had had the chance to speak to Edward about—you know."

"Not yet. But it's very much on my mind."

"It's just that we'd like to set a date, but I feel that I can't do that until the unfinished business with Edward has been confronted and settled."

"You can count on me."

"Thank you, Mr. Barton."

At 1:50 P.M., Dr. Winikus called him. He told Charley that Angelo had had a "small" stroke. Charley said he would be right there. He hung up and was out of the office and into the private elevator to the garage before anyone knew he had gone.

Charley drove himself to Brooklyn in the Chevy van, which he kept in the basement garage of the Barker's Hill building. He was all shook up. He couldn't imagine life continuing on the planet without Pop.

Dr. Winikus was waiting for him in the front room at Pop's house in Bensonhurst. "He's much improved, Mr. Barton," he said. "He had minor motor loss on his right side, but we've had him under sedatives for almost seven hours, and already his movements, although impaired, are discernible. This time tomorrow will tell the story."

"Seven hours?" Charley said. "Why wasn't I told before this?"

"When he became conscious about an hour ago, he asked me to call you." Winikus looked curious as to what the connection could possibly be between this old Sicilian hoodlum and such a man as the Great Organizer.

"I'm his executor," Charley said. "Can I see him?"

"Five minutes. That's all he can take."

Charley went into his father's bedroom. Angelo was propped up on pillows staring at the door. Charley had never seen anybody who looked so awful. Angelo's face had separated into two faces. One was slack, pulled downward by gravity. The other side didn't match at all. "Ah, Mr. Barton," he said weakly out of the left side of his mouth.

Charley shut the door behind himself and pulled a chair up to the bedside.

"Jesus, Pop," he said. "You scared hell out of me."

"Whatta you expect? I'm eighty years old."

"Do you hurt?"

"Where I can feel, I feel great." He sighed. "Except that I'm finally pissed off, a little late. Corrado built a great thing. Then he threw it away."

"Barker's Hill doesn't do too bad."

Angelo smiled scornfully. "You'll never come within thirty percent of what the gambling and shit business made for us. The shit business alone—cocaine, that gold mine bigger than the sun—and he sold it all for a nothing royalty. Why?"

"Maybe he saw coke being legalized. It's very popular on Wall Street."

"Never. He sold out to buy respectability, Charley. Mae planted the idea on him, and once he had bought it it was if he was cursed with it. He threw it away to become an American. It's worthless to us, Charley. We been Sicilians for seven hundred years. Corrado knew that better than anybody. He controlled the most respectable people in the world."

"Take it easy, Pop. What the hell. It's done."

"Mae, that crazy, mixed-up Maerose. She's never gonna make it past St. Peter, Charley. And she is gonna have to pay in this life for all the things she did. What the fuck are we because of her? Like the lost tribe of Israel, scattered and wandering in the wilderness."

He shook his head; then he threw off the despair. "Charley, lissena me. Don't let them take me to a hospital. I hate hospitals. Whatta they got that I can't have here? Round-the-clock nurses, oxygen, portable X ray if that's what Winikus wants, lab tests—we can have it all right here. Okay?"

"I'll handle it, Pop. Don't even think about it."

Dr. Winikus opened the door to signal that the meeting was over. Charley told Angelo he'd be back as soon as he could; then he left the room to talk to the doctor about turning the small house into a miniature hospital.

44

It was a quarter to six when Charley opened the front door at Sixty-fourth Street with his key, tuckered out and ready for an early evening.

He thought he had wandered into the wrong house. The entrance hall was full of uniformed cops and plainclothesmen. He gaped at them. He saw Dick Gallagher, the deputy chief of detectives, whom Charley knew from the old days when Gallagher was a homicide lieutenant. He saw Horace Gavin, agent-in-charge for the FBI, his bald head shining like a spotlight. "What is this?" Charley said. "What's going on here?"

They turned toward him. He heard Maerose scream at him from the top of the stairs, *"Charley!"*

He raced across the entrance hall and up the stairs. Mae was haggard. She stared at him as if she could not believe what she had to tell

233

him. "They took the kids, Charley. The babies. They took them, the twins."

He held her in his arms closely and spoke in a whisper into her ear.

"Where was Al?"

"Al's dead." She began to sob. "Two men. They hit Al; then they slugged me, and when I came to, the cops were there and they told me the babies had been lifted. In the park. In that beautiful park."

"You know anybody?"

"My cousin, Rocco, his son, Beppi."

"You didn't say nothing to the people downstairs?"

"No. I hadda talk to you. But I ain't going along with that *omertà* shit. I just can't figure out how I'm suppose to know hoodlums like Rocco."

Dick Gallagher, allowing a fraction of time for the wife to tell the husband, arrived at the top of the stairs. Two FBI men were right behind him.

"We'd like to talk to you, Mr. Barton," he said respectfully.

Charley broke away from Mary Barton.

"We'll go into the upstairs study," Charley said. "I assume you won't need my wife for this?"

"No, no," the agent-in-charge said.

Mary Barton wandered off toward the nursery. One of the nannies came out to comfort her.

Charley couldn't get himself together. He was shaking as he listened to Horace Gavin. "When they call, we'll be listening, whether here or at your office," Gavin was saying.

Charley stared at him.

"Have you had any hint, any threat, that this might happen, Mr. Barton?"

Charley shook his head.

"We'll get the people. You can be sure of that."

"Never mind them. Get my children back." He sat up straight. He laid the fear on them. "Listen to me," he said. "They want money and we're going to give them the money. Understand that. And until

I have those kids back, you are out of this. Surveillance, contact, pay-offs, everything. You stay out until I have my kids back."

"Within certain parameters, I agree with you, Mr. Barton."

"Forget parameters," Charley said slowly. "I am going to handle this. You are out until my children are back in this house." His voice rose. "Do you understand that? Do you want the president to explain that to the director? You are going to stay out of this until those infants are returned." He pounded on the arm of the chair in an outburst of fear. "It can't be any other way!"

He stood up, turned away from them, left the room, and walked rapidly toward the nursery.

He sat with Mae in their Egyptian pharaoh-style bedroom with its pyramid-shaped bed canopies and its red sandstone walls. "Just believe me, sweetheart," he said. "All Rocco wants is money and he knows we are going to give it to him. He won't lay a finger on the kids. He showed his face to you so you would know that he isn't going to do anything to them. His wife, after all, she had four of her own kids. She'll take care of them and you know she's a good mother."

"Why should Rocco let me make him? Where is the fear if that's what he meant when he showed himself to me?"

"He knows we'll pay. He knows the kids are more important than money."

"But where is the *fear*, Charley?"

"Well, what the hell, Mae—we don't pay and he can send them back to some little village in the old country for the rest of their lives."

She moaned. He held her by the shoulders. "That isn't going to happen, Mae. And no FBI or cops are going to make waves on this. I am going to call the president right now, and he is going to call off all these guys downstairs. It's all gonna work out."

"You think so, Charley? You really think so? You will call the president on this?"

"Watch. And Rocco is too smart to set up the contact with us direct. He'll have a cut-out and the FBI will be whistling Dixie. I don't know how he's going to do it, but we'll be told in a way that nobody but Rocco and us are going to know. He'll tell me how much and I'll get the money together. I'll hand him the money and he'll hand me Rado and Angier. I swear this to you."

Mary Barton's face was all stone. "And when you have them back and they are home and safe, then you give it to my cousin Rocco."

"You can bet your sweet ass on that."

Speaking clearly into the phone so that the FBI monitor wouldn't miss anything, but mostly so that Mae would be reassured that the cops would stay out of it, Charley said, "I hope I haven't broken in on anything, Mr. President, but—"

"What's the problem, Charley?"

"My seven-month-old twins were kidnapped this afternoon."

"My God!"

"I need a favor, Mr. President."

"Anything. Name it."

"I want to ask you if you will tell the FBI to stay out of this until the ransom payment has been made. And if you will instruct them to so advise the New York Police Department."

"Kidnapping is our most heinous offense, Charley. What you are asking is very dangerous. A cover-up."

"It is the only way I can be sure that my children will be returned to their mother safely."

"My people have a lot of experience at this. It's all new to you, Charley."

"I will pay the kidnappers, get my children back, then cooperate entirely with every law enforcement agency."

"You know I'd call out the National Guard for you, Charley. As it is you can have the FBI, the CIA, and the National Security Agency, but—"

"I am pleading with you, Frank."

"Does the media have this?"

"It will certainly be on the seven o'clock news."

"I'll talk to my people." The line went dead.

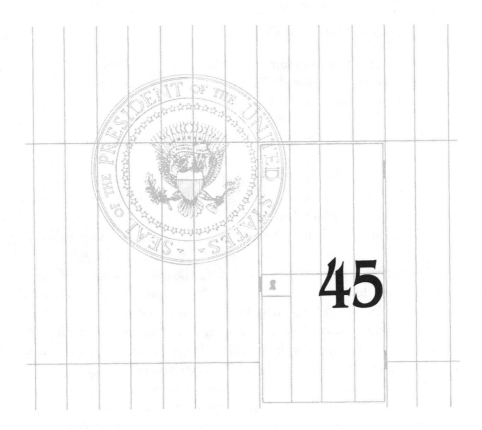

45

The twins were just as happy as they had ever been, under Mary Sestero's loving care in Atlantic City. Rocco played with them in the morning and at night before he went off to the casino and they were given their prebedtime bottle.

"Ain't they beautiful kids?" Mary Sestero said.

"Very rich kids," Rocco said.

"Such beautiful natures. They're always good. They only cry when they're hungry. Mae must be a terrific mother."

"She has baby nurses she ain't even used yet."

When Mary was busy with the twins, Rocco brooded with Beppino about what Angelo had done to Santo.

"How do you know it was Angelo, Pop?"

"I didn't say he done it. He had it done."

"How come you're so sure it was Angelo?"

"Because that meathead, Santo, told me he had gone to see Angelo and he told him that he was gonna take over."

"What a stupe."

Rocco repeated the line Eduardo had told him to stick to. "This whole thing is Angelo's deal."

Beppi wagged his head in admiration. "He's a smart old guy, Pop. He can really put two and two together. When he seen that Santo was fucking up, he had him taken out."

"Big deal," his father said, "so we hadda lift the two kids ourselves."

Four terrible days inched past before the two messages arrived at their separate destinations. Charley didn't go near the office. He tried to comfort Mae. Once every day, he drove to Bensonhurst to check on his father, whose condition, Dr. Winikus said, remained unchanged. On the morning of the fourth day things began to happen for the kids. The fake note went to Mary Barton at Sixty-fourth Street. It said, in newsprint that had been razored out of the *Daily News* pages, KIDS OKAY. WILL CONTACT AGAIN. The FBI intercepted the fake note at the postal delivery station before allowing it to be delivered, but that got them nowhere because it had been sent to divert attention from the real action.

The day the note was delivered to Sixty-fourth Street, Rocco Sestero called his uncle, on Eduardo's private line, at his apartment at 8:47 A.M. and read from a script that Eduardo had prepared. When the telephone rang, Eduardo switched on the tape recorder.

"Uncle Eduardo? Rocco."

"Are they all right?"

"Sure, certainly."

"This is an outrage, Rocco."

"It's business, Uncle. And maybe part of it is what I shoulda got when the old man died. It wasn't right the way Mae got everything."

"Tell me what you want."

"And Angelo had no right to have Santo zotzed."

"Tell me what you want, Rocco," Eduardo said patiently.

"I want what the families paid for the franchises."

"How much was that?"

"Around thirty million. Angelo knows."

"Thirty *million?*"

"In ten thousand denomination U.S. government bearer bonds."

"That's a lot of bonds."

"If there is any left over, make it up in thousand-dollar bills depending on the figure. Have them make the bonds up in stacks of five hundred. Put the packages in cardboard cartons in a new gray Dodge van and tape them shut. Then we want you, and nobody else but you, to park the van under the West Side Highway a block before the Twelfth Street ramp at between ten minutes to seven and seven P.M. next Saturday. Two days from now. You park the van, with the keys in it; then you open the back doors to the van so we can see you are alone and walk away, going toward Tenth Avenue."

"When do we get the babies?"

"You walk around the block. When you get back the van will be gone, but the kids will be inside a Ford Escort parked where the van used to be."

"Be careful, Rocco. That's all you have to do. Be careful with those children."

"We'll be watching you park it. We'll be watching the whole area starting like an hour ago for any scene of FBI people or cops. Okay, Uncle Eduardo?"

"Yes."

Both men hung up simultaneously because they had come to the end of the script.

Eduardo called Charley at the office. They talked in technicalities about the aftermath of the oil company takeover for about four minutes. Toward the end of the call Eduardo said, "My nephew called me."

"How is he?" Charley said.

"Oh, fine. How are you for an old-time power breakfast today?"

"That would be great," Charley said.

"I have an absolutely splendid cook here, so make it at my apartment in a half-hour."

"I'll be there," Charley said. The FBI monitor recorded the call with the other routine business calls that had been made to Charley that morning and entered it in the log for the hourly pickup.

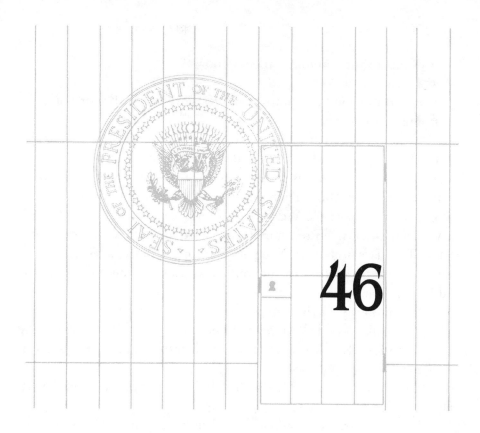

46

Charley entered Eduardo's apartment as bland as a Reblochon cheese. He had repeated the mantra "It's only business" more than three thousand times inside his skull in the past four days. He had said it aloud to Mae over and over again, but she was taking the whole thing as if she had grown up in a square family and didn't know what he was talking about.

After he had taken Eduardo's call at the office, he had gone home, taken Mae into the study, turned on the record player and the TV to foul up any bugs the FBI had put in the room, and told her how Rocco had made his real move. She collapsed in his arms. He held on to her, staggering a little because her dead weight was as unmanageable as a drunk's; then he dumped her on a sofa and went to the bar to get her a shot of brandy. By the time he got back with it, she had come around.

"I gotta go to Eduardo's," he said. "We gotta get the money together. The point is, it's all settled."

"Get a grip on yourself, Charley. You're beginning to sound like some street creature again."

Eduardo had already started the four Barker's Hill brokerages assembling the bearer bonds. He played the tape of Rocco's call back for Charley. They listened intently, side-by-side.

"You know him better than I do, Charley," Eduardo said when they came to the end of the tape for the second time. "How reliable is he?"

"Rocco is good at his work. There's no flash with him. He's steady and he made a good plan."

"How is Angelo?"

"It's slow but he looks a little better."

"How is Mae?"

"Well, you know. Women."

"Maybe you'd better put someone on buying a new Dodge van. Or maybe I'd better call Lee in Detroit and ask him to fly one in to be sure it's gray and brand-new."

"Give him my best."

"That's it then. We'll have all the bonds packaged and assembled by Friday morning. The Dodge van should be here by then. I'll have them load in the basement at Lavery, Mendelson downtown on Saturday morning. They can bring the bonds right down to the garage in their basement."

"That's good," Charley said.

"You'll have the fake demands in the mail Saturday. You and Mae will go off somewhere Rocco tells you to go, and the FBI will follow you out. By the time you get back from wherever it is, I'll have the twins back with their nannies at Sixty-fourth Street."

"Please God."

"Don't believe it that the FBI has been called off this thing."

"No. I only called Heller so Mae would feel better."

"That's it then."

"Except for one thing," Charley said.

"What?"

"Claire Coolidge wants to get married."

"How do you know Claire Coolidge?"

"Eduardo! For heaven's sake! I gave her to you."

Eduardo's eyes flickered, but he gave no other sign that he had heard. "How can I marry Claire Coolidge or anyone else?" he said evenly.

"Not you, Eduardo. She's in love with a fellow her own age. She couldn't find the heart to tell you, so she asked me to tell you."

Eduardo flared. "How does she know you in your new—uh—style?"

"The ballet. Being on the board of the ballet goes with the job I inherited from you. She knows we both serve the same company, so she asked me to tell you."

"I suppose she wants money."

"I don't think so. She just wants to make it as easy as possible for you."

"Who is the man?"

"What's the difference? He's maybe thirty years old. You aren't going to compete with that."

"Well, I have to get used to it just the same, don't I? What do you want me to do?"

"Get used to it; then, after you get that settled, call her and give her your blessing."

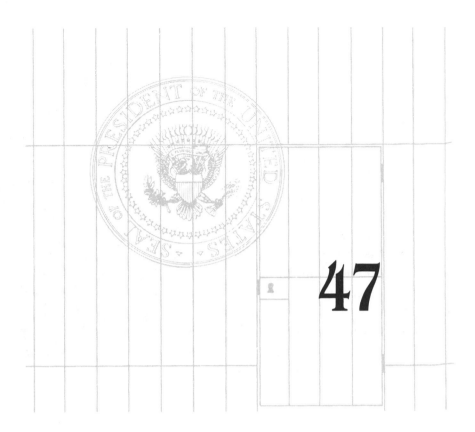

47

The second fake note, spelled out in newsprint, read:

PARKING LOT BRENTWOOD STATE HOSPITAL.
INSTRUCTIONS UNDER REAR FENDER HONDA
ACCORD LICENSE PLATE GFL 8367 AT
TEN MINUTES AFTER NINE SATURDAY NIGHT.
BRING ONE HUNDRED THOUSAND DOLLARS IN
HUNDRED DOLLAR BILLS TO SHOW GOOD FAITH.
BE ALONE.

It was delivered in the mail to Sixty-fourth Street on Saturday just after noon. The note was handed to Charley by Horace Gavin. "My orders are to allow you and Mrs. Barton to go unaccompanied to Brentwood."

243

"At last something is happening," Charley said hoarsely. "Will you arrange permission for the chopper to land on the hospital grounds?"

"I've done that. There's just one thing, Mr. Barton."

"What's that?"

"That seems to be an unusually small demand."

Charley dummied up. "Unusual?"

"You are known to be a wealthy man."

"We can only do what the note says, Mr. Gavin. Now, if you will excuse me, I must make arrangements to get the money."

"We have the money ready."

"Funny money, Mr. Gavin?"

"Standard procedure, Mr. Barton."

Charley raced up the stairs to get Mary Barton. They were downstairs again in seven minutes. The suitcase containing the cash was in the car. Danvers drove them to the heliport. Gavin wasn't in sight. The chopper took them to Brentwood, fifty-one miles away. They touched down twelve minutes after takeoff.

Charley and Mary Barton half ran, half walked to the parking lot, which held several hundred cars. They began to look for the Honda Accord with the specified plates. They searched in every row of the parking lot, but there was no Honda Accord. After twenty minutes of searching, Gavin appeared, coming up the walk from the hospital. "It was a hoax," he said. "There is no such car. In fact there is no such license plate."

Mary Barton, probably because of the tension of playacting until she could get back to Sixty-fourth Street, broke into tears. Charley comforted her.

Eduardo drove up in the new gray Dodge van and parked it well in-between the stanchions under the Twelfth Street ramp at ten minutes to seven on Saturday evening. The place was deserted. At five minutes to seven Rocco drove up in a Ford Escort. He watched his uncle get out of the truck and walk slowly toward him. He just has it, Rocco thought. Every move he makes is classy. From the depths of his pariah complex, Rocco decided that Eduardo had to be the most respectable Prizzi who ever lived. Eduardo reached the car and peered into the backseat. On the floor between the seats were the twins, each one in his own basket, clean and pink, fast asleep or drugged or something, Eduardo thought, but at least they were quiet.

"Good work," he said, standing beside Rocco at the open window. He took a revolver out of his jacket pocket and shot his nephew through the head. He opened the car door, leaned over, and shot him once again for good measure. He shut the front door, opened the back door, lifted the first basket out by its handle and carried it to the back of the van. He opened the back door of the van, put the first basket inside, then carried the second basket from the car to the van, closing and locking the van door when the loading was done.

He got into the van and backed it out of the recess, then headed uptown. He drove through the Midtown Tunnel to Long Island to his summer hideaway at Sands Point, a house that he had not had opened that year because of the preoccupation with the campaign. He unlocked the tall iron gates and rolled into the tree-lined avenue to the main house, locking the gate behind him. He opened the garage door and drove the van inside.

It was necessary to remove the baskets from the back of the van to get the boxes containing the bonds out, and, unfortunately, perhaps in his haste to get the bonds out, but certainly not out of carelessness, he dropped one of the baskets containing a baby. The basket just sort of tilted as if it had a malevolence of its own, and Conrad Price Barton fell a distance of three feet nine inches, landing on the left side of his head on the concrete floor of the garage. Eduardo got the baby back into the basket, packed it into the backseat of a Ford Escort, which was standing by, then transferred the baby in the other basket. The dropped baby was too damned quiet, he thought as he transferred the bonds from the van to the walk-in vault in the cellar of the house. He finished the transfer of the bonds in twenty minutes. He backed the sedan out of the garage, then closed and locked the garage with the Dodge van inside it. He drove with the babies in the back to the Macy-Barton house on Sixty-fourth Street, arriving at ten minutes to nine. He gave the babies over to their happy nannies, then sat in the study, sipping a malt whiskey until Charles and Mary Barton returned from the Brentwood insane asylum.

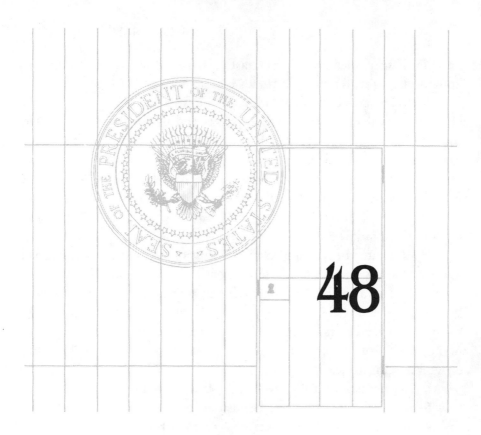

48

When Charles and Mary Barton returned to Sixty-fourth Street that night with Horace Gavin and a special agent, Nanny Bledsoe was sitting in a straight chair in the entrance hall waiting for them. As Mary Barton came in the front door, Nanny Bledsoe said, "The babies are home, madam. They are asleep in the nursery."

Mary Barton sprinted across the main hall and up the stairs.

"Who brought them here?" Horace Gavin asked sharply.

"Mr. Edward Price, sir. He's waiting in the study." Gavin went off to find Eduardo. Charles Barton stared dumbly at Nanny Bledsoe.

"They are fine, sir. Conrad was sleepy but Angier his usual happy, boisterous self. Will that be all, sir?" Charley nodded and watched her climb the stairs to the nursery floor; then, numbly, he went across the drawing room to the study.

246

"You should have told us you were in contact with the kidnappers, Mr. Price," Gavin was saying to Eduardo.

"If I had, the children wouldn't be here."

"If you please, tell me what happened, Mr. Price."

"I had a call last Thursday—I think it was Thursday—to have the ransom money ready."

"What ransom did they demand?"

"Thirty million dollars in U.S. bearer bonds."

"What did you do?"

"I called Mr. Barton. He authorized me to assemble the money."

Gavin glared at Charles Barton. "You knew that wild trip to Brentwood was a phony?"

"I told you at the beginning that I was going to get my children back."

Gavin turned to Eduardo. "Were the bonds marked? Were their serial numbers recorded?"

"No," Eduardo said.

"The bonds are just out there somewhere with hundreds of thousands of other bonds bought last Thursday."

"Yes," Eduardo said.

"All right. I want all the details. I want every shred of information from you about where you made the pickup and a description of the methods and people which turned the babies over to you. Did you recognize the people who held the babies?"

"No," Eduardo said.

A large picture of the ruined and bloody Rocco Sestero was on the front page of the New York DAILY NEWS and the Philadelphia papers that were delivered to the Sestero apartment in Atlantic City on Sunday morning. The FBI and the local police had been there since seven-fifty that morning. Mary Sestero had become hysterical under the questioning, but she held to the story that she knew nothing about her husband's business except that he had worked at the casino of the Mirabelle Hotel. When the police left she turned on her son.

"Angelo Partanna killed your father, whatta you gonna do about it?"

"Angelo?" Beppino said.

"You were here when your father said it! This whole thing, the kids, was Angelo's idea. Angelo set up the whole thing. Angelo was the only one who knew about it, so Angelo had somebody do the job on your father."

"I didn't know. I mean I never figured it that an old guy like Angelo would—"

"He set up Santo, didn't he? You were here. You heard your father say it that Angelo put out the contract on Santo?"

"Angelo gave it to Poppa. Okay. I'm going to New York and give it to Angelo. I know what I gotta do."

Angelo Partanna passed away in his sleep because of heart failure at 1:27 A.M. while his night nurse, Agnes Brady, was making some strong black coffee in the kitchen. At 4:00 A.M. she got out of her chair in Angelo's bedroom to make the regular four-hour check on his vital signs. She put a thermometer in his mouth and picked up his wrist to time his pulse. She knew he was dead. She was dialing Dr. Winikus's telephone as Beppino Sestero let himself into the house by the front door and came into the bedroom. She looked up and had the chance to ask sharply, "What are you doing here?" before he shot her; then he stood beside the bed and shot Angelo twice through the head, crossed himself, and left.

Dr. Winikus heard both shots. He telephoned the police from his house in Brooklyn Heights, dressed, and drove to the Partanna house in Bensonhurst. The police were there when he got there. He identified the bodies at 4:55 A.M.

After the forensic squad had made their measurements, looked for prints, and taken their pictures, the bodies were taken to the city morgue for autopsy. Keifetz, the homicide sergeant, asked Dr. Winikus for Angelo Partanna's next-of-kin.

"I don't know of any," Winikus said. "Do you know who the old man was—or is that before your time?"

"Who was he?"

"That was the right-hand man to Corrado Prizzi."

"Angelo Partanna? That was Angelo Partanna?"

"The only name I have to call is his executor, Charles Macy Barton."

248

"That is his executor? Holy shit, I'm gonna get my name inna papers."

At 9:07 A.M., Sergeant Keifetz called Charles Macy Barton at his office while Barton was in a meeting to reorganize a steel company having seventeen subsidiary companies, identifying himself as NYPD, Homicide. Miss Blue asked the policeman if she could take a message. Sergeant Keifetz said he would prefer to speak to Mr. Barton. Miss Blue said it was impossible for Mr. Barton to come to the telephone. Sergeant Keifetz said the message was urgent and that it involved Angelo Partanna, whose executor, he understood, Mr. Barton was. Mr. Partanna was dead. Mr. Partanna had no survivors known to his doctor; therefore it was necessary that he advise Mr. Barton.

"May we call you back, Sergeant Keifetz?" Miss Blue, having been with Edward S. Price for twenty-two years before she served Mr. Barton, knew Angelo Partanna, who had, from time to time, come to see Mr. Price. It was apparent to Miss Blue that Angelo Partanna had some unusual connection with Barker's Hill if, after years of association with Edward Price, it now had happened that Mr. Barton was Mr. Partanna's executor and that Mr. Partanna was dead.

"Right away, please," Keifetz said. He gave Miss Blue a number.

"Sergeant? Was Mr. Partanna murdered?"

"Yeah."

"We'll get right back to you." She hung up.

Miss Blue sat at her desk and typed a note to Mr. Barton. It said: *"Sergeant Keifetz, NYPD Homicide, called urgently. Mr. Angelo Partanna has been murdered. Sgt. Keifetz urgently wishes you to call him back."* She folded the message slip and took it into the meeting. She passed it to Mr. Barton.

Charley read the message twice before he understood it. The world fell out from under him. He had been waiting for something like this all his life until he had finally decided that it could never happen. That Pop had been over eighty years old didn't change the meaning of what had happened to him. Pop had grown up at the center of this, always knowing that it could happen, never excusing himself from the possibility because he was getting older and older even though he had been the one to see the don die in bed. It was Pop who had made him a man; Pop who had taught him everything. Pop, unassailable, invincible, and everlasting. And somebody had walked into his house in the night and had done the job on him. Business. That fucking business. Maybe Mom was right. Maybe it was better being respectable where the business was only in doing the job on whole companies, then walking away with them and leaving whatever you had to leave behind. Nobody tried to shoot you for it. They gave you testimonial dinners instead. Pop was gone. He had to begin to understand that. Somebody had zotzed Pop.

"Mr. Barton! Are you all right?" The entire table of twenty-six men and women was staring at him.

Charley stood up. He walked unsteadily out of the room, Miss Blue and Carleton Garrone directly following him. In Miss Blue's office, he took Keifetz's number and dialed it.

"Keifetz," the voice said.

"This is Charles Barton."

"You the executor of the late Angelo Partanna?"

"Yes."

"Meet me at the morgue in half an hour. We gotta confirm the identification."

Charley asked for his driver. As they got into the elevator, Charley said to Miss Blue, "Please call Mrs. Barton and tell her what has happened."

49

Keifetz talked to Charley in a small room at the morgue after Charley had made identification.

"I wanna tell you, Mr. Barton, for what it's worth. The autopsy shows that Mr. Partanna had already been dead from heart failure for over two hours before the assailant came in and shot him." Keifetz was a young man who was studying at Delahanty for the lieutenant's examination. He was a dark, affable man to whom every case was another gold star on his personnel record.

Charley made no comment.

"Did you know that Mr. Partanna had been a considerable figure in organized crime in this city?"

"I didn't know that."

"As executor, can you tell me the extent of the victim's estate?"

"We'll have to wait for probate on that." Charley knew that his father's estate would only include the house and his collection of beer steins that Charley's mother had accumulated so she could line them up on the shelved molding that ran all around the dining room. There were his clothes and about four-hundred-odd dollars, all of which he had left to the Salvation Army. All of the money he had accumulated over the years, about three hundred and thirty million dollars, was in numbered accounts in banks in Panama, Hong Kong, and Bahrain, and only Charley knew the numbers.

"How did you come to be Mr. Partanna's executor?"

"When Edward S. Price resigned from our company to seek the nomination for the presidency of the United States—" Charley paused to let that sink into the sergeant's scoring system—"he divested himself of all pecuniary and eleemosynary responsibilities and asked me to take over, as I had taken over his other duties, to represent Mr. Partanna as executor."

"What was Mr. Price's relationship with the victim—if he was the victim's executor."

"I don't know, sergeant. You'll have to ask Mr. Price." Charley put an edge on his voice. "When will the body be released for burial?"

"Give us another day."

"I'll get on with the funeral arrangements then. Good day, Sergeant. Will I tell Mr. Price that you have questions for him?"

"No, sir. That will not be necessary." Keifetz thought maybe he might have gone too far with Charles Macy Barton. He fumbled an envelope and a pen out of his inside breast pocket. "Mr. Barton? I wonder if I could have your autograph for my boy, Brom?"

Angelo Partanna was buried beside Corrado Prizzi and his daughter, Amalia, at the cemetery of Santa Grazia di Traghetto on Staten Island. The church ceremony was attended by the 2,100 former members of the Prizzi family, by 812 members (police/FBI count) or representatives of the *fratellanza* from across the United States, and by members of Black, Hispanic, and Oriental organizations with a light admixture of federal, state, and municipal politicians, church dignitaries, Hollywood celebrities, and great sporting figures, as well as Angelo Partanna's executor, Charles Macy Barton, without his wife, who attended the services and the burial with the other great and near great national figures to pay homage to a dear little old man who no one could ever believe could have been one of those people who had so openly and so colorfully defied Prohibition all those long years ago.

The Bartons rode back to Sixty-fourth Street in one of the undertaker's limousines. Mary Barton had sat out both the church and the cemetery services in the car, with purdah windows, not able to mingle with the other mourners but feeling that she owed it to her husband's father's memory to attend.

"Who did it, Charley?" Mary Barton asked him.

"One of your cousin Rocco's people, I guess."

"You gonna talk to them?"

"No."

"How come?"

"Maybe it's a technicality, but the autopsy showed that Pop was already dead before he was hit. Whatta you want me to tell you?"

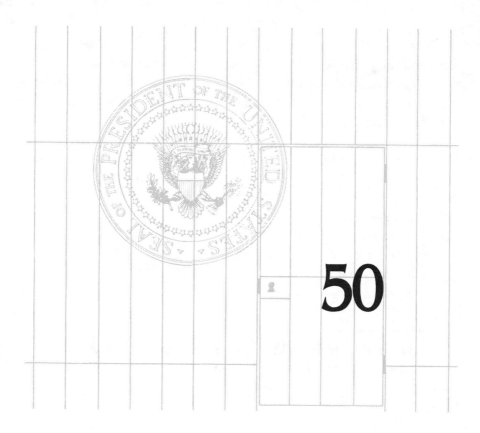

50

On October 28, at 8:50 A.M., the senior nanny, Nanny Willmott, asked to see Mrs. Barton. Mary Barton, in bed, was studying the new fashions in *W*, trying to resolve the political risk of whether or not it would generate more power if she switched dressmakers, weighing what the consequences could be if she put one foot wrong in the delicate but necessary shift of her weight as she climbed higher toward the top of the tree.

"Good morning, ma'am," Nanny Willmott said, curtseying as required, pronouncing "ma'am' as "mom."

Mary Barton put the paper aside. "Good morning, Nanny Willmott," she said. "How are my boys this morning?"

"That's just it, ma'am. In the past week or so, Baby Conrad

254

has been either mewling too much of his time or sleepy when he shouldn't be."

"You mean as compared to Angier?"

"Angier is just right, ma'am, as Baby Conrad always used to be."

"Is it something we should worry about?"

"Not by itself, ma'am. But when I change his diaper, it seems to be that there is something wrong with Baby Conrad's right leg. And although Baby Angier has been pulling himself up in his crib and in his playpen to stand on his two chubby little legs, Baby Conrad cannot stand, ma'am. We've stood him up with his little hands on the railing, but he falls right down upon the mattress."

Mary Barton threw off the covers and got out of bed. "We've got to call the doctor."

"I think perhaps a specialist, ma'am. A neurologist."

"Get him ready. I'll be in with you as soon as I am dressed." Mary Barton picked up the phone and called her husband.

"Charley, the baby—Rado—Nanny Willmott says something is wrong with his right leg."

"Well, Jehoshaphat, Mary, call the doctor."

"Not just the doctor, Charley. You've got to get the best neurologist in the country over here. Nanny Willmott is very worried."

"I'll call you back."

Barker's Hill Enterprises controlled a company that operated 391 hospitals across the country. Charles Barton got its board chairman off the golf course in Palm Springs by grace of an electronic beeper.

"Yes, Mr. Barton?" the chairman said, out of breath.

"Mr. Farb, you can do me a great service. My infant son needs a neurological examination, and I want the best. I want you to get on the phone and in conference with your best people, call me back within ten minutes to tell me the name of the best child neurologist in New York and to say that he is—as you talk—on his way to my house in New York. We're in the book."

"A *house* call, Mr. Barton?"

"The baby cannot be moved. Call me."

Charley called Mae back. "He'll be there in about a half an hour. I don't know his name but he'll tell you."

255

"He makes *house* calls?"

"This one does," Charley said grimly.

"Are you coming over?"

"I can get there in about forty minutes. Now, please—take it easy— we're on top of everything."

Dr. Norman Lesion, who carried an alphabet of degrees and medical honors and who understood tax shelters better than the secretary of the treasury, also could analyze the panic and dismay in Farb's voice from faroff California, and he reasoned instinctively that any medical condition that could shake up a man like Farb this much had to be worth a silo full of money. He sat for a moment in his Mercedes with the MD plates, parked in the No Parking zone in front of the Barton house and calculated to within thirteen dollars and some change what his eventual fee would be. He got out of the car, climbed the broad steps and rang the Barton doorbell at Sixty-fourth Street twenty-three minutes after he had taken the call from Farb. He was led to the nursery, where Mary Barton and the two nannies awaited him. Mary Barton explained the problem. Angier Macy Barton was standing in his playpen, jolly-jaunty, grinning and drooling. Conrad Price Barton lay on his back in the same playpen, listless.

"We'll have him up on the changing table, please," the doctor said. Nanny Willmott made the transfer deftly. She disrobed the baby. Dr. Lesion began his examination, which took him eleven minutes. When it was over, he said he'd like to talk to Mary Barton. She took him into an upstairs sitting room.

"Has the baby had an accident in the past two months or so, Mrs. Barton?"

"No. I don't know. I mean, I can't—not that I know of, doctor."

"Your baby nurses are reliable women?"

"Unquestionably."

"It seems quite certain the baby must have had an accident of some kind."

Mary Barton thought of her cousin, Rocco, and of his hamhanded wife. She thought of Rocco's short, simian arms and his clumsy hands like bear paws, covered with hair. She saw Rocco, again, as he shot Al Melvini.

"What is it, doctor?" she said, wanting to die.

"A child's brain is especially vulnerable during the first few months of life," Lesion said, slowly and carefully. "If an injury occurs at that time, it can result in a dysfunction that mainly affects the motor performance."

"But—"

"It is possible—I cannot say until we run our tests—that your baby is suffering from a form of spastic cerebral palsy"—Mary Barton drew in her breath so sharply as to straighten herself in the chair; she caught her lower lip between her perfect white teeth—"which is characterized by hemiparesis, partial paralysis of the leg on one side. In addition to the weakness, the baby's right leg is thinner and smaller than normal."

"What are we going to do?"

"Motor function can be improved, however, and the success rate is high if the treatment begins early."

"You can make him normal again?"

"It is too soon to say that, Mrs. Barton. Right now, I'd like to have him admitted so that we may possibly forestall epileptic seizures."

"Epileptic seizures?" She wasn't able to follow this man. "Isn't there any way that surgery—"

"It's just too soon to think about surgery, Mrs. Barton. What we must do now is to watch the baby carefully so that we may be sure that there will be no fixed joint and limb deformities—or even a more severe functional disability."

Charley came into the room. Mary Barton introduced the doctor. "It's terrible, Charley," she said. "Terrible."

Charley sat down and stared at Dr. Lesion.

"Somewhere, somehow, there was an accident," the doctor said. "The baby fell, or was dropped, or was struck sharply near the left frontal lobe of his head. There may be clotting. Depending on when the accident happened the infant may be suffering from either acute, subacute, or chronic subdural hematoma." He sighed, wishing he did not have to look at them.

Mary Barton decided she would stay at the hospital in the room with her son. At nine-fifty that night, she and Charles Barton sat in a waiting room that was down the hall from the suite where Baby Conrad had been billeted. They were alone in the room, under harsh fluorescent light, facing each other in chairs, their knees touching.

"Nothing has turned out the way I thought it would," Maerose said.

He reached out and took her hand. "What the hell, Mae—what does?"

"I don't mean just the baby—no one can know what is going to happen to children. I mean everything. We're here and everyone else is gone. My grandfather, my father, your father, Aunt Amalia. They were there, but now they aren't there anymore."

"Well, we're here. And we know mostly what we've got to do."

"It just should have been different. What the hell. Good night, Charley."

51

Charley and Mary Barton were invited by the president to spend election night at the White House, in the Lincoln bedroom. Charley went alone. Mary Barton stayed with the children, beating a path between the hospital and the nursery on Sixty-fourth Street.

It was a fairly late night because Charley waited up with FMH, his staff, and his family for the election returns to come in, or for as long as it took for Gordon Manning to concede. The ticket carried forty-seven states, Manning winning only Rhode Island, Alaska, and his own Connecticut.

The president took Charley aside after the landslide victory had been confirmed. "You had one helluva lot to do with this victory, Charley," he said. "And I want you to know just how grateful I am."

"Thank you, Mr. President."

"We're leaving early tomorrow after they've gotten the photo opportunity out of the way. My asthma is pretty bad, and I have to get a couple of weeks or so at the Arizona chalet." Blister, Arizona, was the site of the "winter" White House, which the president had used regularly all year round during his first term of office. "I won't be seeing you tomorrow, but I want you to know I'll be getting back to you."

"Thank you, Mr. President," Charley said. "Sorry about that asthma."

"We're fifty-three-hundred-feet high out there. Largest ponderosa pine tracts in the world. It's *healthy*, Charley. I get total relief—from asthma, that is. Damn sight better than this place."

"At least you can relax with the knowledge that the campaign deficit has already been handled," Charley said. "It didn't come to anything anyway. Two million eight."

"Don't know what I'd do without you, Charley. And remember, the bed you'll be sleeping on tonight is a historic bed. L. B. Mayer slept in it the first night of the Hoover administration."

Charley went straight home before going to the office the next day. He had breakfast with Mae and tried not to look at her lined, haggard face. He told her of the conversation with the president. She tried to respond with the old-time verve, but she didn't have it anymore.

"Hold out for something big, Charley. Don't let him fob off ambassador to the Court of St. James's."

"London is nice, Mae."

"He should have offered you vice-president before the convention. You got him the information and the money that got him reelected. He's got to pay you off."

"The vice-presidency is where politicians go to die, Mae. I'm a businessman."

"Horseshit."

"So what do you want me to get?"

"Defense?"

"I'm going to listen to what he has to tell me. What's the news on the baby?

"Dr. Lesion is going to have a final prognosis this afternoon at two o'clock." She began to cry silently. She put her head on Charley's chest and sobbed. Charley realized he had never really talked to his wife before. Or any other woman. It was always the same stuff, sex and money. He held her in his arms and said, "Sometimes we should expect the worst, because, if we dared to hope, it would kill us when the truth came in. We have to say it was an accident, Mae. Rocco wouldn't let a thing like that happen on purpose."

"I'm not gonna expect the worst, Charley. What's the use of having what we've got if Rado can't walk like other kids?"

"Mae, lissena me. What I'm trying to say is—don't suffer all this until the doctor tells you that's what's going to be. We'll suffer after that unless we don't have to suffer at all—and it's probably sixty-forty odds—because Lesion has figured out a way to make the baby walk."

She nodded dumbly and wept all over his White House tie.

Following an examination of the Barton baby, Dr. Lesion went through the case with the six assembled interns and residents.

"The bleeding inside the skull seems to have stopped long enough for a fibrous membrane to have formed around the clot," he said. "That was what caused the symptoms to subside. But the hematoma will enlarge when it starts to bleed again. We looked at a pale, irritable baby—weakened by vomiting—with a tense fontanelle. The optic fundi show hemorrhage and papilloedema. Subdural hematoma is confirmed by the needle yield. My intention is to excise the sac; otherwise there will be a scarring of the meninges, which will restrict the growth of the brain, which could result in spasticity and epilepsy. Do you have any questions?"

"Would burr holes be adequate to drain out the hematoma, Dr. Lesion?"

"Not for this patient. Neither will turning the bone flap to evacuate the clot and membrane—or a craniotomy. Since we are going in, we've got to get it all out." He flashed his famous wit at the students. "Modern man doesn't need a brain. He has computers and television."

Loud laughter.

"Will the infant ever regain the use of his right leg?"

"I shouldn't think so. But therapy will help to an extent. It really will."

52

Charley invited S. L. Penrose to New York for a 7:30 A.M. meeting at Barker's Hill offices the day after the surgical procedures on Rado. Penrose never seemed to sleep, yet he always looked watchful and rested. He entered Charley's private office the way he always did, directly from the express elevator that ascended from the garage in the basement. No one could have proved he had been there. Charley locked the doors to his office with an electronic switch. Miss Blue heard the click and wished she could have been a fly on the wall.

"Heller says he wants to show his gratitude," Charley said. "What's open?"

"Justice, the CIA, and Defense."

"What's best?"

"If you can put your own man in Justice, then I think the CIA.

You can control the whole cocaine business from the CIA. And if you can set a friend in Defense, the CIA's big freight carriers can land all kinds of shit at army and air force bases all over the country. No problems with the DEA. They couldn't get near you. Besides, the DEA comes under the attorney general in Justice."

"What else?"

S. L. Penrose grinned. "Hey, that's like a trillion a year, fahcrissake. The *fratellanza* will petition the Pope to get you canonized."

"Forget it. Nobody can get all of it."

"Then there's the secret funds the White House and the CIA control for the Freedom Fighters and their little wars all over the world. At least sixty percent of that is skim. I'm not saying it's skimmed in Washington, but from maker to wearer it's skimmed. After we get through milking the defense contracts, there are a hundred rackets in the CIA. What is the operative word in secret police? Secret."

"Would you take the job?"

"Why not?"

"Could you get confirmed?"

S. L. thought of the National Landscape Association files on the Congress "under the mountain" in West Virginia and of his own almost sacred position amid the power bases. He grinned again. "Why not? But lemme say this, Charley, everything will work better if we have our own man at Justice. Like for one thing, the DEA comes under Narcotics and Dangerous Drugs at Justice. Federal indictments, the Prisons Bureau, the courts, the FBI, organized crime, the Pardon Attorney—they all start there. Justice and the CIA and Defense, with that outtasight budget at Defense—it's like a license to turn the country into a gold mine."

"Eduardo is the natural for a g."

"Nobody better. But he's such a Republican."

"To get a man of Eduardo's caliber, I'll bet Heller would take a larger view."

"What are you gonna take, Charley?"

"Even if I don't take anything, I can try to set you and Eduardo and Defense."

"Who for Defense?"

"Arthur Shuland."

S. L. grinned from ear to ear.

Charley permitted himself a very small smile. "And the families and the Blacks, the Hispanics, and the Orientals will all show their gratitude."

"Don't leave out the Israelis," S. L. said. "They are coming up very strong." He put on a topcoat and a hat. "Do you want to have another meeting tomorrow, or do we have everything wrapped up?"

"Everything is covered," Charley said. "And, besides, Eduardo and I have to go to a very important wedding tomorrow."

After Penrose left, Charley stared out of the window, up Sixth Avenue and across Central Park. He had the feeling that Pop would have been pleased. It had almost all worked out. The don and Mae had got their respectability at the cost of one little kid never being able to be like other little kids. He had been able to take over Barker's Hill, and soon he would be taking over the government of the American people to give them what they absolutely insisted they had to have.

The *fratellanza* hadn't known what they were talking about when they had called Corrado Prizzi the Boss of Bosses. That was one thing you had to say about respectability, Charley thought, it was great for business.

Tomorrow, he promised himself with deep pleasure, I will put the lock on Eduardo.

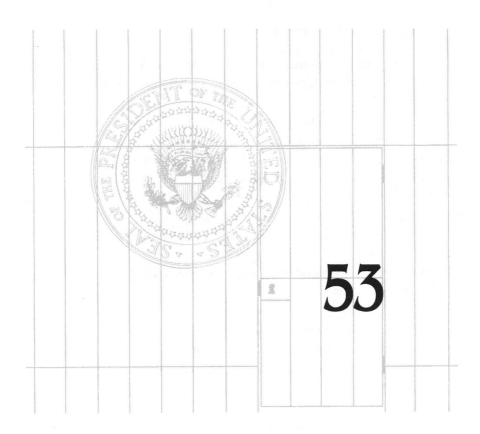

53

Eduardo's stretch limousine, containing Eduardo and Charley, picked up Claire Coolidge at the entrance to her apartment building, and the car moved downtown to City Hall for the wedding ceremony. As Eduardo and Charley had left the Barker's Hill offices, Charley had asked what sort of a wedding present Eduardo was going to give.

"A check," Eduardo said.

"How much?" Charley asked.

"Five thousand."

"Don't give it to her today," Charley advised. "Send it to her with a formal note. It's better to keep a distance between you so as not to embarrass the young man."

"My dear fellow, of course I won't give it to her today."

The bride was so happy that even Eduardo had to decide that it was all worth having to give her up. Charley had a bouquet of flowers for her in the front seat, which he gave to her. She chatted excitedly all the way downtown.

"I don't want you two starchy WASPs to be too surprised when you meet Joseph," she said. "He's Italian way back. One of those dark, romantic Mediterranean beauties. And he loves the ballet."

"I have nothing against Italians," Eduardo said.

"Neither have I," Charley put in loyally. "I have known some very pleasant Italians."

"As a matter of fact," Claire said, "I am actually Italian. My parents are, that is."

"Really?" Charley said. "I would never have thought Coolidge was an Italian name."

"It was Cuchiari," Claire said.

"Boston?" Charley asked.

"Yes, actually. How did you know that?"

"I did some business with people named Cuchiari—in Boston—a few years back."

Joseph, the prospective groom, was waiting for them at the Marriage Bureau office. Eduardo stopped walking when he saw him. Claire, both arms around the young man, was totally unaware of the dismay in the eyes of all three men. The groom was Beppi Sestero, Rocco's son. The three men looked as if they had turned to stone, but Charley got a grip on Eduardo's forearm, and with inbred control in the presence of outsiders, all three men brought off the illusion that the groom was a stranger.

Claire introduced the groom to Eduardo and Charley.

"Edward, may I present the man who is to be my husband in a few minutes, Joseph Sestero." She beamed on her young man. "Joseph, this is the famous Edward S. Price and this"—she held Charley by the upper arm—"is the almost equally distinguished Charles Macy Barton." The men shook hands stiffly. Charley kept talking about what a happy day it was. Eduardo asked for directions to the men's room and excused himself. The bride-to-be kissed and hugged the groom, who had gone into pale greenish colors.

After Eduardo returned, their names were called. In every way it was a sort of famous first in the annals of City Hall marriages. The man who gave the bride away had murdered the father of the groom and the groom had killed the father of the best man, although neither son knew that. It was a sort of Father's Day.

Fifty minutes later, after Eduardo and Charley had wished the young couple Godspeed in their lives and on their honeymoon at the entrance to a luxurious hotel on Central Park South (the bride had to report for rehearsals Monday morning and, it was revealed, the groom had most reluctantly consented to become her manager), the two men drove away after Charley told the driver to take them around the park.

"Did you know about that?" Eduardo asked as the limousine headed toward the Sixth Avenue park entrance.

"I looked at him standing there and I couldn't believe it. Five million men in New York and she picks your nephew."

"What are we going to do about it?"

"I can tell you what you're going to do about it, Eduardo. Now, in this car, right here, you are going to make out a check for fifty thousand dollars for the bride. That's your new, revised wedding present."

"Have you lost your mind, Charley?"

"Do it."

"I'll do no such thing."

"You want to be attorney general? I can do that for you, Eduardo. And I'll do it for you because it's good for business, even though I should have you whacked through the head and dumped in a cement mixer." He stared at Eduardo, laying the fear on him.

Eduardo became alarmed. "Charley, what's the matter? What did I do?"

"We both know what you did. You lifted my two kids for thirty million dollars in bonds."

"Charley! That's crazy!"

"You dropped one of my kids, and he'll never be the same again."

"I dropped—Charley! I handled those kids like they were my own sons. They were little babies! They were breakable! I took every care. If that is what happened, then Rocco did it."

"I'm not going to make you pay, Eduardo. I am going to make you work for me. We are talking business now."

"Charley, you've got to understand—" Eduardo was frozen by the fear Charley was throwing over him. Charley interrupted him.

"Rocco Sestero worked for me. He ran one of my regimes. I knew him. He was a very experienced man, and when he took on a job he always delivered the goods he was paid for just the way they were supposed to be delivered."

"Charley, I swear to God—on my dead mother—"

"Rocco would never have let anyone near him in a setup like that unless he had at least two backup men who would have frisked the man who came to pick up the babies. But you were his Uncle Eduardo, the big man who had almost been president of the United States. So Rocco—Rocco Sestero—a man who knew more about hits than Ty Cobb, went there alone and you took him."

"Charley, listen to me—"

"But there was a sting in it. I told the brokerage house to switch in a whole set of counterfeit bonds that we were going to put up for collateral on a heavy manufacturing deal in Taiwan. That thirty million dollars worth of bonds you think you have isn't worth a dime, Eduardo. Try to cash them and you'll do thirty years."

Eduardo was showing all the symptoms of a heart attack.

"You got pills in your pocket?" Charley asked solicitously. "You want a pill or something?" He jammed Eduardo violently into the far corner of the seat. "All right, you devious shit. Get the top off your fountain pen. Write a check to Claire Coolidge for fifty thousand dollars. I'll see that she gets it."

54

The day after F. M. Heller was seen on the national evening news getting off the helicopter from Andrews Air Force Base, into which he had flown from Blister, Arizona, and being set down in the backyard of the White House, not saluting the Marine guard at the foot of the ramp or waving at anyone, whether they were there or not, he called Charley to set up a private lunch meeting in the family quarters for the next day.

Charley was ushered in, and he and the president were alone. "I don't eat much for lunch," FMH said. "How about you?"

"Usually some fruit and yogurt."

The president nodded to a waiter. "That's what we'll have," he said. He guided Charley to a sofa in front of a fireplace and sat himself in a large wing chair. He patted its arms. "I brought this fellow all the way from Little Germany, Wisconsin, twenty-two years ago, when I came to this town to enter the Senate," he said.

"My dad had a favorite chair," Charley lied.

"Barry Cooper wants to leave. He says the job is only good for two years but a sure burnout for four. He's been here four years and he says he has to leave or lose his temper, which, for Barry, is about the worst crime on the books."

"He's a good man," Charley said.

"He wants to take six months off, then use his experience with some big company. I thought you might help him."

"I'll put my best thinking on it. It's got to be exactly the right job at the very top for Barry."

"But that leaves Barry's job to fill. I had an FBI check run on you, and you're sound, Charley. And you have one helluva fine reputation as an organizer, I don't have to tell you, so confirmation won't be any problem. They respect you on the Hill." The president gazed at Charley as fondly as it was possible for him to regard anything. He nodded his head. "You'll make a great chief of staff. What do you say?"

"If I said yes right now, considering the size of the honor, sir, I wouldn't be saying the right thing. It is just the most overwhelming opportunity anyone has ever had to serve his president and his country. Please let me sleep on it and give you my answer in the morning."

The fruit salad under raspberry yogurt arrived. The two men chatted about the president's health until the waiters left. "The central reason why I need you," the president said, "is that I have to know that the White House and the country are running as smoothly as a watch because this term—my asthma is simply murder in this climate, Charley—I'm going to have to spend more and more time at Blister just to be able to stay on my feet."

"I understand, Mr. President."

"Frank."

"Frank—I meant to say Frank."

"You'll have to run the mechanics of the country, Charley, if I'm to run its policies. What I'm saying is—I really need you."

Charley put out his hand and the president took it. "When do you want me to start?" Charley said huskily.

"How much time do you need to make the move?"

"If I could have, say, about five weeks?"

"Why not? Until just before the inauguration."

"I could live with that."

"How are your two boys?"

"Fine, just fine."

"None the worse?"

"Not at all."

"They still haven't found the money you paid over?"

"Not yet."

"Thirty million?"

"Yes. But I was insured for most of that."

"I have Justice, Defense, and the CIA to fill. Any ideas on that?"

"I will have, I think. But I'll have to brood over that one."

"Let that be your first official recommendation," FMH said. "Your first official recommendation. And let me have it by Monday. They'll be pressing me for announcements."

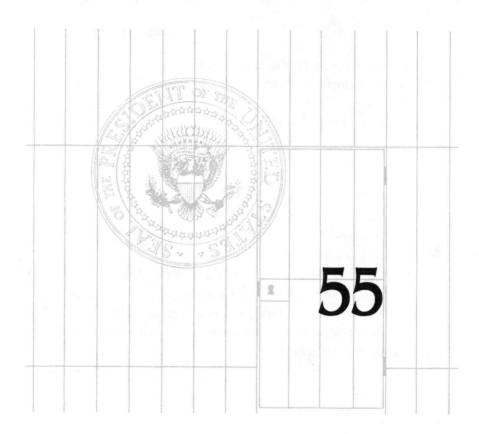

55

Edward S. Price was confirmed as attorney general, Arthur Shuland as secretary of defense, and S. L. Penrose as director of Central Intelligence without a hitch. But the stir of elation was caused by the president's appointment of Charles Macy Barton as his chief of staff, a decision that was internationally proclaimed.

> ### BARTON NEW STAFF CHIEF
> ### GIVES UP $27.1 MILLION
> ### TO TAKE WHITE HOUSE JOB
>
> NEW YORK, December 3—Charles Macy Barton, Chairman and CEO of Barker's Hill Enterprises, one of the world's largest conglomerates, today accepted the key White House post of Chief of Staff, renouncing an annual $27.1 million in salary, bonus, and stock options to serve his country and his President.

President Heller hailed the appointment as "the very pinnacle of patriotism," stating that Barton, known as "the Great Organizer" to millions, had "turned away from wealth to serve his country" and by so doing "has freed me from the routine tasks of running this country so that I may put all my thought and energies into reducing the crippling budget deficit and get on with our nation's crusade to free Latin America from Communism."

(Continued on Page 3)